I0600081

FATAL INVITATION
Copyright © 2025 by S.F. Baumgartner

ISBN: 9798992948370
Library of Congress Control Number: 2025923234

PUBLISHING

Edited by Brilliant Cut Editing and Represent Publishing

Book Cover Design by 100Covers

# FATAL INVITATION

# FATAL INVITATION

## S.F. BAUMGARTNER

# AUTHOR'S NOTE

To all readers, especially residents and those familiar with the state of Florida, I wish to clarify that the town of Pine Grove and a few other locations, as well as Orlando Prime, are purely fictional creations for this series.

All characters and events depicted in this novel are born from my imagination. Any resemblance to actual people, living or dead, or to real-life events is entirely coincidental.

# 5 WEEKS AGO

T*en more minutes!*
In just ten minutes, everything would change.

Sheri Conners leaned against the cool bathroom sink, the hum of flickering fluorescent lights filling the cramped space. The faint scent of disinfectant mixed with the sharper tang of stale mop water, but she barely noticed. All she could think about was what waited beyond these walls. A chance.

Her life as a store cashier? Done. No more punching buttons until her fingertips went numb. No more bagging groceries while customers tapped their feet. No more pasting on that fake smile when someone screamed at her over a fifty-cent coupon discount that wouldn't scan. She could still feel the echo of yesterday's headache from Mrs. Patterson's twenty-minute rant about produce prices, as if Sheri personally set them each morning.

For two years, she'd been invisible behind that register. Just another face people looked through while they counted their change, another voice saying, "Paper or plastic?" that nobody really heard. But not anymore. Still, she wanted that final paycheck. She'd promised her mom she wouldn't leave loose ends.

Sheri smoothed her blouse and studied her reflection. She tugged her ponytail a little higher, added a fresh swipe of lip gloss, and brushed a layer of mascara over her lashes.

Would they like the pink streak? She tilted her head, considering the single highlight that framed her face. Too much? *No, just enough. Shows I'm different. Shows I'm willing to stand out.* Her pulse ticked faster.

Who could believe her luck? One ad, one phone screen, and she was in. No more minimum wage, no more small-town dead end. Her feet wouldn't ache from standing on concrete floors for eight hours. Her cheeks wouldn't hurt from smiling at people who treated her like part of the machinery. *This is it.*

A notification blinked on her phone. Time to clock out. Her heart hammered against her ribs as she stared at the screen. This was happening. After all those nights lying awake, wondering if she'd be stuck here forever, counting register drawers and restocking shelves until she was sixty, freedom was within reach.

Sheri exhaled to steady the flutter in her chest. She grabbed her purse and pushed the bathroom door open.

The store hit her like a wall of sound. Scanners beeped, cart wheels squeaked, and overhead announcements about the daily special grated through their loop. The harsh glare made her squint after the dimmer bathroom lighting. A line of customers snaked from her old register, where Kenny already looked overwhelmed, fumbling with the produce codes she'd memorized.

She walked past checkout lane three without looking back. Past the time clock where she'd punched in and out nearly a thousand times. Past the employee bulletin board with its cheerful reminders about "customer service excellence" and mandatory overtime.

Tomorrow, someone else would be standing behind that register. Someone else would smile and nod while customers complained about prices they couldn't control, policies they didn't make, and wait times they didn't create.

But not Sheri. Never again.

She pushed through the automatic doors and stepped into the parking lot, her chin higher than it had been in months. The afternoon sun felt different on her face, warmer, brighter, full of possibility. She'd done it. She'd found her way out.

# CHAPTER 1

## BODY BY THE LAKE

### ORLANDO, FL

Detective Kylie "KC" Cassidy's phone buzzed, ending her quiet morning. The case report would have to wait, again. She'd chased the same paragraph for the better part of an hour, and now even that small victory was slipping away.

Her mind kept drifting back to the wedding she'd attended with Nathan Tanner, who preferred being called Tanner, over the weekend. Meeting his FBI colleagues had been like stepping into another world, with their easy camaraderie and manner of communicating in half sentences and knowing glances.

Mirror Estate itself offered everything she'd imagined and more. The grand ballroom, the manicured gardens, the under-stated elegance that whispered old money. She'd felt both out of place and oddly at home, especially with Tanner's arm around her waist as he introduced her to his circle like she belonged.

The phone buzzed again. *Time to focus.*

"Cassidy."

"Echo Park. Body found." The voice of her senior partner, Detective Rick Spaulding, came quickly, no preamble, no filler. "I'm tied up at the range for recert. Lieutenant'll give you the details. I'll join you when I can."

"Got it."

The line went dead.

She pushed back from her desk and grabbed her jacket. Before she could sling it on, Lieutenant Andre Coleman stepped out of his office into the squad room, phone in hand.

"Cassidy. Echo Park. Dead body by the lake. Spaulding's stuck on his mandated training."

"I just spoke to him."

"Good. You're working this solo until he gets back. Probably tomorrow or the next day."

*Nice. She'll have a chance to prove her worth.*

"Cassidy?" Coleman added as she stood.

"Yeah?"

"Let's handle this one clean. Echo Park means media. Don't let it get messy."

"Understood."

She retrieved the key. The familiar weight of her service weapon settled against her hip as she headed out. A few weeks in Major Crimes, and she was swamped. This was definitely not Pine Grove, where she'd been the only detective at the sheriff's substation.

The thirty-minute crawl to Echo Park took her through downtown Orlando, past glass towers reflecting the morning sun. At nine in the morning, the city hummed with energy that still felt foreign after small-town policing, traffic lights, construction cranes, the distant rumble of I-4. Everything moved faster here.

Echo Park sat on the city's east side, a man-made lake surrounded by walking trails and benches where retirees fed ducks and joggers logged their morning miles. She'd driven past it dozens of times but never stopped. Now, yellow crime scene tape fluttered between the palm trees like warning flags.

She parked behind two patrol cars and stepped out into air thick with humidity despite the cool temperature. The morning sun cast long shadows across the water, and somewhere a mockingbird ran through its repertoire of stolen songs. A coffee aroma drifted from a vendor cart near the parking lot, mixing with the earthy smell of damp soil and algae.

A crowd had gathered at the tapeline, the usual mix of curious civilians drawn to tragedy. KC counted at least seven people. A jogger in expensive athletic wear, an elderly man with a fishing pole, a woman walking two small dogs, and several others with cell phones raised to capture whatever drama they could post online.

"Excuse me, Detective?" A young woman in yoga pants pushed forward. "What happened? Is it safe to walk here?"

"Ma'am, please step back behind the tape." KC kept her voice firm but polite. "We'll have more information later."

"But I walk my dog here every morning," the woman persisted. "If there's a dangerous person—"

"We're handling the situation. Please give us space to work."

KC ducked under the tape.

Ignoring her words, the crowd pressed closer. The man with his phone raised high was clearly recording, probably already posting to whatever platform would give him his fifteen seconds of internet fame.

"Officer Wilson!" KC called to the uniformed cop standing guard. "Move them back another twenty feet. And remind anyone filming, this is an active crime scene."

"Yes, ma'am."

She followed the worn path toward the lake's edge, where Officer Martinez waited near a stand of palmetto scrub. The morning light filtered through the canopy overhead, casting shifting patterns on the sandy trail. The Spanish moss draped from ancient oak trees swayed, and the air grew cooler in the shade.

"Detective Cassidy?" Martinez approached, his face pale under his tan. "Body's just beyond those bushes. CSU's already here."

KC pulled on gloves as she stepped off the main trail. Her boots crunched on fallen palm fronds and scattered shells left by visiting families. The peaceful setting, complete with a wooden bench overlooking the water, made what waited ahead feel even more obscene.

The body lay on its side near the base of a massive cypress, head turned away from the path. Hard to tell the age or gender from this vantage point, but the pink oversized T-shirt and skinny shorts suggested young, possibly female, though she'd not be foolish enough to assume. Brown hair had been cut short, the edges jagged and uneven.

But most peculiar was the mound of fresh earth piled beside the body in what looked like a hastily scraped depression. As if someone had dumped her there and gathered dirt to cover her but never finished the job. Was the person planning to come back and complete the burial?

A CSU tech passed by with his camera.

"Get everything, wide, mid, tight, before the ME moves in. Footprints, tire tracks, whatever's here."

"Yes, ma'am."

KC crouched at a respectful distance. No obvious signs of struggle. No defensive wounds on the visible arm. The body's position looked almost peaceful, as if she'd simply lain down and never woken up. But death had its own smell, and she caught it beneath the morning freshness, something metallic and wrong that made her stomach tighten.

"Who's first on scene?"

"That would be Officer Wilson."

She headed back to Wilson, who was helping push the onlookers farther back.

"You're first on scene?"

"Yes, ma'am."

"Who found her?"

"Guy walking his dog. Cyrus Jagers. Gulf War vet. His

German shepherd sniffed her out around nine fifteen. He said he knew that she was gone. Didn't touch anything. Called it in."

"Where is he?"

"In the squad car with his dog."

As she made her way over, she passed trampled grass, a crushed soda cup, and a cigarette butt half buried in sand.

Cyrus Jagers sat in the back with the door open, dog sitting by the car.

"Mr. Jagers? I'm Detective Cassidy. Can you walk me through what happened?"

The man stepped out, lean and solid despite the lines in his face, posture straight as a rail.

"Eeyore, my German shepherd, and I walk here most mornings. He went into the brush, started barking. I thought he'd found a turtle or something. When I got closer, I saw the body. Pale. Neck didn't look right. I've seen enough dead to know."

She glanced at the German shepherd. *Interesting name for such a massive guard dog!*

"Did you see anyone else? Any vehicles?"

Jagers crossed his arms. "Didn't notice anybody else or vehicles."

"Thank you." She fished out her card. "If anything comes to you later, give us a call."

He accepted it.

"Officer Wilson will take your contact info if he hasn't already. You're free to go."

"Kylie Cassidy?"

She half-shifted back to the man. "Yes?"

He studied her for a beat, as if seeing her for the first time. "Oh… nothing. Nothing at all." He tucked the card into his pocket.

KC frowned but didn't pursue it. She had more urgent business than puzzling over a stranger's odd reaction. However, he'd had a slight accent. British, maybe. She shook her head, refocusing.

"Are you the detective?" The voice cut through from the crowd. A man in his twenties aimed his phone camera at her.

"May I help you?"

"Todd Rowe, *StreetBeat News*. Can you confirm there's a dead body here? Victim's identity?"

"Sir, please step back behind the tape. Now."

His questions triggered a chorus from others, shouts about safety, muggings, danger.

She focused on Wilson. "Keep them back. Find a few uniforms and start canvassing. Talk to the regulars, see if anyone saw something. Start with that group."

"Yes, ma'am."

The ME van's low rumble intruded. A CSU tech was snapping away.

"Bag that soda cup. That cigarette butt too."

"Will do."

Luna Hunt, the death investigator, approached with gloves snapping into place. She and KC had worked several scenes together.

"Morning, KC. CSU clear me?"

"Go ahead."

The investigator crouched, studying limbs, fingers, positioning. "Recent. Rigor just starting. No visible ID."

Gloved hands gently turned the head.

The face that emerged stopped KC cold.

She recognized this girl.

# CHAPTER 2

## RECOGNITION

Yes, the victim had been a cashier at Pine Grove Market. Most evenings when KC stopped for groceries, Sheri was behind the register. Barely out of high school, just coming out of her goth phase. A pink streak in her otherwise dark hair, not loud, just enough to say she was trying to stand out without all the weight of black.

Now her hair was hacked short and brown, the pink had grown out in the weeks since KC last saw her, leaving only jagged ends that spoke of scissors wielded without care. The morning mist that clung to Echo Park's lake surface suddenly felt suffocating. The air tasted of wet earth and something else, something that made KC's stomach clench. Death, subtle but unmistakable, threaded through the pine needles and morning dew.

*"KC, Jill Conners says her daughter, Sheri, is missing." The dispatcher's voice echoed through the Pine Grove substation, urgent and tinged with the kind of worry that small towns carried differently from cities.*

*KC was packing her desk, cardboard boxes stacked like*

*tiny monuments to a career she was leaving behind, when someone hollered from the break room.*

*"Betsy, it's her last day! Give it to the new guy!"*

*KC didn't argue. She sealed another box instead, the sound of tape ripping through the silence like skin tearing. It made sense. She was leaving Pine Grove, wouldn't be there to see it through. Let someone else chase the shadows.*

Now, those shadows had followed her here.

"No ID—" Luna Hunt's voice cut through KC's reverie.

"It's Sheri Conners." How strangely steady her voice sounded. "From Pine Grove."

Luna glanced up from where she crouched beside the body, her latex gloves already stained. The morning light on the silver in her hair made her look older than her thirtysomething years. "You knew her?"

"She worked the register at Pine Grove Market." KC exhaled. "About twenty. Sweet kid. Always asked about my day like she cared about the answer."

Had a full laugh, quick and bright, bubbling up when elderly Mrs. Patterson forgot her grocery list for the third time in a week. She'd seemed like one of those kids content where she was. But maybe that smile, that gentle efficiency, had been the face she put on while she dreamed of something better.

"Wonder how she ended up here." Luna slid her hands over the body with practiced precision.

*My thoughts exactly.* KC stepped closer, the damp grass soaking through her shoes. The park stretched around them, serene and oblivious. Joggers would be here soon, dog walkers, families with strollers. This peaceful morning sanctuary would become their nightmare.

"TOD?"

Luna pulled out a liver thermometer with the casual grace of someone who'd done this dance too many times, on too many bodies that had once been people with grocery lists and favorite songs. She checked the reading, frowned, and checked again. "Based on rigor and lividity, between six and ten hours."

KC again knelt at a respectful distance, her knees sinking into the soft earth. The death smell was stronger here.

"Looks like she was dumped here sometime overnight or early this morning," Luna continued.

"Any visible trauma?"

"None that I can see. No obvious wounds, no defensive marks on her hands or arms. Fingernails are clean." Luna maintained the careful neutrality of someone delivering bad news in small doses. "We'll know more on the table."

She then took out a portable scanner. "I'll pull her prints now. Even if you're sure, we need it official before we make the notification."

KC studied the scene with trained eyes. No blood pool darkening the earth. No drag marks scored the grass. No trampled vegetation suggesting a struggle.

Luna gestured with the handheld device. "Hit. Sheri Conners. Driver's license photo matches what we've got here."

Before KC could absorb it, voices rose from beyond the tape, louder, sharper than the earlier gawkers.

"Detective Cassidy! Can you confirm the victim's identity? Is she local or a tourist?"

"Any suspects? Are you looking for a serial killer?"

"Detective! Are city parks still safe?"

A cluster of journalists pressed against the tape, local newscasters, camera crews, and at the edge, Todd Rowe of *StreetBeat News*, angling his phone for a clear shot. News vans were rolling in, their satellite dishes rising against the pale morning sky.

The crowd of onlookers had thinned, replaced by a new swarm, a different kind of chaos.

KC raised her voice, calm but firm. "Please stay behind the

tape. No comment at this time. Our Public Information Office will release a statement later."

Rowe wasn't deterred. "Detective Cassidy! How many bodies so far? Are you warning the public?"

Blocking out the noise, she refocused on the body. There was work to do. The girl on the ground mattered more than headlines.

Sheri lay on her side, knees drawn up slightly, arms loose at her sides. Like she was sleeping, if you could ignore the waxy pallor of her skin and the unnatural stillness of her chest.

"She didn't die here."

"Correct. She was dumped." Luna rocked back on her heels, peeling off her gloves with sharp snaps. "This is just where someone wanted her found."

Or where someone wanted her hidden. KC scanned the tree line. Echo Park wasn't exactly off the beaten path, but it wasn't Times Square either. Early morning joggers, maybe a few fishermen. Someone could dump a body here and reasonably expect hours before discovery.

But they'd placed her carefully, almost tenderly. Not thrown or dragged, but arranged. Like they cared about how she looked, even in death.

KC rose, brushing dirt from her knees. She stopped a CSU tech with a camera. "I want all the footage we can get, parking lot cameras, street cams, traffic feeds from the main road. And canvass the neighborhood. Someone might have seen a vehicle."

"Yes, ma'am." He walked away.

She then turned away from the body, from the girl who would never again ask about her day or separate eggs from bread. The sun climbed higher, burning off the mist and revealing the lake in all its postcard perfection. Ducks glided across the surface, leaving V-shaped wakes. Somewhere in the distance, a lawn mower started up, the sound absurdly normal.

Now, the hard part. The notification. "Can I see her driver's license again?"

"Sure." Luna handed her the device.

Sheri lived with her mom, so this would be her mom's address too. KC had made death notifications before. But this time felt different. This time, she could picture the woman who would answer the door.

Before leaving the scene, KC took a slow, methodical walk of the area, attuned to details the chaos of first response might have missed.

She moved beyond the body, past the CSU markers, scanning the tree line where the ground sloped toward the water. The breeze stirred the undergrowth, rustling leaves against damp soil.

Something pale caught her eye, just at a clump of scrub near a low-hanging pine. KC crouched. A folded piece of paper, edges soft with moisture, lay partially obscured by fallen leaves and pine needles.

She didn't touch it. Instead, she straightened and signaled to a nearby CSU tech.

"Marker here. Let's get photos."

The tech hurried over, dropping the evidence marker and snapping shots from multiple angles.

Only when the last frame clicked did KC pull on fresh gloves and pick up the paper, unfolding it just enough to see.

Her pulse quickened.

It was a Missing Person flyer. Sheri's face stared back at her from beneath a soggy crease, her details printed in smudged ink.

Had the killer left this on purpose? Or had it been dropped by accident?

# CHAPTER 3

## CONFIRMATION

### PINE GROVE, FL

K C tightened her grip on the steering wheel as Pine Grove materialized through the windshield. Weathered storefronts and cracked sidewalks she'd walked as a kid now rushed past in a haze of exhaust fumes. Some people remembered childhood in colors or songs. KC remembered it in the hum of hospital lights and Aunt Mae's perfume. Some things never left the body, even if they were too young to remember.

The address on Sheri's license pulsed in her mind like a migraine. The yellow house on Maple Drive wasn't the same as before. Paint curled away from the porch railings in brittle strips, and a plastic wind chime knocked against itself in the humid breeze, each hollow note like a countdown. KC had barely shifted into park when the screen door groaned open.

The woman who emerged bore little resemblance to the Jill Conners from the Christmas tree lighting just weeks ago. Gone was the animated face that organized the cookie exchange and chatted about the next community event. This Jill moved like someone carrying invisible weights, her eyes sunken into dark circles, worry lines carved deep around her mouth.

"KC, you're back!" Jill froze in the doorway. Then her shoulders sagged, and she stepped aside as if the fight had drained out of her completely. "Please tell me she's okay."

"We have some news." KC's throat tightened. "Maybe you should sit down."

Jill's hand flew to her mouth. Her head began shaking in small, desperate movements. "No, no. Please, no."

Her knees buckled.

KC lunged forward, catching Jill's trembling weight, and guided her toward the faded floral couch. The cushions exhaled stale air and the faint scent of vanilla candles. "I'm very sorry."

Jill collapsed forward, burying her face in her hands as a raw sob tore from her chest, the sound of a mother's world cracking in half.

KC allowed the grief its moment while scanning the living room. A shrine of photographs covered one wall: wedding portrait, family photos, birthday parties, Sheri's school pictures tracing the years from gap-toothed kindergartner to radiant high school graduate. The wedding photo caught her attention. Jill in white lace beside a man with kind eyes and Sheri's stubborn chin.

"But... but didn't you move to Orlando?" Jill's voice came out thick and broken.

"Yes, I am with Orlando PD."

"I don't understand." Jill fumbled for tissues, blew her nose with shaking hands.

"We found her at Echo Park this morning. When you're ready, we'll need you to make an official identification." KC paused. The wedding photo was still in prominent display, probably not divorced. However, she didn't want to assume. "Jill, is there anyone else you can call? Sheri's dad?"

Fresh tears spilled down Jill's cheeks. "He passed when Sheri was ten. My folks are gone. My sister lives in Kentucky with her family. And Brian. Oh dear..." The wail that followed seemed to come from somewhere deeper than her lungs.

KC waited through the storm. "Who's Brian?"

Struggling for composure, Jill wiped her nose. "Her boyfriend. Well, she said they broke up recently. But they've been together for a long time."

KC pulled out her phone, fingers poised over the notepad. "What's Brian's last name? Do you know where I can find him?"

"Shipley. Brian Shipley. He goes to UF."

University of Florida, about two hours from Orlando. She'd need to track him down. Maybe he knew more than he realized.

"Tell me about Sheri's last few days."

Jill closed her eyes as if rewinding through memory. "She told me she had this amazing opportunity but wouldn't give me details. Just said she'd know more after some meeting."

"When was this? And when was the meeting supposed to happen?"

"She told me the day before she…" Jill's voice caught. "Before she didn't come home. The meeting was supposed to be after her shift the next day. I don't know where." Her voice turned bitter. "I was afraid it was some scam and warned her, but she just shrugged me off. Said I worried too much."

"All right if I take a look at her room? And do you know if she had a laptop? Tablet?"

Jill shook her head. "Go ahead. The room on the left upstairs. And no, she doesn't—didn't—have a laptop or a tablet."

Rather unusual, but not unheard of. If Sheri's room was upstairs, the room right next to the living room had to be Jill's.

The house's modest footprint became clear as KC mapped the layout. She crossed to the staircase that faced the makeshift dining table and climbed to the small landing above. At the landing, a sliver of hallway split into two doorways. One room facing the stairs was a small room with a queen bed, a guest room, maybe.

A visual sweep dissected Sheri's sparse room in an instant— queen bed with rumpled sheets, dresser against the far wall, vanity by the window. KC crouched, peered under the bed. Nothing.

The dresser drawers yielded only clothes, neatly folded. She approached the corner shelf. Tracked a finger along a couple of snow globes, paperback novels with cracked spines, cheap jewelry. Her gaze moved to the walls, bare, no photos, no personal touches that might reveal who Sheri really was.

No laptop. No tablet. No charging cables snaked across the nightstand. Not even a smartphone charger was visible.

Back down in the living room, she handed over her business card. "If you think of anything else, anything at all, please call me."

Jill's fingers closed around the card like a lifeline.

KC lingered at the door, one hand on the knob, unwilling to leave Jill alone with her grief. She reached for her phone and pressed 1, speed dial to Aunt Mae.

"Kylie?" Aunt Mae, the only one to call her Kylie, answered on the first ring. "Are you all right?"

"I'm fine. But I need a favor. I'm at Jill Conners's place. It's Sheri... She was the victim we found—"

"No, no!"

"—this morning. I don't think Jill should be alone."

"Of course not! I'll be there in a jiffy."

"I knew I could count on you."

"I'll take care of it. We'll bring food, sit with her, whatever she needs."

The tension in her shoulders loosening, KC exhaled. "Thanks, Aunt Mae."

"Go catch that killer. We've got this."

She stepped back toward Jill. "My aunt will be here soon."

Jill nodded.

KC started to go, then paused at the threshold. "By the way, have you seen Brian since Sheri went missing?"

"Yes, he came by that weekend. Sweet boy. He helped me

make the missing person flyer. Posted it all over social media and around town." Jill's voice softened with the first hint of warmth since KC had arrived. "He's been calling every week to check on me."

"Did Sheri ever mention why they broke up?"

Jill's face clouded. "She wouldn't talk about it. Just said it was complicated."

# CHAPTER 4

## DIGITAL BAIT

The moment KC stepped into the Pine Grove station, the familiar scent of burnt coffee and lemon floor wax assailed her.

"KC!" someone called from across the bullpen. "Heard you were back."

A couple of deputies offered warm nods or quick smiles. KC returned them with a slight wave, all while scanning the room for changes, counting what remained the same.

Deputy Erin Garcia approached her. "How's the big city treating you?"

"Busy. How are things here?"

"Same old, same old." Erin leaned in and whispered, "Did Sheriff say anything about the promotion?"

Erin had passed the detective test and other hurdles. And she was a strong contender for the second detective position. KC had given the Sheriff her recommendation before she left.

"I haven't talked to him since I left. Don't worry! He's probably waiting for the final approval from the board." KC looked toward her old office. "Is he in?"

"Yeah."

"Hang in there!" She headed to the detective's office.

"Detective Cassidy." Jed Hutchins stood up.

"KC's fine. Looks like you inherited my old desk."

"Sheriff said it had good mojo. Not sure I believe in that, though." He laughed and sat back down.

She gave a polite smile and sat. The worn chair creaked under her weight. "Let's talk Sheri Conners."

"What about her?"

"Her body turned up in Echo Park."

"No kidding." Hutchins moved his mouse, clicked a few times. "Here it is. She was reported missing. I did the usual. Chased down some leads. No usable video, no witnesses. Her phone pinged on Highway 9, but then nothing."

*That's it? A phone ping and you waited?* KC's jaw tightened, but she nodded. *Maybe if you had investigated instead of filing paperwork, she might not have ended up dead in Orlando.*

"Anything else?" The words came out tighter than she intended.

"Not really." He shrugged, the gesture dismissive. "I didn't know her. Didn't have much to go on. How'd she end up in Orlando?"

She glared. *You're asking me?* Her fingers pressed against her thighs. "That's the question, isn't it?"

Highway 9 was a forty-mile stretch. Had he even driven it? Checked the businesses along the route? She gripped the chair arms, forcing her voice to stay level. Antagonizing Hutchins wouldn't bring Sheri back or solve this case. "May I see the file?"

"Of course! It's all in the system. I can log you in at one of the desks out there."

"Mind if I get a copy?"

Hutchins arched a brow. "Technically, you're out of jurisdiction. But I'll print you what we've got. Just don't take it to the press."

"Wouldn't dream of it." *What little there is to take.*

The old printer wheezed to life in the background as he tapped keys. "It should be coming out now. I trust you still know where it is."

She stood, forcing another smile. "Unless you moved it. Thank you for your time."

Time to do the job that should have been done weeks ago.

KC tossed the folder onto the passenger seat and pulled out of the substation lot, steering toward Pine Grove Market. With one hand on the wheel, she tapped her earpiece.

"Cassidy to Rios."

The line clicked. "Talk to me."

"Hey, Janelle. Just checking on anything from the Echo Park scene."

Janelle Rios, a civilian with an impressive cybersecurity background, held down the intel desk in Major Crimes.

In KC's short time there, she'd learned two things quickly: Janelle moved information faster than most cops moved coffee, and if you wanted results yesterday, you asked her. Major Crimes unit in a big city came with perks KC never had back in Pine Grove.

"You're hoping for a miracle, huh?" Janelle's voice sounded chirpy as usual. "Okay, let me pull it up."

KC waited through a few clicks and a sip of lukewarm gas station coffee.

"Fingerprints from the flyer are still in the queue. CSU ran partials, but nothing popped on the initial scan. They're trying to clean it for another pass."

"Any trace? Hair, fibers, soil, whatever?"

"Collected, not processed. Lab says the earliest results won't hit the system until tomorrow unless something flags hot."

"Autopsy?"

"Slated for noon tomorrow. Dr. Patel got that one. She's got two others, both gang related, so you're third in line."

KC exhaled through her nose. "And surveillance?"

"Officer Yee viewed the Echo Park feed this morning. Said it showed nothing useful. Just park traffic, no obvious drop, no fight. He filed the report ten minutes ago."

"Can you send me that report?"

"Already did. Check your inbox."

"You're the best."

"I know. And I didn't even roll my eyes when I said it."

KC cracked a smile. "I owe you caffeine."

"Put it on your tab."

She ended the call and merged onto Main, the light beige siding of Pine Grove Market coming into view. No break-throughs yet. But all it took was one thread.

A moment later, she walked into the familiar store. With her badge on display, she approached the teen idling at a checkout station. "Manager here?"

He jerked his head toward the customer service counter. "Back there."

KC headed to the counter and approached Tracy, the manager. Unfortunately, she didn't have much to offer. "Sheri didn't talk to many people, but I seen her and Tess together a few times. She's on break now."

"Thank you."

KC found Tess in the break room, fiddling with her phone. The young woman couldn't be more than twenty, with dark eyeliner and chipped purple nails.

"Hi. I'm Detective Kylie Cassidy."

Tess glanced at her, stood up at once. "You probably don't remember me. You came to my high school once. For career day? You were still Deputy Cassidy then."

*Wow, that makes her feel so old!* "Pine Grove High?"

"Yeah! You talked about how you caught some guy by tracking his social media. It was cool." The young woman set down her coffee mug. "I mean, I thought so. I'm at Orange Technical College now. Just started their Veterinary Assisting program. It's supposed to take, like, ten months, but I might go for the vet tech degree after, if I don't flunk out first."

KC made the appropriate supportive sounds. "Sounds like a solid plan." She gestured for Tess to sit and followed suit. "I'm looking into Sheri Conners's, uh, disappearance."

"Oh, yeah. That's super weird. She said she had this new gig. Said she would give me all the deets so I could get on it. But then, she just up and—poof—gone."

"Okay, so she mentioned a job opportunity?"

"Yeah, what I said. She only had one phone screen with this dude."

"Where did she find this opportunity?"

Tess shook more sugar into her mug and tested it. "Not sure, but I think she responded to something on TikTok or Instagram."

"You're thinking she saw a video on TikTok or Instagram offering some job opportunities?"

"No. Have you seen any TikTok videos?"

"A few."

Tess gave her a pitying look. "Okay, well, they don't *say* it like that. It's more like there's this superslick video, right? Someone's all like, 'I made four K in three days just using my phone,' and then they're in a car or on a beach or whatever. Real flex-y." She bounced around in her seat, with too much energy to be "flex-y." "And the caption's all, 'Comment yes or DM me if you want in.' You know?"

This girl didn't need more sugar added to her caffeine.

"So she commented or messaged the poster."

"Yeah. And then they hit you back, like, 'We're only taking a few more people,' which is total cap, but Sheri thought it was legit. Said it was like a remote assistant thing, posting content, moderating lives, basic stuff."

KC rubbed her temples. Total cap? Must mean, total BS. *Man, I'm getting old.*

"Did she ever tell you the name of the company?"

Tess stirred her drink. "Nah. She just said it was like a start-up or something. Honestly, I thought it was sus, but she was hyped."

*Sus? Ah, suspicious!*

"Do you remember what the person looked like in the video? Or the account name?"

*Ting, ting, ting.* The spoon in Tess's hand jittered against her cup. "No clue on the name, but the girl in the video was super pretty, like, influencer pretty. You know the type, lashes for days, neon nails, that baby-voice thing they do."

KC arched a brow.

Tess waved the spoon, arcing a spray of coffee across the table. "It's a thing."

"Did she say anything else about this company? Or job?"

The girl sipped her drink, a crease between her brows. Maybe she realized she added too much sugar, or maybe she was trying hard to think. "Nope, just that someone was going to meet her after her last shift." She glanced at her phone, swigged the rest of her coffee, and sprang up. "Sorry, break's over. I gotta get back to work."

"Thank you." KC handed Tess her card. "Call me if you remember anything else."

Walking back to her car, KC felt the familiar chill that came with recognizing a pattern. A beautiful influencer. A too-good-to-be-true opportunity. A young woman who trusted the wrong person.

How many other Sheri's were out there, scrolling through their feeds, about to comment yes on the wrong video?

# CHAPTER 5

## THE TOWN CAR

Pine Grove Market's parking lot shimmered beyond her windshield. According to Tess, someone would be meeting Sheri after her last shift. Hutchins claimed no usable video, but KC would bet he hadn't looked beyond the obvious places.

She shifted her gaze to Landen Family Drug Mart next door. Time to do the legwork that should've been done weeks ago.

"Hey, KC! Don't tell me your aunt is sick." Tucker, who'd inherited the store from his father, had gone to school with her.

"Nah, she's fine. How's business?" She scanned the store, a few customers were browsing the aisles. A mom and a child sat by the pharmacy window waiting for prescriptions. The pharmacist spotted KC and waved. She returned the gesture.

"Can't complain. Small-town folks are still loyal to locals." Bent forward, he folded his arms near the register.

"Didn't expect to see you on register?"

"Just so she can go on a break." He swapped places with a teen. "So, can I help you find something?"

"Actually, I'm hoping you could check your records to see who was working the afternoon Sheri Conners went missing. That would be—"

"I was here. I remember."

She snapped her gaze toward him. "You do?"

"Yup, but only because of the town car."

"Excuse me?"

"I didn't see her come out of the store. Only that she got into a town car. Black. Shiny. You know, she wasn't in school when we were there. So, I didn't know her. But I saw her around. If it wasn't for the town car, I wouldn't have noticed."

"Did you catch the plate?"

He shook his head. "Sorry, didn't think anything of it until I saw the flyer."

"Do you have cameras out front?"

"No, we have one in here and one out back by the pharmacy. It's the drugs we need to be concerned about."

"All right, thanks."

Memory said the gift shop across the street had a camera.

After saying goodbye to Tucker, KC crossed Main Street to Pine Grove Treasures. The bell chimed as she entered, and vanilla candles mixed with the scent of Florida-themed merchandise.

"Can I help you?" A woman in her fifties approached from behind a postcard display, her Midwest accent unmistakable.

KC showed her badge. "Detective Cassidy. I'm hoping you can help with an investigation."

The woman's smile faded. "I'm Linda Morrison. I've only had the shop about eight months."

"I'm looking into the disappearance of a young woman who worked across the street. About five weeks ago. Do you have security cameras outside?"

"Yes, but the footage isn't stored here. Guardian Security handles all that." Linda gestured toward a small camera above the door. "They keep everything for sixty days, although I can access it online here."

"Can you give me their contact information? I'll need to request the official footage."

"Of course." Linda handed her a business card from behind the counter. "Such a worry for her family. Any word on where she might be?"

KC kept her expression neutral. "We're still investigating."

Linda then led her to the cramped office and logged into the security portal. Within minutes, they were watching grainy footage of Sheri walking to the curb and climbing into a black town car.

The bell dinged.

"Excuse me." Linda wedged by. "I need to tend to a customer."

"No problem." KC pulled out her phone and took several photos of the screen, focusing on the license plate. The resolution wasn't great, but it might be enough to start a search.

She rewound the footage, watching Sheri's confident stride to the curb. No hesitation. No fear. She'd been expecting this ride.

But what kind of employer sends a town car to scoop up a twenty-one-year-old in Pine Grove?

And why was she now dead, thirty-five miles away?

# CHAPTER 6

## UNTIL THE NEXT CALL

After reviewing the footage at Pine Grove Treasures, KC sat in her car debating her next move. The grainy stills weren't much, but they were something. The boyfriend would have to wait. How could it be approaching 4 p.m. already?

Time to regroup at Aunt Mae's.

Several minutes later, she parked on Aunt Mae's driveway. She'd driven past her old bungalow and caught herself glancing at the driveway where her car used to sit. How many mornings had she rushed out of that front door, coffee in hand, late for some case or another?

She got out and went around to the back. Sir Nick was already stationed behind the screen door, paws braced like he'd been assigned sentry duty.

KC punched in the code and let herself in. As soon as she stepped inside, the Doberman pressed into her with a full-body lean, tail thumping hard enough to rattle the umbrella stand.

"Easy, boy." She dropped her bag by the door and kneeled to rub behind his ears. "You act like it's been a year."

The house smelled faintly of garlic and lemon oil. She got

up, followed the scent into the kitchen, flipped on the lights and headed straight for the fridge with Sir Nick close on her heels.

A foil-covered plate waited dead center on the top shelf with a sticky note. "Heat for 1:30. Eat like a human."

How did she do that? Aunt Mae seemed to know where KC would look when she got to town. Anyhow, she dutifully removed the foil, put the plate in the microwave, set the time, and pressed start.

While the lasagna spun in the microwave, she pulled out her phone and dialed Janelle. Sir Nick stood by her, eyeing the magic machine and hoping some goodies would come his way.

"Nothing yet." Janelle spoke before KC could.

"Oh, come on. Give me something."

"What can I tell you? Prints are still waiting to be processed. CSU logged the flyer, the scene, the soil samples. Everything's bagged but not analyzed. Tox screen hasn't dropped. You're still slotted for autopsy tomorrow. Have you looked at the video and the report? That should keep you occupied for some time."

KC winced. "Sorry, got sidetracked. I'll do it later. Speaking of videos, I have some stills from a surveillance camera. Sending them to you now." She texted them to Janelle. "Do you think tech can clean them up?"

Janelle didn't answer for a moment. "I don't know. I'll send them over, but I wouldn't hold my breath. You know the backlog, and they're really bad shots."

Not what KC wanted to hear. "Can you submit them, anyway?"

"Of course."

"Oh, can you also call Guardian Security and request the footage?" She gave the details.

"Okay. Anything else?"

"That's it for now. Thanks." She ended the call and grabbed the plate from the microwave. She set it on the table, took out a fork, and sat.

Sir Nick looked at the plate with pleading eyes.

"Sorry, not for you. I haven't eaten anything since breakfast." She ate with her right hand and petted the dog with her left. "I miss you too. So, what do you think? How did Sheri end up in Orlando? Hmm, I miss this. Really should come back more often."

Sir Nick stood by her legs, begging.

"Told you, no. What? You think the boyfriend had something to do with it? But there's that sketchy job. You know, I should check with Aunt Mae. See how Jill is doing." She took the last bite and lowered the plate to the floor. "Here you go. Clean it up."

Then she dialed Aunt Mae.

"Hey," Aunt Mae answered.

"Just checking in. How's Jill?"

"She's still quiet. But she's not alone." A pause. "She keeps holding the flyer. Doesn't say much. Just… holds it. I've alerted the church women's group. They'll be bringing meals and coming to sit with her."

"Thank you!"

"Of course. That's what we do in this town. We take care of each other. Oh, I told her you'd find whoever did this."

KC winced. Her aunt shouldn't have made that promise. "I'll do my best."

She ended the call and set the phone aside. Sir Nick plopped down with a sigh, resting his head on her foot. "So what do we have so far?" And what should she do next?

Her phone buzzed again. Tanner.

"Hey."

"Tell me you're not living on gas station peanuts."

"Better. Aunt Mae's lasagna."

"You're in Pine Grove? Did you take a day off?"

"No." She went on to explain the case without getting into

details. "I got some grainy photos off a security feed. I'm not sure how soon I can get these cleaned up."

"No visible plate?"

"Can't read it. Lab's got a line out the door."

"Let me ask Deanna."

"It's not your case or even a Fed case."

"Yeah, well, she knows people in the lab world. Maybe she knows who you need to ask. I'm texting her now."

She didn't argue, and they chatted until another call came in. Deanna. "She's calling me now."

"Talk to her." He clicked off.

She switched to the other call. "Hi, Deanna."

"KC, send the photos to Jack Stamps." Deanna didn't bother with greetings.

"Who's he?"

"The lab guy with Orlando Prime."

"You mean the new one?" The governor had already set up Prime units, elite crime-fighting units, in Miami and Tampa. Orlando Prime was the newest expansion.

"Not that new anymore. In operation for about two years now. Anyway, he's got some experimental cleanup software. Said he'd be happy to test it."

"Are you sure?"

"Positive. I was on the phone with him when Tanner texted. His team was chasing some serial killer. He wanted to know if we've ever come across—never mind that. I think they report directly to the governor. Their jurisdiction is quite wide. And not a favor. Professional curiosity is all. I'm texting you his phone and email. Send him the photos, and he'll let you know."

"Wow! Thank you!"

"Sure thing."

They ended the call. KC picked up the plate from the floor and put it in the dishwasher. She had just pulled the lid off the

Keurig and was about to put in a new K-Cup when her phone buzzed again.

Dispatch.

"Cassidy."

"Detective, we've got a body. South trailhead near Lake Jesup. Uniforms are on-site."

*So much for coffee!* She took a quick scan to make sure she didn't leave anything. "Text me the location. I'm en route."

# CHAPTER 7

## THE PATTERN EMERGES

### ORLANDO, FL

The smell hit KC the moment she stepped out of her car, wet earth and something that made her stomach clench as she clipped her badge to her belt.

A curtain of humidity clung to the air, heavy with the scent of dewy grass and cypress mulch. The rhythmic squawk of a distant hawk echoed above. Otherwise, the clearing was quiet, eerily so. Crickets chirped from the nearby brush, oblivious to the crime scene unfolding beyond the barricade tape.

Uniformed officers milled about, careful not to step past the perimeter markers. Yellow tape fluttered at the edges of the dense woods where Spanish moss draped from ancient oaks like ghostly curtains.

A white tent had been partially erected around the excavation site, though the wind kept flapping the tarp against the frame like a restless warning. Disturbed earth and scattered pine needles marked where the dog had clawed at the shallow grave, exposing what lay beneath.

KC approached the first officer standing guard with a clipboard.

"Detective Cassidy, Orlando PD." She flashed her badge. "Who found her?"

Her phone buzzed, but she ignored it. She never took calls while walking a fresh scene, too many details to miss.

"Family with a dog. Father and his eight-year-old daughter were throwing a Frisbee when their golden retriever took off into the woods and wouldn't come back. When they went looking..." The officer shook his head. "Kid didn't see much, but the father's pretty shaken. We've got them waiting in one of the cruisers."

He thumbed toward the lot. "Body was buried in a shallow grave about twenty feet off the path. Dog must've caught the scent. Been in the ground maybe four, five days from the looks of it."

KC nodded, scanning the underbrush, the brim of her ball cap shading her eyes. She made a slow, deliberate path toward the taped-off scene. Leaves crunched underfoot. A mosquito buzzed past her ear. Her gaze swept the surroundings: access points, possible drop zones, tire impressions in the soft dirt where the ground sloped toward a service road.

Then movement caught her eye.

A figure ducked beneath the tape from the perimeter's far side, his stride confident. Crisp button-down rolled to the elbows, and a clean-shaven face too polished for local law enforcement.

KC straightened. "Excuse me—" Her hand brushed her badge.

He raised a black leather credential holder, flipping it open without slowing. "Commander Frank Travers. Orlando Prime."

Her eyebrows shot up. The commander of the elite Prime Unit? She put the man in his mid-forties and fit.

He crossed the space between them with practiced ease and extended a hand. Blue eyes sharp, the creases between them intense. "Detective Kylie Cassidy, right? Been meaning to meet the woman who got Jack all worked up."

She took his hand, still processing. "Please call me KC. I presume you mean Jack Stamps. But what do you mean, 'worked up'?"

"Yes, our Jack. I understand you sent him stills from surveillance footage. He ran them through his software. He was able to see a couple of letters and a number—"

Only a partial.

"—but that was enough. We had another partial. He uses some fancy terms, something to do with the angle, pixels, or whatever. Bottom line, we now have a plate."

KC frowned. "You lost me. What other partial?"

He pursed his lips, his gaze drifting toward the white tent. "Our team is chasing a serial killer. We flag any bodies with organs removed. About your victim, since we haven't gotten any notification, I assume no autopsy yet."

A serial killer? Her pulse quickened. "Correct. It's scheduled for tomorrow. The ME investigator didn't mention any missing organs."

"They're smart. They close up the wounds. A cursory exam wouldn't tell the investigator anything until the body is on the table." He scanned the scene even as he talked, visibly taking in details with the same methodical approach she used. "So, KC, Jack told me the surveillance footage was from a shop in Pine Grove. Isn't that a bit out of your jurisdiction?"

"Yeah, the victim was from Pine Grove. She was a missing person there, so I went to talk to the detective, hoping for some leads."

"And?"

She hesitated. "Let's just say, the file is pretty thin. Since that's my hometown and my old beat, I, uh—"

"Did what the other cop should have done. Commendable."

Heat crept up her neck. "Are you suggesting it was some organ harvesting operation, sir?"

"We don't know yet. So far, we only have three bodies. This morning's will make four. And we don't know about this one."

"All missing organs? Any leads?"

He did that lip-pursing again, his attention divided between her and the crime scene. "Why don't we walk the scene here together? I have no intention of bigfooting your case—er, cases. But the one body this morning, it's ours. I've cleared it with your lieutenant. I thought he'd have called you by now."

Something cold settled in her chest. *Cleared it.* Past tense. Decision already made. She'd been standing here thinking they were collaborating, maybe even that her work had impressed them enough to bring her in. But they'd already decided, before he'd met her, before he'd seen what she could do.

Of course, Coleman would have called. She'd been so focused on the scene that she'd ignored... She pulled out her phone. Yep, Coleman had left a voicemail, and so had Jack.

"Excuse me a moment." Her thumb swiped the screen with more force than necessary. Coleman's message was short and to the point—hand it over to Orlando Prime. Jack's voicemail mentioned he'd gotten a plate and the commander might be contacting her.

While Coleman's message confirmed what she'd feared, the commander drifted toward where most of the activity was clustered. Her case. Her body. Her town, her leads, her surveillance footage that cracked it open. And now they were just... taking it.

The bitter chill in her throat had a name: Cheated.

She forced herself to speak evenly. "Yes, sir. Let's do this together."

He nodded. Military bearing. Politician hair. "Lead the way, Detective."

KC lifted her chin and started toward the white tent, praying the body wouldn't tell the same story as the others. Because if it did, she'd just lost her first real case to a serial killer, and there went the chance to prove she belonged here.

# CHAPTER 8

## THE HANDOVER

K C ducked under the tent flap, and the smell hit her like a punch, decomposition mixed with damp earth. The smell never got easier. Four days in Florida humidity.

Luna was already there, kneeling beside the shallow grave. She looked up, ponytail swaying as she adjusted her position. Her face brightened when she saw Travers. "Commander! I wasn't expecting to see you here. Is this your case?"

"Don't know yet." Travers crouched beside Luna. "For now, it's Detective Cassidy's case."

"Okay, so far, we've got a female, late teens or early twenties. Been here four to five days, give or take. No ID on her. CSU says, no bag or phone nearby."

KC pulled out her notebook. "Luna, you said four to five days. Can you narrow that down? I need to know when she was last seen alive."

"Not externally." Luna adjusted her gloves. "No ligature marks. No defensive wounds I can see. There's some bruising around the ribs, but hard to tell the cause until we get her on the table."

The woman's skin was mottled, bloated in some areas,

sunken in others. Hair tangled with pine needles and soil. What had brought her here? Who was missing her right now?

"Would you notice if something were done surgically?" Travers asked.

Luna nodded. "Of course, Commander. Let me check for any postmortem incisions."

Luna's hands stilled over the abdomen. She leaned closer, adjusting her angle to catch the light. "KC, look at this."

KC moved to Luna's shoulder. A thin line, barely visible, ran horizontally across the lower torso.

"This isn't decomposition patterning." Luna traced the air above the mark without touching. "See how straight it is? And here—" She pointed to tiny marks along the line. "Suture points. Someone opened her up and closed her back up. Clean work too."

KC's pen stopped moving across her notepad. Another one.

Travers straightened and cursed under his breath. "That matches our guy."

She stepped closer to Luna. "You can't confirm there was a surgical procedure out here, right?"

"No, not until the ME gets her on the table." Luna documented her findings, then shrugged. "Could have been anything."

Voices rose outside. The tarp shifted as a breeze carried snippets of conversation.

"...Orlando Prime is here. You think it's connected to the Echo Park girl?"

"...that's Commander Travers. Get a shot—"

The familiar voice made her turn. Todd Rowe again, the *StreetBeat News* guy, standing just outside the tape, phone held high like a weapon.

"Detective Cassidy!" he called out. "Any comment on the connection between this body and Echo Park?"

Travers stepped forward, his height and presence enough to make Todd flinch. "Back behind the tape. Now."

"But, Commander, Orlando Prime doesn't usually respond to—"

"We're done here." Travers's voice carried the kind of authority that ended conversations.

Rowe hesitated, then backed away, phone still recording.

KC's jaw tightened. "He's been dogging me since Echo Park."

"He can keep dogging. Just not here." Travers turned to Luna again. "Timeline on the autopsy? If this matches our pattern, we'll be taking over tomorrow."

"Yes, sir. I'll bag and transport as soon as CSU is done."

He nodded, then faced KC. "It looks like this is our guy, but I'll wait for the ME confirmation."

KC clung to hope. Her gaze drifted back to the shallow grave. Two bodies in one day. One fresh and one decomposing. Why was there a missing person flyer at Echo Park and not here? Was that a mistake or a deliberate distraction?

She knelt beside the grave again. "Luna, can you get me a close-up of that incision line before you transport?"

"I'll email them tonight." Luna held up her portable scanner. "And got a hit on the prints. Celina Bishop, twenty-one, Orlando address. Driver's license photo matches what I can see of facial structure."

KC photographed the scanner screen and stood, brushing pine needles from her pants. Travers had stepped away, speaking into his phone, his back to them.

She scanned the scene again. Tire impressions. Partial footprints. Broken ferns where someone had dragged or carried weight. She snapped a few photos with her phone before CSU flagged the area. Everything might matter later.

A breeze rustled through the pines as Travers finished his call and returned. "As soon as the ME confirms, I'll let your lieutenant know." He started to leave, paused, pivoted. "Good job on that surveillance footage."

As she followed him out of the tent, the press shouted questions again. Travers sidestepped them with an occasional "no comment." KC took the opportunity to slip by the crowd.

The sun was almost gone now, the trees casting long shadows across the forest floor. Crime scene lights created an artificial day within the darkness.

KC had Celina Bishop's address pulled up before she reached her car. If the autopsy confirmed missing organs tomorrow morning, Travers would take over by noon. She started the engine. Time to find out who wanted Celina Bishop dead and why.

# CHAPTER 9

## A WEEK OF SILENCE

The building manager's office smelled like instant coffee and disappointment, but Diane Palmer's first words cut through the mundane atmosphere like a blade.

"Celina looked thrilled about something the last time I saw her." Palmer adjusted her bifocals as she squinted at KC across the cluttered desk. "When I asked what had her so happy, she said she'd gotten this great job offer."

KC looked up from her notepad. "What kind of job?"

"That's just it. She wouldn't say. Said it was confidential, but that it was going to change everything for her."

Something cold twisted in her gut. This sounded like the same scheme Sheri had fallen for. Different towns, same pitch. Someone out there was good at making young women disappear. "What else can you tell me about her?"

"Apartment 204. Sweet girl, never any trouble. Rent always on time, never complained about the neighbors." She paused, looking up from the laptop. "Is she in some kind of trouble?"

KC kept her expression neutral. "You said she was excited when you last saw her. When was that?"

"Oh, let me think." Palmer tapped her pen against the desk, a nervous habit that matched the coffee rings staining the wood surface. "Maybe five days ago? She was getting her mail." A small gasp escaped her mouth. "Oh, she asked about getting the bathroom faucet fixed."

"Did you fix it?"

"Sent Miguel over the next day. Yes, he closed the maintenance report but noted the tenant wasn't home. She was probably at school or at work." Palmer's face creased.

KC made a note. Five days ago would put it close to the time of death. "Other than that, notice anything else?"

Head shaking, Palmer shifted in her chair, the vinyl squeaking. "She was one of the quiet ones. Never had parties, never played music too loud. The kind of tenant you appreciate but don't think about, you know? Good tenants sort of disappear into the background."

"Any recent changes in her routine? New visitors? Anything out of the ordinary?"

Palmer rocked back in her chair. "Not that I noticed. She kept to herself, mostly. Sometimes I'd see her coming home late from classes, but that's about it. You should ask her boyfriend. He would know. They live together."

"Boyfriend?" The word came out sharper than KC intended. Could be a real lead.

"Yes, hang on." Palmer tapped some keys. "Kevin Rankin."

"You have a phone number?"

Palmer gave it to her.

"Can you describe him?"

"Tall guy, about Celina's age. Dark hair, kind of stocky build. Wears work clothes daily, those heavy boots, uniform shirts."

KC scribbled more notes. "When did you last see him?"

"You know, I haven't seen that truck around for a week or so. I just figured they were both busy with work and school."

"Did they seem to have any problems? Arguments, anything like that?"

"Not that I ever witnessed. They seemed like a normal couple. He'd help her carry groceries sometimes, that sort of thing." Palmer leaned forward. "Is something wrong? Has something happened to Celina?"

KC avoided the question. "This boyfriend. Do you know where he works?"

The manager consulted the laptop. "Says here, Oakwood Heating and Air."

KC closed her notepad. "Is there anything else you can think of? Any detail, no matter how small?"

Palmer was quiet, staring out the window overlooking the parking lot. "No, nothing comes to mind."

KC stood. "Thank you."

A few minutes later, KC sat in her car, tapping the steering wheel. The numbers on the apartment door refused to change. The brass 204 glinted against the stucco as the sun dipped lower, throwing long shadows across the second-floor landing. Even from the parking lot, she could see they weren't quite lined up. The building was trying a little too hard to look put together.

No flickering light behind the curtains. No movement in the breezeway. Just the slow crawl of twilight across the two-story beige stucco building that stretched before her in a tired afterthought, its outdoor metal stairwells zigzagging up to the second floor as if the fire escapes had given up caring.

The Florida winter air carried that strange Orlando mix of cooling concrete and lingering heat trapped in the pavement. Palm fronds rustled overhead, their sound similar to paper shuffling through empty offices. Behind the building, a narrow hedge ran along the property line, neat but tired. A playground stood just beyond it, empty this time of night, one swing shifting in the breeze like it hadn't been used in a while.

No security cameras that she could see. Minimal lighting, just enough yellow bulbs to keep the complex from being completely dark, but not enough to make anyone feel truly safe.

The kind of place where people minded their own business until someone vanished.

While she waited, she switched gears back to Sheri's case. Time to make the call she'd been putting off.

She dialed Brian Shipley's number and waited through three rings.

"Yeah?" He sounded tired, strained. Background noise suggested he was in a busy place—voices, footsteps, the distant beep of medical equipment.

"Brian Shipley? This is Detective Kylie Cassidy. Orlando PD. Do you have a moment?"

"Is this about Sheri? Did you find her?"

Hmm. Either he hadn't heard about Sheri's death yet, or he was a great actor.

"Her mom mentioned she had a job offer?" KC scooted back in the seat. "Any idea?"

A pause. Then just breathing. "I haven't talked to her for a couple of months. She was acting kind of secretive before she vanished. And she was always chasing these big dreams. Modeling, acting, influencer stuff. I just…" His voice dropped lower. "I can't talk right now, seriously."

"Where are you?"

"At work. Shands Hospital. Gotta go—"

"Okay. We'll…" Click.

She set the phone beside her. The question hung in the air. *Did you find her?* Like he was expecting bad news but hoping for good. Or like he knew what had happened and was playing dumb.

The shadows had lengthened while she'd been on the phone. Porch lights were starting to flicker on across the complex, casting yellow pools on the concrete walkways and metal stairwells. Somewhere nearby, someone was cooking. The smell of onions and garlic drifted through the cracked window, soft and sharp against the humid Florida air.

Finally, a dusty blue pickup turned into the lot, the Oakwood Heating and Air logo on the side.

Kevin Rankin.

He stepped out. The truck had seen better days with dents in the bed and a windshield spider-webbed from too many Florida storms. His boots hit the ground with a heavy thud, steel-toed work boots scuffed from their share of crawl spaces and attics. He looked up at apartment 204, shoulders hunched.

Thirty seconds later, a silver sedan pulled into the lot and parked two spaces away.

A woman stepped out, in jeans and a T-shirt, bag slung over one shoulder. Mid-twenties, maybe. Dark hair tied in a ponytail. She moved with the purposeful stride of someone who belonged here, but her posture suggested this wasn't a casual visit.

Kevin looked over and saw her. Waved. Then they moved toward each other.

KC sat up straighter. Too casual. Too timed. One week without contact, and now he was back with a different woman?

# CHAPTER 10

## PRESSURE POINTS

The Hub was quieting down, but Frank Travers wasn't finished.

He stepped inside the bullpen, damp from drizzle and road dust, and beelined for the evidence board. The converted warehouse space was empty now, industrial pendant lights casting long shadows across exposed brick walls. Desks sat abandoned, half-drunk coffee cold beside silent monitors. His team was either gone for the day or out chasing leads.

The evidence board held five photos pinned in two neat rows. Kasey Gallo, Monica Lewis, Rosa Ortega from the earlier cases. Then Sheri Conners and Celina Bishop from this week. Not all blonde, but all young. All college age. All dead.

He pulled his jacket off, tossed it over the back of his chair, and sighed into the seat. The leather creaked under his weight. He rubbed at the base of his neck where tension had knotted itself into a permanent ache.

Officer Keller appeared in the doorway, gesturing someone forward. "Commander, Miles Green to see you."

The public information manager, still in his shirtsleeves and windbreaker, gestured toward the conference room. His tie hung loose, and sweat beaded along his hairline despite the evening chill. He looked like a man who had his car keys in one hand and a migraine in the other.

"Frank, you got a minute?" He started toward the glass-paneled room.

Frank pushed back from his desk and followed Miles upstairs and into the conference room. "Didn't you clock out two hours ago?"

Miles shut the door with more force than necessary. The sound echoed against the brick walls and high ceiling. "I was halfway to the parking garage when the mayor's office called. Said, WFTV is getting pushback from their city desk. One of the journalists at the afternoon crime scene didn't like being stonewalled, so they went digging. Now, someone upstairs wants answers."

"Let them want."

Miles paced to the window overlooking the parking lot. Rain streaked the glass, distorting the streetlights into amber smears. "Frank, they're already whispering about a serial. I only knew of two… three now, counting today. Is it true?"

Frank had worked hard to keep a lid on the cases. If Miles only knew about two, then the containment was holding, for now. Frank sank into a chair, posture stiff against the day's pressures. "We may, but I don't want any of this to get out."

Miles crossed his arms. "Do we have more than three bodies?"

"Maybe."

"Come on." Miles widened his stance. "You gotta give me something. The media's going to run with it whether we confirm or not. I need to know what I can say before I get ambushed again."

"We haven't confirmed anything. No autopsies, no lab work, no suspect. Until we do, the official line is that it's an active investigation. That's it."

"And when the governor's press secretary calls?"

"Tell them we don't speculate. We investigate."

Miles exhaled hard through his nose, his breath fogging the window. "The mayor's going to want more than that by tomorrow morning. Channel 6 is running teasers about a possible connection."

Frank leaned back in his chair, studying Miles's reflection in the dark window. Twenty years of wrangling reporters, and Miles still let politics get under his skin. "Then tell him to call me directly."

The guy obviously wanted to argue, jaw clenched, hands balled into fists. "Fine." He pivoted his glare to Frank. He must've thought better of arguing. "But if this leaks and it's chaos by sunrise, I'm sending them your way."

"You always do."

Miles left the conference room, muttering something under his breath that didn't sound flattering. Keller escorted him back toward the entrance.

Frank returned to his desk and opened his tablet but found himself staring at the evidence board instead. Five victims across three months. The earlier three had seemed random, different locations, but all within their jurisdiction. Kasey Gallo, found in a drainage ditch on Orlando's east side. Monica Lewis, discovered in a vacant lot in Orange County. Rosa Ortega, pulled from a lake just inside Seminole County.

And now, with Sheri Conners and Celina Bishop…

He brought up the case files on his tablet, cross-referencing details. Same age range. Same general build. Similar cause of death, pending final autopsy results. The geographic spread was deliberate, scattered across their territory to slow down pattern recognition.

Someone was hunting college-aged women. Someone smart enough to know how law enforcement worked.

Beyond the kitchen and courtyard, the low hum of machines drifted from Jack's lab, steady, tireless, like the man himself.

A soft knock interrupted Frank's thoughts. Keller appeared in the doorway again, this time with a different visitor.

"Assistant State Attorney Watkins." Keller's tone suggested he'd rather escort a raccoon than the man now stepping inside.

Gavin Watkins walked up as if he owned the place. His suit was pressed, his smile practiced, and his cologne unable to conceal his whiskey breath.

Frank stood.

"Frank." Watkins extended his hand, a politician's grin spreading across his face. "Heard you had a scene today."

Frank shook his hand. Outside, the soft tap of rain against the windows muffled the distant hum of traffic on Highway 50. "Are you here on an official visit?"

"Official. The mayor's office has been getting calls. Rumors are making their way up to Tallahassee. Governor's team, maybe even the AG."

Frank sat back at his desk and gestured for Watkins to sit. "They think we've got a repeat offender?"

"They're asking. And the state attorney wants to make sure we're not caught flat-footed if this explodes."

"Well, we don't know what we've got yet."

Watkins moved his feet, his leather shoes echoing against the polished concrete floor. "That's why I'm here. To ensure this investigation stays airtight from the beginning. No missteps, no weak evidence, no missed warrants. I can help with that."

Watkins was sweating despite the air-conditioning, and his hands trembled as he adjusted his tie. Something was off with this ASA.

Frank braced his elbows on his armrests. "You okay?"

Watkins attempted a smile. "It's been a rough week. My son's been in and out of the hospital. It wears on you."

"I'm sorry to hear that. Hope it's nothing serious."

"Thank you. We've got it managed."

Frank nodded.

"So, about the cases? Anything you can tell me?"

"Nothing really. It's early in the investigation yet. We'll be sure to have the paperwork in order."

Watkins straightened his jacket. "I've been asked to offer legal oversight. With the press circling, it wouldn't hurt to have someone in the loop."

Hands locked over his torso, Frank sat back. "Right."

Watkins gave a faint, humorless chuckle, but his eyes didn't match.

Frank didn't push, but the tension settled in the air like humidity before a storm.

"Offer noted." He crossed one knee over the other, the tablet beckoning. "Now, unless you're going to suggest a drink, I've got to get to this document."

"This is going to explode, Frank. Public wants answers. And the mayor wants assurance that someone competent is at the helm."

The governor wouldn't have asked Frank to lead the team if he hadn't thought Frank was competent. But he swallowed the remark. "Then it's a good thing I'm not going anywhere."

Watkins turned to leave, his cologne lingering in his wake.

The desk phone rang.

Lt. Andre Coleman.

# CHAPTER 11

## THE APARTMENT

The last of the daylight was fading, rain turning the pavement slick as KC approached the pair standing in the parking lot. Kevin Rankin faced the woman. The woman was talking. "...you sure?"

The woman stopped as soon as KC held up her badge. "Detective Cassidy, Major Crimes. Kevin Rankin?"

He frowned. "Yes?"

KC eyed the woman. "And who's your friend?"

He swiveled his head to glance at the woman as if he had just noticed her. "Oh, this is Lisbeth, Celina's, uh, my girlfriend's sister."

Lisbeth edged in closer. "Is this about Celina?"

"What made you think that?"

"Well, I can't get a hold of her. She didn't answer my text or call. We were supposed to plan a trip home to Charleston."

KC inhaled. Her gaze flew from Lisbeth to Kevin, then to the keys dangling in his hand. "Mind if we talk inside?"

"Yeah, sure." He let Lisbeth go first, waiting for KC until she gestured him on ahead.

She followed them up a narrow exterior staircase to the

second floor. The walkway creaked underfoot. Apartment 204 was at the end, a plastic doormat curling at the edges. He unlocked the door and stepped aside, holding it open with a nervous gesture.

The inside hit her like a still frame from someone's paused life. The place was tidy. A mug still on the table, a jacket draped over the back of a chair. The whiteboard calendar on the wall was filled with neat handwriting, class notes, deadlines, a red-circled reminder. "Call back re: job?"

It smelled faintly of lavender and something warmer, lived-in. She tilted her head toward the couch and chair. "Maybe we should sit?"

The two exchanged nervous glances, then sat on opposite ends of the couch. Lisbeth laid her purse on the side table. KC sat on the chair.

"I'm sorry to have to tell both of you. A body was discovered earlier today. We believe it's Celina Bishop."

"No!" Lisbeth put a hand on her mouth.

He froze, then shook his head. "No, no, you're wrong. She's fine. She just needs to cool off. She'll be back. I was going to apologize. I was going to tell her I loved her. She just needed space. Probably went off somewhere…"

"I'm sorry." KC sat stiff while he continued his rant.

When he accepted the truth, he put his face in his hands and sniffed. Unless he was an Oscar-winning actor, his denial and grief were genuine.

Lisbeth, on the other hand, was quiet, tears pooling in her eyes, burgundy throw pillow hugged in her lap.

KC gave them a moment, rose, drifted through the apartment like a shadow. She'd check the bedroom later. The living area and kitchen looked undisturbed. Lots of magnets on the refrigerator door, a save the date from an engaged couple, another calendar, nothing written on it, photos, friends, family.

When she returned to the chair, the two were composed

enough. She faced Kevin first. "Did you not notice she was missing?"

"Nah, we had this stupid fight. Can't even remember what about. She gets like that. All hot and angry. So, I just went to crash at a buddy's. I gave her a day to cool off. Then I kept texting her and called, but she didn't answer. I just thought…" He slammed a fist on the couch. "I should have come and checked."

"Don't blame yourself. There's nothing you could have done. Did she mention any job offer?"

He jerked his head up, frowning. "Don't think so. Why? Did something happen at work?"

"When was the last time you saw her?"

"Like six days ago. Been crashing at my buddy's, then pulling doubles, need the OT. This gig pays overtime, you know? I kept texting her."

"Right. So, you had a fight. You took off, tried to contact her, but she didn't respond. What made you show up this evening?"

He shrugged. "I figured she was ghosting me, so I'd swing by. Maybe we could work it out."

"All right. I'll need your friend and this job's contact information."

He rattled off the names, reading numbers from his phone while KC jotted them down. She capped her pen and shifted in her chair, studying Lisbeth's face. The woman had been quiet during Kevin's breakdown, too quiet for someone who'd just lost her sister. "What brought you here tonight, Lisbeth?"

"Like I said, we were supposed to plan a trip home. She wasn't texting me back or answering my calls. So, I thought I'd stop by. I was working evenings, and today is my day off."

"Where do you work?"

"Orlando Hospital. I'm a nurse."

"Did she ever mention a job to you?"

Lisbeth squeezed the throw pillow to her chest. "Not exactly. But… I might've sent her something. A video."

KC tilted her head. "What kind of video?"

"One of those TikToks." Lisbeth let the pillow drop on her lap, slid a finger along its tasseled side. "It was dumb. A modeling side hustle kind of thing, you know, the usual spam that pops up. I thought it was a scam or a joke. I sent it to her as a laugh."

KC's pen hovered above her notebook. "How long ago?"

"A week or two ago."

"And did she respond?"

"I think she just liked the message." Lisbeth twisted tassel strings. "I didn't think she'd do anything with it."

KC's heartbeat picked up. This sounded like the same tactic. "Anything else come to mind? Any other unusual behavior? Arguments? Secrets?"

Lisbeth opened her mouth, then closed it. "No. Nothing."

Kevin ran a hand over his hair, grabbed the back of his head. "She didn't tell me about that video."

"I didn't think it mattered," Lisbeth said. "It was just a video."

"I assume she had a laptop and a phone. Any other electronics? Tablet?"

He lowered his hand, kneading his neck. "No tablet. Just a laptop and a phone. The laptop should be on her desk."

When he pointed to a desk in the corner, KC glanced at it. Nothing was on top. She'd check the drawers before she left. "One more question. There's this whiteboard calendar. There's also a calendar on the fridge door—"

"Oh yeah. That's just for show. I mean, it's there so we can see the dates, especially in the future, easier. Just flip the pages."

She stood up and went over to the desk. The only drawer wasn't big enough for a laptop. She opened it anyway with her gloved hands. No laptop. Just some pens, miscellaneous stationery items. "I'm going to check the bedroom. Maybe the laptop is there."

There was just one bedroom off to the side. The bed was made. No laptop. She peeked under the bed. Nothing. The closet yielded only clothes, shoes, and a suitcase. It would be safe to assume Celina had her phone with her and perhaps her laptop as well. Or did the perp ask her to bring the laptop to get rid of the evidence? Sheri didn't have a laptop, according to Jill. Not a pattern yet.

Back in the living room, the two of them hadn't moved, like they were hoping they'd wake up from this nightmare.

She slipped her card from her coat and set it on the coffee table. "If anything else comes to mind, either of you, day or night, call me."

She moved toward the door, pausing only when Lisbeth spoke again.

"Detective—"

KC turned.

Lisbeth's grip on the pillow tightened. Her mouth opened as if she might confess something else. Instead, she said, "I hope you find out what happened to her."

KC met her gaze. "So do I."

But as she stepped back into the thick, humid night, KC didn't believe for a second that Lisbeth had told her everything.

And whatever she was holding back, it mattered.

# CHAPTER 12

## THE CALL

The rain had stopped, but moisture clung to the steering wheel as KC gripped it, engine idling. Exhaustion pressed behind her eyes like a dull blade.

Missing laptop. Suspicious TikTok video. Lisbeth's hesitation. The sister was hiding something.

Her phone buzzed against the console. A voicemail. She must have missed it. She swiped to listen. Aunt Mae's voice drifted through the speaker. "Just checking in. Jill's holding up okay. The ladies brought food over. We all had dinner together. You need anything, you call me, honey."

KC's mouth curved into her first smile of the day. Aunt Mae never failed her.

Time for the station. Time for paperwork. She dropped the phone and drove out of the lot.

A little while later, she parked and got out. Fluorescent lights hummed over half-empty desks when she pushed through the station doors. The front desk officer sat hunched over crossword puzzles, pen tapping against his teeth. Phones rang unanswered in the background.

Major Crimes looked like a ghost town, except for one figure bent over case files.

Spaulding sat at his desk, trail mix scattered beside an open folder, salt crystals dusting his fingers as he flipped pages.

"Thought you weren't back till tomorrow."

He wiped his hands on a napkin, then flicked a sunflower seed shell off the case file. "Recert wrapped early. Figured I'd check on our overachiever. How'd it go with the body?"

KC snorted and sank into her chair. "Two bodies. But we may be losing them to Orlando Prime." And she briefed him on what had transpired.

He crunched on trail mix. "All good. They want it, they can have it."

While he might feel indifferent, she was miffed. She opened her phone and navigated the department's internal roster, only Travers wasn't listed. Not under OPD anyway.

She dug deeper, pulling up a public press release from two years ago. Francis M. Travers, a retired navy commander, tapped by the governor to lead a newly formed Orlando Prime, reporting directly to the governor with a dotted line to the mayor's office. No formal law enforcement background. No political ties. Just twenty years of decorated service and a reputation for getting results.

"Seriously, who *is* this guy?" She rotated the screen toward Spaulding.

He leaned in. "Travers? Ex-navy. Heard he was a good guy."

KC blinked. "So… not police?"

"Not technically, but if you ask me, he's the kind of guy who makes brass nervous. Probably why they put him in charge of the elite team."

KC closed the screen. "Then I really better not screw this up."

She dropped her notebook beside the keyboard, the thud echoing through the quiet bullpen.

"File that report yet?"

She sat up straighter. Lieutenant Coleman stood in his office doorway, coat draped over one arm, car keys catching the overhead light. The stance of someone who'd been watching for a while.

"Working on it now, Lieutenant."

Coleman stepped back, flicked on his office light. "Then let's hear it while it's fresh. Both of you."

She exchanged glances with Spaulding, who scraped his chair back with a metallic screech. They filed into Coleman's office, the air thick with old coffee and cleaning solution.

Coleman settled behind his desk, hands folded like he was about to hear a confession. His face revealed nothing, not curiosity, not impatience. Just waiting.

She started with Sheri Conners from Pine Grove. She'd gone out for a death notification, only to find the local detective hadn't lifted a finger. So she did it herself. Talked to the boss, coworkers, shopkeepers, and finally, a grainy town car on surveillance footage, all the legwork that should have been done weeks ago.

Then Celina Bishop. Another young woman, another job offer, another family destroyed. Similar age, similar circumstances. Both girls' electronics missing. Both found in isolated locations. Two cases that sang the same deadly song.

Coleman's expression never changed. He might have been listening to a weather report.

When KC finished, silence stretched between them like a taut wire.

At last, he braced his elbows on the desk, chair creaking. "You went to Pine Grove alone?"

"I needed to make the notification. Thought the local had more on the Missing Persons file." She shrugged. "Turns out I was wrong."

"And Frank, uh, Commander Travers showed up at your second scene because of a surveillance photo?"

Heat crawled up KC's neck. "The photo was grainy, terrible quality. I know how backed up we are, so I called, uh, a friend. Long story short, she hooked me up with Jack. I had no clue he was with Prime then. He has some experimental program and managed to enhance the image, got a partial plate. Apparently, Prime has another partial that matches."

Spaulding hooked an ankle over his knee, foot bobbing. Salty fingerprints smeared the front of his button-up. "She worked both scenes while her senior partner was off playing with paper targets. No backup, no support. Just good instincts."

"That's enough." Coleman waved toward the door.

They stood and walked out of the office. She frowned at the glass partition. Beyond it, Coleman reached for his desk phone, fingers already dialing.

"Makes me want to be a fly on that wall," Spaulding muttered, gaze fixed on their lieutenant's lips moving in conversation they couldn't hear. "And you, way to impress the brass!"

KC settled at her desk and opened her laptop. Paperwork first. File the reports while everything was fresh. But while her fingers hovered over the keyboard, her gaze drifted back to Coleman's office.

His free hand drummed against the desk blotter. The way he'd called the commander "Frank" earlier—were they friends? Was Coleman singing her praises right now or handing off two cases that had grown too big for Major Crimes?

The cursor blinked on her blank screen, waiting.

# CHAPTER 13

## MOVING BODIES

F ollowing the freeway sign, KC took the campus exit. Ninety minutes of freeway had dissolved into winding back roads that cut between dormitories and lecture halls. "We're close."

Spaulding's granola bar crackled as he tore it open next to her. "See? When you show off like that, we're stuck with the cases."

"You'd rather us sit on our tush?"

"Just teasing!"

The previous evening, when Coleman came out of his office, she expected him to remind her to hand over the files to Prime. Instead, he told them, "You two continue to work the cases. Just share intel with Prime. They'll do the same."

Spaulding finished the bar. "Kid's probably in Philosophy 101 right now."

"While his girlfriend's in the morgue." Her coffee had gone cold somewhere around mile marker forty-three, but she took another sip, anyway. The bitter sludge matched her mood.

"How did he seem when you talked to him last night?" He brushed crumbs off his jacket.

"He was at work and couldn't talk. I told him I'd be in touch. He's premed. Patient transporter at Shands. Moves bodies around all day, then comes home to study anatomy. I emailed his dossier to you." She checked the GPS as they passed a cluster of brick buildings.

Students hurried between classes under colorful umbrellas, backpacks slung over shoulders.

He tapped his phone, pulled his reading glasses from his shirt pocket, and read. "Brian Shipley, junior, no records, 3.9 GPA. Kid's smart."

"Makes me wonder if it has something to do with why Sheri broke up with him. You know, like she's going nowhere, but he's gonna be a doctor."

"Wants to be a doctor. There's a difference. Let me see here." He kept scrolling. "So, Sheri was going to college but dropped out after a semester. Know why?"

"I'm gonna guess money. Jill, her mom, works in the high school office."

"Is he expecting us?"

"No, speaking of. Call Janelle and ping his phone again. Just to make sure he hasn't bolted."

He dialed Janelle and made the request. Moments later, he ended the call. "Okay, Brian's phone is still there. What do you say, we wait till Prime asks before we turn over anything?"

"You're asking lil ol' me?" She batted her eyes at him. "*You're* the senior detective."

He sighed. "If they play nice, we play nice. Otherwise, we gotta watch out for ourselves."

The morning haze had burned off by the time they found visitor parking near Brian's lecture hall. Students walked in clusters, clutching iced coffees, earbuds in, focused everywhere but ahead.

KC parked in a visitor slot near Brian's building. She turned off the engine.

The clock on her phone read 10:40 a.m. when they entered the corridor outside the psych building.

The hallway roared with voices, zippers, and phone alerts. She stepped aside to avoid a pair of students arguing over a group project. The air smelled faintly of sweat, vending machine coffee, and synthetic berry vape.

She leaned against the cool cinderblock wall, arms folded, watching the rows of identical doors like something might burst through them at any second.

Spaulding stood beside her, scanning the stream of students beginning to trickle out of the psych lecture.

"Blue hoodie, black backpack." He tapped her arm. "Nine o'clock."

There, Brian: tall, thin, all caffeine and anxiety. Odd that he moved slower than the others, his eyes down, earbuds half in.

They approached.

Badge out, KC stepped forward. "Brian Shipley?"

His head snapped up. "Yeah?"

"Detective Cassidy. We spoke last night on the phone. This is Detective Spaulding. Mind if we ask you a few questions?"

Brian's expression shifted. Hope flared, then fear. "Did you find her?"

Spaulding motioned toward the entrance. "Let's go outside and sit."

They moved to a shaded bench on the quad, tucked under a giant oak tree with limbs wide enough to shelter half the lawn. A few students lounged nearby, sipping energy drinks. Others tossed Frisbees. But the spot was in its own quiet corner.

Brian sat forward, elbows on knees, hands laced like a prayer. "She's gone, isn't she?"

She nodded once. "Her body was found yesterday. I'm sorry, Brian."

Stillness settled over him. No gasp, no tears, just the slow collapse of someone absorbing a weight they'd half expected. His knuckles whitened. "I-I figured. But... I didn't want to believe it."

Spaulding took the softer tone. "We know this is hard. We just need a few answers. Help us understand who Sheri was with, what she was involved in."

Leaning closer, KC pressed, "When did you last see her?"

A glance upward. "About two months ago. After Thanksgiving." His voice was hoarse now. "I was home for the holiday. Before I left on Sunday, I ran into her at the store. She said she had something exciting lined up, new job, something big, but she wouldn't tell me more."

"You two were dating then?" she asked.

"We were. Off and on for years." A pause. "She broke up with me in the summer."

"Any reason why?" She kept her tone neutral.

Brian swallowed. "At first, I thought it was the same old deal. She just needed space and would text me again. It was like that. I might comment on a post, and she'd get back with me. But this time, she ghosted me." His gaze drifted away. "She used to be a good student, had dreams to be a vet. But she didn't get the money she needed. Commuted to a local college for a semester. Couldn't hack it."

"Then why make the flyer?" Spaulding asked. "Most guys don't paper a town for an ex."

"Because of Mrs. Conners." Brian flexed his hands, locked them together again, and braced his chin on them. "She was so worried. And it's not like Sheri to disappear like that. The cops didn't do squat."

Heat rose from her belly, and KC pushed it down. If she were still at Pine Grove, she would've done a thorough job.

"About that new job. Did she mention a video or a contact person?"

"Nah, like I said, she wouldn't tell me. Believe me, I asked."

Spaulding studied the young man, then asked, "Any idea why one of your flyers was found close to the body?"

Brian blinked. "Where?"

"Echo Park."

"Echo Park?" Back against the bench, he stared. "She was found *there*? What was she doing there? I haven't been to Echo Park in forever. I have no idea how a flyer ended up there."

Brian probably wasn't the perp, but until the ME gave a more definitive time of death, she couldn't ask for his alibi. "You work at Shands?"

"Yes."

"What do you do?"

He shrugged. "Pushing gurneys, wheelchairs. Basically, moving patients from one place to another. Nothing exciting, but I get to know the doctors."

"Right. Angling for that recommendation letter to med schools." Spaulding smirked.

Brian rose. "I have a class in five minutes. I need to go."

She wanted to say they weren't done yet, but a glance at Spaulding told her they were.

They stood.

"Thanks for your time, Brian." She held out her card. "If you think of anything else, call us."

Brian stuffed it in his pocket and took off.

KC stared at his retreating figure. "He's hiding something."

"Of course. He was fine until we asked him about his job—"

"So why'd you let him leave?" She followed him toward the car.

"My dear padawan, lawyers never ask questions they don't already know the answers to. Let's find out more about his job first."

KC slid into the driver's seat. "A premed student who moves bodies for a living. Guess we'll see what else he knows about death."

# CHAPTER 14

## PATIENT TRANSPORT

The corridors of Shands Hospital twisted like arteries, beige walls closing in with each turn. KC's shoes squeaked against the waxed linoleum as she followed Spaulding past gurneys lined against walls and wheelchair clusters that blocked their path.

The elevator's mechanical wheeze competed with overhead pages that crackled through speakers, calling doctors to codes she didn't understand. Beneath it all, the sharp bite of industrial disinfectant burned her nostrils, a smell that promised sterility but delivered only the memory of sickness.

At the reception desk, an elderly volunteer pointed them toward Patient Transport. "Down that hall, make a left, and through the double doors."

KC's badge caught the fluorescent light as they badged their way past security checkpoints. In the transport station, orderlies pushed wheelchairs, transport workers checked clipboards, and elevators pinged arrivals.

Gina Kemp barely looked up from her screen when they approached her desk, her fingers moving to minimize whatever she'd been reading. Her navy scrubs had seen too many wash cycles, and when she raised her head, her dark eyes held the practiced wariness of someone who'd fielded too many questions from too many officials.

"How can I help you?" Her tone suggested she'd rather not.

Spaulding slid his phone across the counter, Brian's employee photo glowing on the screen. "He works here, correct? Are you his supervisor?"

Kemp's expression shifted. She set down her tablet with deliberate care. "Brian Shipley. Yes, he's part-time." Her fingers moved across the keyboard with the efficiency of a life spent behind a computer screen. "He's not scheduled today."

"We know." KC leaned against the counter. *Hmm, Kemp's shoulders tensed.* "We're hoping you can tell us about him. His work ethic, any issues, how long he's been here."

"Solid worker. Shows up on time. Does what's asked." Kemp's gaze returned to her screen, as if the computer held more comfortable truths than their faces. "Started last fall. Beginning of the semester, I think."

The smell of cafeteria food drifted from somewhere deeper in the hospital, overcooked vegetables and industrial coffee. KC's stomach churned, perhaps from hunger or the sterile atmosphere.

Spaulding shifted his weight, the movement drawing Kemp's attention back to them. "Does he have friends here? Anyone he hangs around with?"

"I manage schedules and assignments, not social lives." Kemp's fingers drummed against her desk, a nervous habit she probably didn't realize she had. "Maybe the floor nurses would know better."

"What kind of assignments does he typically get?"

"Everything. Pre-op, post-op, ICU transfers, outpatient discharges." She shrugged. "Wherever we need bodies."

KC rose on her toes, craning to glimpse Kemp's screen. The

supervisor angled her monitor away like she was guarding state secrets.

"Any particular assignments in the last few days?" KC pressed.

Kemp's jaw tightened. "Nothing unusual. Standard rotations." She studied their faces, calculating how much truth to reveal. "You think he's involved in something serious?"

"Just being thorough. If anything comes up, here's my card." KC slid it across the counter.

Kemp examined the card as if she was memorizing it, then slipped it into her scrub pocket. "You'll be the first to know."

"We'll need his work schedule for the last two months," Spaulding added.

Kemp's grunt could have meant anything. Her fingers attacked the keyboard with renewed vigor, and the printer behind her desk whirred to life. She spun in her chair to retrieve the paper.

Kemp handed Spaulding the fresh printout. Two months of Brian Shipley's life reduced to columns of dates and shift codes.

They headed toward the exit.

A nurse maneuvered a mobile computer station through the maze of equipment. Silver threaded through her dark hair, and laugh lines mapped the corners of her eyes. She wore the comfortable confidence of someone who'd navigated these halls for years.

The nurse nodded as they passed. KC took the opening.

"Excuse me." KC glanced at the woman's badge. "Joanne, do you know Brian Shipley?"

"Brian? Sure, sweet kid. But he won't be in until this evening. He usually works the later shifts."

Spaulding approached the computer cart and ran his hand along its sleek edge. "Nice setup. I remember when everything was clipboards and carbon paper."

Joanne laughed, the sound cutting through the hospital's

mechanical hum. "Those were the days when your back didn't ache from hunching over a screen." She patted the monitor. "Technology, a blessing and a curse rolled into one."

"How well do you know Brian?"

KC stepped back, pulling out her phone as Spaulding worked his charm. Three missed messages from Janelle lit up her screen. The first confirmed Sheri's autopsy had been moved up. Preliminary results matched the previous Prime victims. Same methodology, same precision. The second contained Lisbeth's background information, files that would take hours to digest properly.

The third message made her breath catch. Commander Travers was glad they'd be working together. The files on the previous victims would be forthcoming.

Really? Spaulding suggested Prime wouldn't share.

"You're gonna want to hear this."

Spaulding's voice pulled her back. She pocketed her phone. "What've you got? Because the commander said they would send over the files."

"I'll believe that when I see it." They resumed walking toward the exit, their footsteps echoing in the wide corridor. "But get this. Brian has a cousin working as a medical intern. Rotated through here last year, now he's over at Orlando Hospital."

The familiar tingle of a lead developing skittered through her. "Name?"

"Joanne couldn't remember. But she saw something interesting. Brian's cousin meeting with a former transplant surgeon in the parking garage. Some heated discussion that didn't look particularly friendly."

"When?"

"Few weeks ago. And here's the kicker. A couple days later, she witnessed Brian and his cousin arguing. Loud enough that she remembered it."

Former transplant surgeon. The pieces were starting to form

a pattern, even if she couldn't see the complete picture yet. With a bait video and two dead women, this wasn't amateur hour. This was organized, methodical. Professional.

"The surgeon have a name?"

"Terry Chandler."

KC filed the name away as they approached the hospital's main entrance. The automatic doors sensed their presence, sliding apart with a mechanical wheeze akin to the elevators they'd left behind.

Sunlight hit them like a physical blow after the hospital's artificial twilight. KC fumbled for her sunglasses, blinking away the brightness that seemed too sharp, too clean for the kind of story unfolding around them.

"Any idea why Chandler lost his license?"

Spaulding held the printed schedule between two fingers, treating it like evidence that might crumble if handled roughly. "Joanne said it was kept quiet. Internal investigation, sealed records."

"We'll have to dig."

The parking lot stretched before them, asphalt shimmering in the heat. Somewhere in this maze of concrete and steel, crucial conversations had taken place. Deals had been struck, arguments had escalated, and people had made choices that led to several women dying.

KC squinted through her sunglasses at the hospital behind them. From the outside, it looked like any other medical center, all clean lines, professional signage, the promise of healing contained within modern architecture. But some of the most dangerous predators operated in plain sight, hiding behind credentials and public trust.

# CHAPTER 15

## BETWEEN THE LINES

The lunch rush had long cleared out by the time KC and Spaulding found a booth at a Mexican spot tucked between a barbershop and a pawnshop. Ceiling fans churned the thick air, heavy with garlic and fried plantains. KC pushed the last taco around her plate, while traffic crawled through the shimmering asphalt outside.

A month into their partnership, she was still adjusting to having someone read her moods. Spaulding finished his last bite and hesitated before reaching for her untouched taco. Back in Pine Grove, no one questioned her eating habits. "You gonna eat that?"

KC slid it over. "Knock yourself out."

He bit in. "All right. Let's hear it. You've been chewing on something since the nurse at Shands dropped that cousin bomb."

KC leaned back, fingers tapping her cup. "It's not about Brian. Not really. It's Lisbeth. Something doesn't sit right."

"Celina's sister?"

"She's hiding something. I can feel it."

Spaulding wiped his fingers. "You think she knows more than she said?"

"She's a surgical nurse. Janelle ran her. Clean record, twenty-five, no priors, good employment history. If she's hiding something, it's not on paper."

He crumpled the napkin and tossed it onto his plate. "Let's shake her tree."

About an hour later, they were back in Orlando. They found Lisbeth in a modest two-story apartment building on the city's east side, half a mile from the hospital. She answered the door in gray scrubs, makeup half done, hair still up in clips.

"Detectives." Her tone was polite but wary, her eyes downcast. "I'm heading in soon."

KC tucked her hands in her pockets. "You're not taking a leave?"

Lisbeth sighed. "I will, when... I haven't told my parents yet. How do you tell them they won't see their little girl again?"

Tears pooled in her eyes. She took a deep breath.

"If you're not ready to call them, we can reach out to local law enforcement and ask them to notify your parents in person. It's standard. You don't have to do this alone." Spaulding inched closer inside. "Mind if we talk inside?"

At her headshake, they followed her into the apartment. The space smelled like lavender detergent and strong coffee, with an undertone of the antiseptic clinging to her scrubs. A long wooden coffee table. Two chairs flanked the couch. A TV perched on an entertainment center opposite them. IKEA pieces, positioned like a showroom display.

Everything felt temporary, as if Lisbeth hadn't committed to living here. The blue couch looked like a pullout bed. Maybe Celina stayed here when she needed distance from Kevin. KC and Spaulding sat on the couch, Lisbeth on a chair.

KC's slacks rasped against the cushion. "You live alone?"

"Yes." Lisbeth's voice caught, and she pressed her lips together. She pivoted her gaze to Spaulding, avoiding KC's penetrating stare. "My folks live in Charleston. Are you sure you can handle telling them?"

The woman's breathing came out shallow, controlled. Her nurse's training kicking in, managing her crisis like she would a patient's.

"Yes, we'll handle it."

"We just had a few follow-up questions and figured it might be easier without Kevin here." KC redirected the conversation.

"All right."

"What was Celina like? Just trying to get a better picture of her."

Lisbeth's face softened. "Smart. Determined. Stubborn as hell. She was always trying to fix something, even when it wasn't hers to fix."

"Was she happy with Kevin?"

Face tipped downward, Lisbeth rubbed her chin. "I think so. But Celina could be private. She didn't always tell me things until after they went sideways."

Spaulding braced his notepad against the armrest. "What about work? Was she studying anything?"

"She was in the College of Education. She wanted to be a teacher, but she took the semester off."

"Any idea why?"

"No, my parents blamed Kevin."

"And you?"

She shrugged. "I don't know. I mean, she broke up with him. He can't have that big of an influence."

KC scooted backward enough to get the cushion to relax its grip on her slacks. "You're a nurse, right? At Orlando Hospital? Which department?"

"Scrub nurse. Mostly general and ortho. Sometimes transplant."

Spaulding tilted his head. "Ever cross paths with a surgeon named Terry Chandler?"

His question came out casually, but KC caught him glancing at her, checking her reaction. A month in, she was still getting used to this coordinated dance. Back in Pine Grove, she'd worked most cases alone. Here, everything required silent communication, reading each other's cues.

Lisbeth blinked, her pupils dilating. "Yes, actually. A few years ago." Her left hand gripped the arm of her chair, knuckles going white. "He's not here anymore, though."

"You worked on any of his transplant cases?"

"Two, maybe three."

There it was—the shift, a flicker in her eyes. Something held back. "You okay?"

A terse nod.

"Listen, sometimes the smallest thing, something you think doesn't matter, could be what we need. Let us decide if it's relevant."

Lisbeth hesitated, her fingers playing with the fold in the chair arm. The apartment felt smaller, the afternoon light filtering through the blinds casting prison-bar shadows across the floor. Then her shoulders sagged as if an invisible weight had become too much to bear.

"Some rumors started among the surgical staff. Most nurses ignored them—no proof, no pattern, just whispers during shift changes. But I saw something I couldn't explain, something that's been eating at me ever since."

Spaulding slid his elbow off the armrest and straightened. "What?"

"There was this teenage boy. Sixteen. He was in bad shape, congenital heart defect. Needed a new heart. I checked his registry number out of curiosity one night. He wasn't anywhere near the top ten. But then…" She swallowed. "Two days later, I was told to prep him. That a heart was available."

"No timely relative passing?" KC asked.

Lisbeth's quick headshake jostled her hair clips. "I asked.

They said no. Just that a match had been found. The whole thing felt fast."

"Did you report it?"

Her cheeks colored. "Who would I report it to? There was no mistake on paper. It looked clean. But something felt... wrong."

"You were a scrub nurse, not a detective." Spaulding leaned forward, his voice gentler than KC had heard it before. "You noticed something was off. That matters."

KC exchanged a look with him. "You think someone moved him up the list?"

"I don't know. I just knew something wasn't right." Lisbeth glanced at her phone. "I'm sorry. I really need to leave."

They stood.

As they stepped back into the hallway, the institutional fluorescent lighting harsh after Lisbeth's dimmer apartment, Spaulding muttered, "It's time to chat with the disgraced doc."

"Good idea. Let's see if Janelle has his LKA."

"You call her, padawan. She likes you. She'll find the last known address for you." He snatched the key fob out of her hands.

"Hey!" She made to grab it back.

He pressed the button to unlock the doors, keeping it away from her. "I'll drive. You drive like we're in a school zone."

"No, I don't." She hated Orlando traffic.

"You hesitate at green lights."

She feigned irritation. "It's called being cautious. A car in cross traffic might not have cleared the intersection yet."

"Yeah, right." He slid into the driver's seat.

# CHAPTER 16

## BEHIND THE SMILE

The fourth floor of the Apex Surgical Solutions building smelled faintly of coffee, printer toner, and professionalism. KC paused just inside the glass doors, eyes scanning the clean lines and cool neutrals of the lobby, frosted glass, chrome fixtures, framed FDA clearance certificates, and surgical instruments in sleek display cases.

"Corporate," Spaulding muttered beside her. "But not evil corporate. Just... middle-management corporate."

KC said nothing, but her gaze lingered on a titanium clamp mounted in a backlit case like it was fine art. A receptionist looked up, smiled with efficient politeness, and picked up the phone. A minute later, a young man in a tucked polo and khakis escorted them past cubicles and conference rooms, one wall of which was covered in color-coded sales projections and a marker-scrawled FDA timeline.

They found Terry Chandler in a modest private office overlooking a parking lot dotted with palm trees and Camrys.

Fifty-two, according to Janelle's dossier. He looked every bit of it. What hair remained was more gray than brown, his hairline receding like a shoreline at high tide. His skin sagged under the eyes, but his button-down shirt was crisp, his voice even.

He stood as they entered. "Detectives, to what do I owe the pleasure?"

"I'm Detective Spaulding." Spaulding took the lead. "This is Detective Cassidy. We're following up on a case that may have medical ties. Just getting some background information."

"Of course." Chandler gestured to the two visitor chairs, then sat behind his desk. "I try to be helpful when I can. Especially to the police."

Calm. No tension in the shoulders. No nervous tapping of his pen. Either he had nothing to hide... or he was practiced at hiding it.

Spaulding held the business card he had taken from the reception counter. "Surgical Device Consultant. So, what do you do?"

"I consult on surgical equipment, train teams, help roll out new tech, bridge the gap between engineering and the OR. Apex handles devices from planning to post-op support, so I stay pretty busy."

Spaulding feigned interest. "Sounds cool. Do you need sales experience? Medical expertise?"

Chandler hesitated. "No sales experience. But I practiced medicine for over twenty years, most of them as a surgeon."

"Ah, so what made you decide to quit?"

Chandler rocked back in his chair, smile polite. "Oh, being a surgeon isn't as great as it sounds. The stress. It was time to step away."

Twenty years of surgery, and he walked away from it all for corporate consulting? She'd read Janelle's dossier, the malpractice suits, the impairment issue, privileges revoked after that incident at Orlando Hospital. License pulled by the state board. Chandler hadn't "stepped away" from anything. He'd been pushed out, his career ending not with retirement but with disgrace.

She let out a breath. "Must have been quite an adjustment, going from life-and-death decisions to... what, PowerPoint presentations?"

A muscle twitched in his jaw. "The skills transfer more than you'd think. Precision. Attention to detail. Problem-solving under pressure." He straightened a pen on his desk. "Plus, I still get to help save lives, just from a different angle."

Spaulding braced his elbows on his knees, hands locked by his chin. "Any regrets? About leaving medicine?"

"None." The answer came too fast. "It was the right decision at the right time."

KC tilted her head. "Sounds like a good gig."

"Less stressful for sure." Chandler's smile didn't quite reach his eyes. His fingers tapped once against the desk before he caught himself. A flicker of something—resentment, maybe—passed over his face and vanished just as fast.

The man was selling contentment, but the pitch felt hollow. She filed away each microexpression, each tell. The way his shoulders tensed when they mentioned his surgical background. The practiced responses sounded rehearsed.

The pristine office, the perfectly arranged desk, the wall of certifications, everything designed to project competence and trustworthiness. But beneath the corporate polish lay a man trying to rebuild the credibility he'd lost in an operating room.

They moved on to questions about the victims, Celina Bishop and Sheri Conners.

When he showed no sign of recognition, Spaulding sat up and slid his phone from his pocket. "We just got another name to run by you. Louis Shipley."

Janelle had sent them basic information on Brian's cousin. He would be their next visit.

Chandler's pupils dilated slightly. A microexpression crossed his face, surprise, then something else, calculation.

"Louis Shipley," Chandler repeated, buying time. His fingers drummed once against the desk before he caught himself. "That name... sounds familiar, but I can't place it."

"Take your time." She waved at him as if granting permission. "Sometimes these things come to you."

Chandler's eyes shifted left, accessing memory, according to her training. But when he looked back, his expression was neutral. "No, I'm sorry. I meet a lot of people in this business. The name might be familiar from a conference or something, but I can't put a face to it."

"He's a medical intern." Spaulding tucked his phone away. "Works at one of the local hospitals."

"Then it's possible our paths crossed. I interact with a lot of hospital staff. But I can't say I remember him specifically."

KC tilted her head. "What about outside of work? Maybe through friends, family?"

"I don't think so." But uncertainty carried in his voice, like a man walking on ice he wasn't sure would hold.

Spaulding didn't push. KC didn't either.

They stood to leave, polite handshakes exchanged. Chandler walked them out, offering a practiced, "Let me know if you need anything else."

Once they were back in the elevator, KC rested against the wall. "He's hiding something."

Spaulding nodded. "He recognized the cousin's name."

"I'd bet good money he's not just pushing surgical tools and booking conference calls."

"Unfortunately, we need some solid evidence. Time to dig into his and Louis Shipley's backgrounds. Phone calls, texts, everything. There's got to be a connection somewhere. Chandler and the victims. Chandler and the Shipleys."

"Louis Shipley is our next stop. Maybe he won't be as

elusive." She took out her phone, opened Janelle's email. "Janelle got us the address."

Before they could reach the lobby, Spaulding's phone buzzed. He checked the screen, jaw tightening.

"Another body. Lake Eola area."

KC tensed. "If the MO matches, that's six victims. Three in two days." The numbers hit like physical blows. "Louis Shipley will have to wait. Let's get to the scene before anyone else contaminates it."

"Sure. You just don't want Prime to get there first."

He wasn't wrong. She wanted—no, needed—to claim the case before it slipped away. These cases were like a puzzle, and she was obsessed with solving them.

*Careful! Don't let the old wiring take over. Not now.*

# CHAPTER 17

## JANE DOE

Flashing red and blue lit up the scene when KC and Spaulding pulled up near the Lake Eola area, not far from the band shell. The humid night air carried the murmur of voices and the metallic crackle of police radios.

A thin crowd had formed behind the yellow tape, most holding up phones or murmuring behind cupped hands. Police radios crackled, dispatchers' voices breaking through the static with coordinates and codes.

KC scanned the bystanders and groaned. Todd Rowe was there, smartphone in one hand, mic in the other, narrating for his livestream.

"*StreetBeat News.* Sources tell us this may be the third young woman found under suspicious circumstances in the last two days. We'll bring you exclusive updates as we get them."

"Unbelievable," KC muttered as they ducked under the tape. "This guy was at the first two scenes. Does he camp out with a scanner taped to his ear?"

Spaulding shrugged. "I've seen him before. He's annoying, but harmless. I'm sure he listens to a scanner, or he's got a deal with a dispatcher who owes him a favor."

"Detectives!" A uniform, who looked no more than twenty—or maybe KC was getting old—lifted the crime scene tape.

They ducked and went inside. KC asked, "Who was first on scene?"

The officer nodded toward another officer. "Crane, over there."

They found the officer corralling a group of onlookers, reminding them to stay behind the tape. Spaulding cleared his throat. "What do we have?"

Crane gestured toward a shallow greenbelt just off the sidewalk, where Luna crouched near the tarp-covered form.

"Jogger spotted her. Didn't touch the body, called it in. No ID, no phone, no bag. Scene was quiet when I arrived. Doesn't look like this is where she was killed."

KC's gaze swept the perimeter. The bushes weren't disturbed, no signs of a struggle, and the woman's position looked... arranged. Staged.

"Jane Doe." Luna peeled off her gloves, studying the body with clinical detachment. "Can't tell you her age here, based on this condition. Facial recognition's out. We'll need dental comparison, possibly DNA if we can get familial markers."

She gestured at the victim's hands. "No viable prints here, but back at the lab, we can try dermal rehydration. Might get enough ridge detail for AFIS."

KC crouched beside the body, fighting the urge to breathe through her mouth. Even outdoors, the sweet-sick smell of decomposition mixed with the clean scent of lake water and damp earth. The skin had a gray tinge, mottled and bloated in places. Clothes intact, but nothing personal.

Beside her, Spaulding scanned the body. "She was moved."

"I concur," Luna confirmed. "Lividity doesn't match the position, and the leaf litter doesn't line up." She indicated the torso, just under the ribs. "Look here. Not obvious, but there are recent scars. Jagged. Crude. Could be surgical, but if so, not by anyone with steady hands."

KC glanced at her partner. Was he thinking the same thing? Could be the same perp.

He edged in for a closer look. "Can you tell if they were postmortem?"

"Can't tell now. The ME will be able to tell you more once she's on the table."

The commander told Luna to mark the bodies priority at the scene yesterday. KC widened her stance. "Would this trigger priority?"

"Already done." Luna's fingers tapped on her phone. "Prime's got the juice to fast-track it."

"Can you tell TOD?"

"ME will be able to give you a better estimate. I'd say about seven days. Could be longer."

Sheri was a recent death. Celina's body was about four days old. And this Jane Doe could've been killed seven or more days ago. If the pattern held, they would have three or four days before the next victim.

Spaulding pushed to his feet. "We need to work fast if we don't want another one."

"My thoughts exactly." KC rose as well.

"You done with the body? I think they're ready to transport." Luna held off the techs with a hand.

"Yeah, go ahead." Spaulding stepped away.

The metallic zip of the body bag seemed to echo across the water, final and absolute. KC moved aside to let the techs work and waved goodbye to Luna.

"Find out who owns the building. I'll go talk to the jogger." Spaulding turned, then turned back. "And see if the guy from *StreetBeat*'s still sniffing around. He might've seen something or filmed it."

KC found Officer Crane standing sentry. Young guy, probably still learning the neighborhoods. "You walk this beat?"

"Yes, ma'am." He wiped sweat from his forehead despite the cool air.

"So who maintains this stretch? City or parks?"

Crane shrugged. "Parks guys come through sometimes, but honestly? Could be either. I just keep people from camping here."

"Security cameras?"

"One down the block." He pointed. "That's it, far as I know."

"Where's CSU?"

"Pulling in now."

She followed his gaze. Then the truck was parked, and Spaulding headed toward it. That was a fast interview with the jogger. She left him to touch base with CSU and called Janelle instead.

"Can you pull property records on a building near Lake Eola?" She said as soon as Janelle answered. "Looks like it's been vacant a while. See who owns it, past and present, and flag anything sketchy. And we need the traffic cam footage down the block."

A sigh came through. "I knew it was wishful thinking. I was hoping you wouldn't call to request anything before I leave."

"Oh, you hurt my feelings."

"Yeah, right. Address?"

KC rattled off the address. "Will you—"

"ASAP, I know."

"Thank you so much. You're the best."

She ended the call and scanned the crowd for Rowe. Off to the side, easy to spot, filming. KC approached before he could slip away. "Impressive response time, Rowe. You moonlighting as a dispatcher?"

He didn't look up from his phone. "Public airwaves, Detective. Anyone can listen."

"So you were here when the body was found?"

"Same time as your boys in blue." He met her eyes, smug. "But I wasn't recording the ground."

"Can I see your footage?"

He eyed her like she was insane. "Do you have a warrant?"

She blew out a breath. "I just want to see it, not confiscate it."

"Still, First Amendment, Detective. No warrant. No footage."

"Yeah, sure. Did you see anything or anyone before the first unit arrived?"

He fiddled with his phone for a beat. "Not yet. But people talk. You'd be amazed what you can overhear with the right mic."

"And what did you hear?"

He shrugged. "Nothing useful."

He wasn't going to volunteer anything. She'd have to check *StreetBeat*'s stream later. Maybe Rowe recorded something or someone without knowing it.

KC lingered, looking past the body toward the lake. Beneath the voices of the crime scene team and the gentle lapping of water, the distant hum of traffic reminded her that life continued beyond this circle of death. The water was calm, picture-perfect, if you didn't know what had just been dropped at its edge.

The night breeze carried competing scents—rotting vegetation from the lake, the metallic tang of blood, and something else. Something that made her want to shower.

Spaulding returned, pocketing his phone. "Just like Crane said, the jogger didn't touch or see anything. A uniform took his statement. I asked CSU to check tire tracks."

As they talked, CSU techs scattered around, taking photos and measurements, collecting evidence. The techs loaded Jane Doe into the van.

Somewhere out there, he was already choosing his next

victim. The thought made her skin crawl—not the cool night air, but the certainty that they were always one step behind.

# CHAPTER 18

## THE INTERN

By the time they reached Orlando Hospital, the sun slanted through the lobby's floor-to-ceiling windows, casting geometric shadows across the polished terrazzo floors. The familiar cocktail of disinfectant and anxiety hung in the air, punctuated by the distant chime of elevator bells and the soft squeak of sneakers on linoleum.

KC and Spaulding waited outside the staff lounge, a utilitarian space tucked behind radiology. She tilted her watch into view. They had checked with the administration. Shipley would be off in five minutes.

A few minutes later, Louis Shipley appeared, white coat, stethoscope around his neck, hair too styled for someone finishing a twelve-hour day. The guy belonged in a residency recruitment ad.

"Louis Shipley?" Spaulding held up his badge. "Detective Spaulding, Orlando PD. This is Detective Cassidy. We need a few minutes of your time."

Louis swept his gaze over the two of them, his expression shifting from tired to wary. "Seriously? Do you guys talk to each other down at the station? Because I just went through this whole song and dance with two other detectives like an hour ago."

"What other detectives?" KC stepped closer, watching his face.

"I don't know, some guy and a woman. Said they were with Prime."

KC and Spaulding exchanged a glance. So Prime had already gotten to him.

Spaulding nodded. "Even so, we'll need to ask you a few questions."

Louis shifted his weight, rolled his eyes, but opened the lounger door. "Look, can we make this quick? I've been on my feet for twelve hours."

The staff lounge felt like an afterthought tucked behind radiology, fluorescent lights humming overhead, casting everything in harsh relief. The microwave's digital clock blinked 12:00 in perpetual confusion, while a half-stocked vending machine offered stale sandwiches behind scratched plexiglass. The table bore the scars of countless hurried meals and spilled coffee.

Louis dropped into a molded plastic chair that creaked under his weight, the kind designed more for easy cleaning than comfort. His white coat hung open, revealing scrubs with vomit stains, and when he cracked open the sports drink, the carbonation hissed in the quiet room. "So?"

"Your cousin, Brian Shipley. You met his girlfriend, Sheri Conners?"

Louis took a long pull from his sports drink. "Ex-girlfriend, last I heard. Though with those two, who knows? They break up, get back together, break up again. It's like watching a soap opera." He paused, studying their faces. "Wait, why are you asking about Sheri? Did something happen to her?"

"When's the last time you saw her?"

"I don't know, maybe a couple of months ago? Brian brought

her to some family thing at my mom's house. She seemed… I don't know, distracted. Kept checking her phone."

No hesitation. It appeared the guy didn't know about Sheri going missing and her subsequent death. One look at Spaulding told her he agreed.

She flipped a page in her notepad and shifted gears. "Tell us about Terry Chandler."

Louis groaned, head falling back against the chair. "Not this again. I spent twenty minutes explaining this to your Prime buddies."

"Humor us."

"Fine." Louis straightened up, his tone shifting to the practiced cadence of someone who'd already told this story. "Chandler approached me at some alumni mixer about two months ago. Seemed to know way more about me than I knew about him, where I was doing my internship, what my specialty interests were, even mentioned my undergrad GPA, which was weird."

KC arched a brow. "What exactly did he offer?"

"Called it 'device consultation'. Said medical device companies needed people with fresh perspectives, recent training. Claimed I could make more in a weekend than most interns see in a month." Louis shrugged, rocked back, and lifted the plastic chair's front legs off the linoleum. "Sounded like a scam."

"But he was persistent?"

"That's putting it mildly." He let the chair drop back into place. "Guy wouldn't take no for an answer. Kept saying I had the 'right profile,' whatever that means. Started feeling less like a job offer and more like a sales pitch."

"Was that all your interactions with him? Did he email you? Text you?"

"No email. No text. I don't want to associate with a disgraced doctor."

Spaulding shifted in his seat. "We have a witness who saw you two arguing."

Louis hesitated, then sighed. "It wasn't a full-blown argument. He didn't like being turned down. Got pushy."

"Pushy how?"

"He kept saying it was a once-in-a-lifetime opportunity. Kept name-dropping surgeons he used to work with."

KC's eyes narrowed. "And you're sure that's all it was?"

Louis crossed his arms. "Look, I didn't take the job. I haven't talked to him since. If you think he's involved in something shady, that's on him, not me."

They gave him a few more softball questions, watching his reactions, but it was clear. Louis didn't know anything beyond his brief encounter with Chandler. His annoyance seemed real. So did his confusion.

As they stepped out into the fading daylight, the cool air wrapped around them. The parking lot stretched before them, half empty now as the evening shift settled in.

"He's not our guy," Spaulding echoed her thoughts.

She nodded. "But Chandler just got more interesting. I get the feeling he had something specific in mind for Louis."

"Yeah, and probably other interns or residents too." Spaulding's phone buzzed. He swiped the screen. "Prime sent over the files, like the commander promised."

"Finally." She headed toward the passenger side. "You think the earlier victims led them to Louis? Maybe they found the same connection we did, through Brian. But I only sent them Sheri's file this morning, and Brian didn't mention Prime visiting him."

Spaulding braced himself against the hood, scrolling through his phone. "Maybe these files will tell us our next step." He straightened and opened the door. "Assuming Louis is telling the truth, what would Chandler want with him? Can't be consulting."

KC slid into the passenger seat, working through possibilities. How was Chandler involved? And who was he working for? Because whatever this was, it was bigger than one disgraced doctor operating alone.

# CHAPTER 19

## THE OUTLIER

Back at the station conference room, KC stood in front of the whiteboard, the fluorescent lights humming overhead and casting harsh shadows across the timeline she'd been building. The smell of stale coffee mixed with industrial disinfectant. The red marker's plastic cap pressed ridges into her palm as she gripped it too tightly.

She shifted from the case files spread out on the table like puzzle pieces that didn't quite fit, their manila edges catching the sterile light. She uncapped the marker, the small pop echoing in the quiet room, and drew a short line between each name. The marker squeaked against the whiteboard's surface.

"Sheri Conners." She tapped the photo with the marker's tip. "Dead maybe forty-eight hours before we found her. Celina Bishop, about four days prior."

Spaulding braced against the table, arms crossed, his shirt wrinkled from the long day. The metal table's edge must be biting into his hip, but he didn't shift. "And our Jane Doe? ME said roughly seven days."

KC stepped back, eyeing the timeline, the marker cap clicking between her fingers. The red lines gleamed, dark and congealed under the harsh lighting. "Then look at Prime's victims. Kasey Gallo, two months ago. Monica Lewis, one month. Rosa Ortega, two weeks." She capped the marker with a sharp snap. "It's accelerating."

Spaulding pushed off the table. "Intervals are shrinking. From a month to weeks to days."

"We've got maybe two, three days before another girl turns up, if the pattern holds." The words tasted bitter in her mouth, clinical and cold when they should have carried more weight. Another life reduced to data points on a timeline.

Spaulding flipped through Kasey Gallo's file. Pages rustling, he thumbed past autopsy photos and interview transcripts. His eyes narrowed, his brow creasing deeper with each page.

He slid the folder toward her, his sleeve catching on the table's edge, his finger underlining one line. "Here, ER visit. Six months ago. Cut her finger on a glass. Needed sutures."

KC leaned in. "Treated by… Louis Shipley?"

"Under an attending. But the doc signed off early. Shipley handled discharge, maybe the dressing."

Her gaze lifted from the page to meet his. "You think Prime found that in the hospital system? Used it to trace contact?"

"Could be. If they're digging through victims' histories, that's a smart breadcrumb."

Her jaw tightened, her head dipping. Her shoulder blades tensed. "So that's how they got to Shipley first."

Before Spaulding could reply, both their phones buzzed on the table, the vibration rattling the metal surface. KC snatched hers, the smooth plastic warming in her palm as she read the preview.

ME LAB

Got a print hit off your Jane Doe.

Her pulse quickened. Finally, a break.

She tapped the call icon and faced the window, where the

evening light was fading into that gray hour between day and night. She identified herself when the call connected, her free hand already reaching for a notepad.

A chipper voice answered, too bright for the gravity of what they were discussing. "Hey, this is Erin at the ME lab. Rehydration worked on the fingers. AFIS came back with a match."

KC grabbed a pen, clicking it once out of habit. "Name?"

"Kathy Foley. Forty-six. Print's on file from a Department of Education background check. Teacher."

KC scribbled the information, her handwriting getting messier as she wrote faster. "Missing person report?"

"Nothing we could find. No active flags."

"Next of kin?"

"We're pulling that now from her school records. HR has her emergency contact on file. We'll forward it to your analyst."

"Janelle left for the day. Could you please send it directly to me?"

"Sure thing."

"Thanks, Erin." KC hung up.

Spaulding watched her, expectation lifting a brow. "We got her?"

"Kathy Foley. Forty-six. Taught in Orange County. No missing report filed."

He frowned, running a hand through his hair. "Foley... Name doesn't ring a bell."

Forty-six? The number hit her like a cold slap. That didn't fit the pattern.

The others were twenty-something. Young. Disposable, to someone like this. But forty-six? That was off.

Her pulse ticked faster at her wrist, a steady drumbeat against her skin. Something about it itched at her brain, a splinter working its way deeper under the surface.

*No. I need to go back. Start from the beginning. Look at the files again. Every timeline. Every detail.*

She strode to the whiteboard, the red lines now mocking her careful organization. The fluorescent light above flickered once, casting momentary shadows across the photos.

One wrong variable meant the whole equation didn't work. She hated when the pieces didn't fit.

"Hey, KC!"

She startled, her shoulders jerked. The pen slipped from her fingers, clattering to the floor.

Spaulding's hand was on her arm, his eyes searching hers. "You all right? You blanked out there. ME office emailed you the file."

She blinked, shaking her head to clear the fog. *Too close. He's noticing.*

"I'm fine. Just thinking." She bent to retrieve the pen, using the moment to compose herself. When she straightened, she swiped to her email and tapped the screen-share icon. Then, the plasma screen on the far wall flickered to life. Erin's message filled the display with that familiar blue glow.

KC clicked the attachment, and the emergency contact information appeared in stark black letters against the white background.

EMERGENCY CONTACT: GAVIN WATKINS
RELATIONSHIP: SPOUSE

The silence stretched for three heartbeats.

Spaulding let out a low whistle. "You've got to be kidding me."

KC looked up, the screen's glow washing his face. "What? You know him?"

He nodded, his expression darkening. "Assistant state attorney. Works downtown. Didn't even know he was married."

KC pulled up the HR records on her phone, scrolling through the employee information. "HR says he's divorced."

"Then why would she still list him as her emergency contact?"

"Maybe she never got around to changing it. And maybe she ignored the annual HR update request. Wouldn't be the first."

Spaulding's jaw worked before he spoke. "Think he knows? About her being dead?"

KC studied Kathy Foley's school photo on the screen, a woman with kind eyes and graying hair. "Doesn't sound like he's even noticed she's gone."

That settled between them. A woman dead for a week, and her emergency contact, her ex-husband, hadn't filed a missing person report. Hadn't even called to check on her.

Spaulding stepped back from the screen, running both hands through his hair now. "This just got complicated."

KC stared at the latest victim's photo, this newest face on their timeline who didn't fit the pattern, who connected their case to the state attorney's office, who'd been forgotten by the very person who was supposed to protect her.

"Yeah," she whispered. "And personal."

# CHAPTER 20

## NO WAY BACK

The surgical device brochures were still scattered across his desk when Chandler grabbed the flask from his bottom drawer. Twenty minutes later, he sat on the dock's edge, the taste of cheap whiskey mixing with the metallic fear coating his tongue. His consultant office felt like a trap now, all those legitimate medical devices covering for what he'd really been cutting.

The bottle tipped in his hand as he slumped on the dock, his other palm scraping splintered wood. Somewhere behind him, a bullfrog croaked in the reeds. Chandler didn't flinch. His focus was fixed on the dark ripple of water just beyond his dangling feet.

He took another swig. Warm. Harsh. Didn't matter. The flask trembled as he lowered it.

"I used to save lives," he muttered.

No one answered.

The burner phone buzzed in his jacket pocket, three short vibrations. He pulled it out with damp fingers. The screen lit his reflection in blue, exaggerating the bags under his eyes.

The wind picked up, carrying a faint smell of mildew and gasoline. Somewhere across the lake, a dog barked once, then went quiet. No choice. He had to tell him. He tapped the only number stored in this burner.

"This better be urgent," the voice answered.

"Two detectives came by, asking questions." Chandler took another pull from the flask.

"Timing's unfortunate. We have another client tomorrow."

"Tomorrow? I need time to—"

"Time's up, Doctor. High-profile patient needs a kidney. You know what that means."

"You can't be serious."

"Dead serious. And if you're thinking about backing out, remember we know where you live. We know your routine. We know you come to this dock every night to drink yourself stupid."

Chandler looked around the empty shoreline, suddenly feeling exposed.

His throat worked. He spat into the water and scowled. *I've done enough, haven't I?*

But he didn't dare convey his thoughts. "But what should I do about the detectives?"

"They're fishing. If they have anything solid, you'd be in handcuffs."

Not reassuring. "They'll be back. What if... what if they find out about that woman?" They told him he'd be saving lives, and he'd believed them.

Until they brought him the unconscious woman. The pulse had been so faint he'd almost missed it, a flutter under his fingertips that made his training kick in. Without thinking, he'd reached for the crash cart, hands moving toward the defibrillator paddles....

*"What are you doing?" the guard had snapped.*

*"She's alive. Barely, but—"*

*The gun barrel pressed against his temple before he could finish the sentence. "Step away from the equipment, Doc."*

*"I need to try to save her. Give me ten minutes, maybe fifteen—"*

*"Your job to save lives will start soon enough." The metal chilled his skin.*

So, he'd stood there, hands at his sides, watching her breathe her last breath. Every instinct screamed at him to act, but the gun was absolute.

The irony wasn't lost on him, forced to watch a woman die, then hooking her up to machines to keep the organs viable, and then harvesting organs to save someone else.

"Find a patsy. The kid who refused to join would be a good one."

Shipley? No, he couldn't do that. Chandler saw the promise in that intern. "But, but… how?"

"You're a talented doctor. I'm sure you can think of something." Click.

Chandler let the phone fall to his lap. His head tilted back, eyes searching the stars through the cloud cover. His breath escaped in a thin, shaking sigh.

"What have I gotten into?"

The pills had started innocently enough, postsurgical pain relief after he'd thrown out his back during a twelve-hour operation. But twelve hours had become sixteen-hour days, and one pill had become three, then six.

The malpractice suits had piled up like surgical sponges, forgotten, overlooked, left to fester. Trembling hands during procedures. Missed diagnoses. One patient had nearly died because he'd been too high to read an EKG properly.

Orlando Hospital's report to the board had been clinical, devastating: "Substance abuse rendering Dr. Terry Chandler unfit for practice." Twenty years of medical school, residency, building a reputation, gone in a single hearing.

The consultant job had offered him salvation at first. Still medical, still using his knowledge. But forty thousand a year instead of four hundred thousand. Living in a studio apartment instead of his old colonial. Shopping at discount grocery stores.

When they'd approached him about getting his license back, he'd wanted to believe so badly it hurt.

He rubbed his face with both hands, then looked at the scars across his knuckles, faint reminders of a cleaner time. A steadier time.

He was so stupid to believe their promise of redemption. They pitched it like charity. He should've known better.

A bubble popped somewhere beneath the dock.

He fiddled with his burner phone. His reflection frowned at him from the black screen. Older. Broken. A man pretending he still mattered. "How am I going to fix this?"

The trees whispered. The lake breathed.

The woman's intense eyes seared his memory. His hands went to his pocket and retrieved the card she'd given him. He tossed the burner phone into the water and pulled out his personal phone. Maybe this would be his real redemption.

His fingers traced the detective's card, Kylie Cassidy. The woman who'd looked at him like she could see straight through his consultant charade to the man underneath. While Spaulding asked the obvious questions, Cassidy watched his hands, his eyes, reading the tells he thought he'd buried.

He'd thrown away his medical license, his marriage, his self-respect. But maybe, just maybe, he could throw away his fear too.

The flask felt heavier in his other hand. He could finish it, let the lake take both him and his secrets. Or he could dial the number printed in neat black letters.

The burner phone disappeared beneath the surface with barely a splash.

# CHAPTER 21

## SILENCED

KC stared at the screen, the glow washing her surroundings in pale light. The office was quiet now. Spaulding had left an hour ago, having made plans to do the notification first thing tomorrow. But she hadn't moved since.

She scrolled through the case files again. Sheri Conners. Celina Bishop. And Kathy Foley. And the ones from Prime.

It still didn't add up.

All the victims, except Foley, fit a type, targeted with surgical precision, no signs of struggle. Foley, though... Her wounds were jagged. Messy. Amateur.

Either she wasn't part of the same string, or someone had slipped. KC rubbed her temples. This compulsion was something she'd learned to keep buried, but cases like this made her wonder if she should stop fighting what might actually help.

She leaned back, stretching her arms overhead as the ache behind her eyes pulsed. That's when her phone buzzed. She answered without checking the screen. Tanner's ringtone.

"Hey, Deanna told me Jack thanked her for connecting you two. A serial, I heard." Tanner sounded tired.

"I should thank her." She relaxed, dropping her pen on the desk. "Do you know Commander Travers?"

"I know of him. I believe Ron and the commander know each other. They worked together way back. Some joint operation, I think. Why?"

"He's the leader of Prime. Technically, these cases are theirs. But Coleman got Prime to let us continue working the cases."

"Any chance—"

A ding indicated another call on her phone. Unknown number, but the number looked familiar. "Sorry, got another call."

They said goodbye, and she picked up the other call. "Cassidy."

A beat of silence. Then: "Detective. This is Terry Chandler. You were in my office earlier today."

Her spine straightened. "Right. How may I help you?"

Silence. She checked the screen to make sure the call hadn't dropped.

Then: "I… There's something I need to tell you."

"About?"

"This whole thing."

Her brows knitted. *This whole thing.* "Uh, care to elaborate?"

"Not exactly. But… I think I can help you understand what's happening."

She narrowed her eyes at the files still open on her screen. "I'm listening."

"Not over the phone. And I would need protection."

Her heartbeat picked up. Only certain people would want protection when they offered to meet with police. "All right. When?"

"Tomorrow morning. Can you meet me at my house? I can't be seen walking into a police station."

"Sure. Eight thirty work?"

"I'll be waiting."

He hung up without saying goodbye.

She stared at her phone. Before Chandler got his license revoked, he had been a great surgeon. His specialty, if she recalled correctly, was organ transplants. And their cases involved victims with organs removed. Chandler would have the skill, but she couldn't see him as the mastermind.

Was he turning himself in? Would he flip on his partner or partners?

**WEDNESDAY**

The next morning, Spaulding was already in when she arrived. She briefed him while they were getting their cups of coffee.

"He said he had something to tell us. About 'the whole thing,' whatever that means. And he can help us understand what's going on? Wouldn't say more over the phone."

Back at their desks, he leaned back. "Funny what guilt does to people."

"So, we're on the same page. He also asked for protection."

"Sure sounds like he wants a deal, immunity." He sipped his coffee. "Still want to hear what he's got. Even liars leave a breadcrumb."

"He sounded tense. Not high, though."

Coleman walked in. "Spaulding, Cassidy, my office."

They glanced at each other, got up, and followed the lieutenant to his office.

"Don't bother sitting. I said you could continue working the cases. And I also said to share your findings with Prime. Or did I forget to mention that?"

KC remained quiet. Spaulding was the senior detective. She let him answer.

"Right, yeah, you did mention that. It's just—we haven't really found anything worth sharing yet."

Coleman looked from one to the other. "Is that right? Why did I get a call about Brian Shipley? Seems you two interviewed him but somehow forgot to let Prime know."

"Loo, they interviewed Louis Shipley without telling us," KC blurted.

She could hear Spaulding taking a breath.

"Cassidy, let me tell you. Prime is the elite unit here. These cases are theirs technically. Since you're the one who has the in with the Pine Grove victim, you two are staying in the loop. That doesn't mean you are in charge."

Chastised, she looked down. "Yes, sir."

"Now, any update?"

They told him about Chandler's call.

"All right. Get out of here. Check in with Prime. And Cassidy, I fought for you. Don't make me regret it."

"Yes, sir. Thank you, sir."

She walked out. Only after she sat at her desk did she realize Spaulding was still in the office. She looked back to where he and Coleman were talking.

A moment later, he walked out, grabbed his jacket. "Let's go."

She hurried after him. "What was that?"

"Nothing." He patted her shoulder in passing. "Don't let it get under your skin. He's just venting. You know how it is. Pressure from up high."

They pulled up to Chandler's studio apartment ten minutes early. It was a far cry from his previous mansion in his file.

Spaulding knocked. No answer.

"He said he'd be here." She checked her watch.

They tried his office. His cell. Nothing.

"I'll get Janelle to ping his phone. I don't like this."

Spaulding leaned against the doorjamb. "Think he got cold feet?"

She shook her head. "No. This feels wrong."

Her phone buzzed.

Janelle texted: Device offline. Last location: Maple Ridge Docks.

Her stomach dropped.

He read the screen over her shoulder. "Let's move."

They hit lights but not sirens. The sharp tang of brine struck her as they stepped out of the car, salt air mixing with diesel fuel from the fishing boats. Water lapped against the pilings below while gulls wheeled overhead. The dock boards were slick with morning dew, creaking under the weight of uniforms and yellow tape that fluttered in the harbor breeze. A uniform waved them off, but Spaulding flashed his badge.

"Detective Spaulding, Detective Cassidy, Major Crimes. What's going on?"

"You guys got here fast. We just called it in." The officer pointed beyond the dock. "Dockworker found the body when he came in, about forty minutes ago. Man in his fifties. No ID. Wallet's missing. Key fob was in the car."

KC didn't need to see the face.

She knew.

They got closer to check. Seagulls had already found him. She waved them off, the birds lifting with indignant shrieks before settling on nearby posts to wait.

The body was in the driver's seat, folded awkwardly against the wheel, neck askew, skin already losing its color.

Chandler's face, blank and empty now.

He was supposed to talk.

He'd called her.

He'd tried to do the right thing, or something like it.

And now he was just another dead man.

# CHAPTER 22

## THE WRONG HAND

Spaulding stood inside the yellow tape, arms folded, the breeze tugging his jacket hem. The tang of saltwater curled through the air, clinging to the back of his throat. Crime scene techs photographed Chandler's body, slumped over the steering wheel in the driver's seat.

From where he stood, it looked like suicide. Gun in Chandler's right hand, temple shot, the man's head tilted against the side window. A phone face up in the passenger seat. But something felt off. Spaulding had learned to trust his instincts, and right now, they were screaming.

While KC interviewed the worker who found the body, Spaulding scanned the area to get a feel for the crime and spotted a few security cameras. Hopefully, the footage would give him something to work with. He couldn't examine the body before the ME investigator released it, but he could assess a staged scene.

The driver's door hung open. Was Chandler planning to leave after the supposed suicide? That made no sense.

"Excuse me."

He backed away when Luna walked by.

"You're here already." She crouched beside the open car door.

"We were supposed to meet him this morning. Now he's morning cargo."

"You knew him?"

"Yeah. Former transplant surgeon. Got his license pulled a few years ago."

Luna began her examination. "I can see the entry wound. Temple shot, close range." She pulled out her GSR test kit. "Let me check for gunshot residue."

She swabbed Chandler's right hand, then processed the sample.

He rocked back on his toes, tension already tightening his muscles. "What's the verdict?"

"Positive for GSR. Looks to be self-inflicted."

She reached across to the passenger seat and retrieved the phone. "You'll want to see this."

Spaulding touched the screen with a gloved finger. It woke, no PIN, no security. Strange for a paranoid ex-surgeon who'd been scared enough to call for protection. A suicide note filled the display. "I'm sorry. I didn't mean for anyone to get hurt."

If Chandler had changed his mind about talking, wouldn't he have mentioned it in the note? And if he'd already decided to kill himself, why call to set up the meeting? Why seek protection?

"Time of death?" he asked.

"Hmm, between seven and midnight last night. We'll narrow it down once the ME gets him on the table."

"This is connected to the other female victims."

"Prime?"

He nodded.

She stood. "I'll flag it for priority."

"Hey, Luna. Can I take a look at the body?" KC approached. Must've finished with the dockworker.

"Be my guest!" Luna stepped aside.

KC leaned closer to the driver's seat, examining Chandler's position.

Spaulding stood to the side. "Anything good from the dockworker?"

"Chandler was a regular here. Liked to come either early morning or late evening to smoke, sometimes drink." She crouched, still studying the body. "And the dock manager let me see the security footage. Chandler was heading to the parking lot, then everything went dark. Between 8:01 and 8:08 last night."

"Convenient," Spaulding muttered.

"I asked CSU to look for tire tracks and dust the car for prints." KC straightened, her brow creased. "But this is staged."

Spaulding looked up from the phone. "What made you say that?"

"Chandler was left-handed. I noticed when he signed paper-work during our first meeting. Gun's in his right hand." She gestured toward the body. "Besides, he called me yesterday. Genuinely wanted to talk. Sounded scared but determined. People don't arrange meetings, then off themselves."

"You're right." Luna crossed her arms. "We'd have caught it eventually, but good call. Now that I'm looking at it again, the angle's wrong. A left-handed person would position differently."

Spaulding's jaw clenched. Their first lead just disappeared. "This is a professional hit. Someone who knew enough to plant GSR but missed the handedness detail." He bagged the phone, then peeled off his gloves. "Better update Prime before we get reamed again."

Back at the car, he slid into the driver's seat and punched the number for Prime. When someone answered, he asked to speak to the commander.

"Sorry, the commander is not available. This is Detective Quinn Sterling. Can I help you?"

He covered the mouthpiece. "Do you know a Detective Quinn Sterling?"

KC shook her head. "I only met the commander. And I emailed and texted Jack, their forensic specialist."

He spoke to the phone. "Is Jack there?"

"Yes, let me transfer you." While she did that, Spaulding handed over his phone and started the engine. "You talk to Jack. Put him on speaker."

"This is Jack."

"Hey, it's KC—Cassidy—from Major Crimes."

"Oh yeah. Sending me more footage?"

She chuckled. "Not really. Come to think of it. I have a question. Spaulding and I are at Maple Ridge Docks. I was looking at the security footage, and several minutes were dark. You have any magic tricks?"

"It depends, but not likely. You can always check cameras down the block, around the area. Might give you something."

Pulling from the lot, Spaulding mouthed, *Great idea.*

"Thanks. We'll do that. Just wanted to flag it for the commander. Chandler's dead. Staged to look like suicide. ME's got the body."

"Okay, I'll ping the commander. You do know I'm just a lab rat. When the evidence gets here, then I'll know who this guy was."

"Sorry, he was a former surgeon, a person of interest in the serial case."

"Oh, wow! The plot thickens."

Spaulding stopped at a light. "This is Spaulding. We'll send over the report once we write it up."

"Copy that," Jack replied, typing audibly in the background. "Hey, while I've got you. You still want that town car plate from the Pine Grove footage?"

KC sat up. "Yes. Do you have a hit?"

"Oh, I ran it through every database short of NORAD. Pulled partials off the video you sent. Cross-referenced with DMV records, rental agencies, and a couple less-than-legal registries I'm not supposed to know about."

Her right hand making a circling motion, she rolled her eyes. "That's great, Jack. Could you give us the name?"

"Texting you now. Plate number and registered owner."

Spaulding grinned, starting to like this guy. "We need to find that car."

"Working on it. They're savvy in hiding themselves. I saw the car go into a garage and never come out. I've got eyes on traffic cams, and I'll ping local PD if it shows up again. Just say the word."

"We're saying it. Keep us posted."

"You got it. Oh, guys, a traffic cam just picked up the town car. Sending you the location."

# CHAPTER 23

## INCONSISTENCIES

Frank stepped into the medical examiner's office. Fluorescent lights buzzed like angry wasps over stainless steel tables. He tried not to wrinkle his nose at the scent lingering in the air, somewhere between bleach and something metallic, like the memory of death hadn't quite cleared.

Dr. Bill O'Bannon stood behind his desk, a bald, slim man. They had met before. His crisp white coat was unbuttoned, pressed shirt beneath. Another white coat was present. A petite woman rose from one of the guest chairs and approached Frank. Asian, making her age difficult to gauge. Could be thirty or forty.

"Commander, thanks for coming." O'Bannon offered his hand.

They shook.

O'Bannon gestured toward the woman. "Dr. Alana Shay. She did the post on Katherine Foley. Please sit."

Frank had only met Foley once, years ago when she and Watkins were still married, but the ID of their Jane Doe still hit him hard. He shook Shay's hand and sat in the other guest chair.

This was his first time in the ME office. Various certificates adorned the wall behind the ME desk. "You said it was important."

"We believe it is."

The ME slid a sealed folder across the desk. Frank let it sit there.

"We've found some inconsistencies between this and the other cases."

"Inconsistencies?" Frank opened the folder and scanned the header. Foley, Katherine L., age forty-six. Public school teacher. Orlando County District. "What kind?"

"Given the advanced state of decomposition, our best estimate on time of death is about seven days," O'Bannon began. "Cause of death is exsanguination due to a blunt-force head wound. So, the inconsistencies. There's a depressed fracture to the occipital bone. Er, in plain language, she had a fracture at the back of her skull, and it triggered bleeding in her brain. The bleeding was so severe she died in just a few minutes."

"Okay?" And this was significant, why?

"Toxicology came back clean. No paralytics. No anesthetics." Shay sank back in her chair, elbows on the armrests, fingers laced by her chest. "She was conscious at the time of injury."

This was different from the other cases. The other women had been sedated. But there was more, wasn't there?

"She also had multiple contusions across both forearms." Shay's index fingers tapped each other. "Linear bruises. Some defensive wounds. Torn nail beds. Her hands showed signs of impact. She fought back. Unfortunately, no usable DNA recovered."

Frank shifted in his chair. This was a deviation. "As I recall, there were no defensive wounds on the others."

"Correct." O'Bannon took over again. "The other victims showed no struggle. No resistance. They were drugged, incisions clean. Surgical precision. Foley... was different."

Frank turned the page, scanning the surgical notes. Sutures

jagged. Extraction performed postmortem. Heart, kidneys. "Am I mistaken to think this was done by an inexperienced practitioner?"

"You're not wrong. The organs were nonviable. Dead tissue. No signs of perfusion. We believe she died minutes before the organs were removed. We noted the jagged scars. Again, another inconsistency. The sutures on the others were all precise and uniform."

"Anything else?"

O'Bannon looked at Shay, who shook her head. "I believe that's all. Mind you, even though the sutures were jagged, the person who did this still had medical training, either inexperienced or impaired."

"Thank you, doctors." Frank stood and gave them a final nod.

He stepped out into the heavy morning air, the automatic doors hissing closed behind him.

The parking lot stretched wide and mostly empty, its asphalt warming under the sun. He walked toward his SUV, the distant traffic muffled by the surrounding buildings. With each step, the clinical chill of the autopsy suite gave way to the rising heat and the weight of what he'd just learned.

He slid into the driver's seat. Once the engine started, he tapped the phone icon and called Eli Feldman.

"Frank," Eli answered, his voice calm and deliberate, the faint hum of background noise suggesting he might already be in the Hub.

"You at the Hub?" Frank left the lot.

"Just got in. Anything new?"

"I just left the ME's office. Kathy Foley doesn't match the others."

A pause. "Say that again?"

"Cause of death was a head wound, blunt-force trauma to the

occipital bone. She bled out fast. No sedation. Tox screen was clean."

Eli was quiet for a beat. "And the organs?"

"Removed after death. Jagged sutures. ME said either inexperienced or impaired. Both the heart and the only kidney they took weren't viable."

"Or someone did it under duress."

Frank hadn't considered that. "Could be. Also, defensive wounds, bruising, torn fingernails. You think your profile needs refinement? Or are we looking at a copycat?"

"I'll need to review the body photos again. But on the copycat theory, organ removal was withheld from the media. If this is someone else, either they have an inside source, or they're close to the real thing."

Frank stopped at a sign, turning over possibilities. "An insider? I don't like the thought."

"Frank, given the cause of death, the nonviable organs, the head wound, and the age gap from the other victims, it smells like a cover-up."

A cover-up. Frank could see it, a doctor trying to erase his own crime or someone paying a doctor to make it disappear. For now, he'd treat it as a regular homicide.

"Listen, I'm on my way back. Everyone in?"

"Far as I can tell. The kid in the lab has been going on about some detective and a photo of a town car. And he told me just to call him Jack. Said he wouldn't know to answer Stamps."

Frank smiled. "Yeah, that's Jack. He's an acquired taste. Competent, though. Put me on speaker, please. And I know about the town car."

"Sure." A click, and the background commotion of the Hub filled the SUV.

"Damon, Claire, go pay Gavin Watkins a visit." Frank paused, then added, "Handle it carefully."

"The ex-husband?" Damon Cruz, Frank's second-in-command, spoke with that familiar Marine-sharp edge.

"He's the ASA, yeah. I know Gavin. The detectives should have already informed him, but…" Frank let that hang. "Go in under the guise of following up. See if anything shakes loose— bad blood, recent arguments, anyone with motive. But tread lightly. Work the Foley case like any other homicide, just remember who you're talking to."

Chairs scraped the floor, commotion rising.

"On it." Claire Santos's voice sounded far away.

A pause. Then another voice cut in from the side, Jack's.

"Boss?"

"Yes?"

"KC and Spaulding called a little while ago. They found Chandler dead in his car. Staged to look like suicide—"

Frank frowned. "Chandler?"

"Yeah, a person of interest in the serial case, according to them."

"Terry Chandler, former renowned surgeon." Quinn Sterling, the team's IT specialist, chimed in. "You didn't hear about the scandal a few years ago? Substance abuse. Malpractice. Something like that."

A surgeon. Dead. Staged. This was connected to their serial case. But how?

"Also… remember that town car from the Pine Grove footage?" Jack was back. "Got a hit off a traffic cam, twenty-five minutes. Sent the location to the detectives."

"Send it to me." Frank needed to chat with KC, anyway.

# CHAPTER 24

## KOZLOV

KC's phone dinged with Jack's text as Spaulding accelerated through the intersection, their city-issued Tahoe's air-conditioning working overtime against the oppressive heat. One look at the address told her they wouldn't make it in time, not with downtown traffic already backing up like arterial plaque. "It's, like, ten blocks away."

Spaulding eased off the gas. "It might be gone by the time we get there."

"I'm sure Jack has set an alert for it. Let's update the loo. What next? Go see Gavin Watkins? We were supposed to do the notification first thing this morning."

"Yeah. Can you find out if he's working today?"

KC made the call to the lieutenant on speaker. They updated Coleman, let him know they had also looped in Prime. Then she found Watkins's number. A quick call to the state attorney's office confirmed the ASA was working.

They made their way downtown, tension riding quiet between them. No sirens. No adrenaline. Just the thick weight of what they had to do. Jill's reaction to hearing of Sheri's death was still fresh in her mind. Would KC ever get used to this part of the job?

Downtown shimmered in the Florida heat, the courthouse and state attorney's office squatting like stone sentinels under the midmorning sun. She adjusted her lightweight blazer as they stepped out, the air sticky against her skin.

They pushed through the heavy glass doors. The lobby buzzed with the familiar courthouse energy, lawyers clutching briefcases, families huddled on benches, the low murmur of plea bargains and postponements echoing off marble walls.

Her trained eye swept the space, cataloging exits and noting the nervous energy that permeated buildings where justice was dispensed in measured doses.

Cold fluorescent lights buzzed overhead. A uniformed officer manned the entrance, nodding as they flashed their badges. "Go on through, Detectives." They bypassed the metal detectors and headed straight for the elevators.

As the elevator rose, her dark-haired reflection stared back at her from the brushed metal, composed, sharp-eyed, but already calculating the next steps.

Watkins was just returning to his office when they stepped off the elevator. Briefcase in hand, pinstriped suit still crisp despite the muggy air outside. Forty-nine, according to his dossier, average height and build.

"Counselor." Spaulding followed Watkins to his office.

Watkins pivoted at the door, glanced from Spaulding to her. He flicked his gaze to their badges and frowned. "Detectives? What case are you here for?"

"Mind if we step in?"

He opened his office door and stepped aside to let them in. Not a big office, but sufficient. She and Spaulding sat in the guest chairs. A card was lying on his desk. She caught the name, Kozlov, before the ASA pocketed it.

Where had she seen that name before? KC's mind riffled

through the past week like files in a cabinet, reports on her desk, names mentioned in passing, witness statements. Kozlov. Typed on a document? Handwritten in notes? The memory hovered just beyond reach, like trying to remember a dream after waking.

Watkins set his briefcase on the desk, retrieved some legal documents and moved them aside, then lowered himself into the leather chair behind the desk. "So, what case?"

Spaulding took the lead. "We're not here about a case, Counselor. I'm sorry to inform you, but your ex-wife was found deceased yesterday."

Did he look... scared? No, perhaps he was shocked. Then again, as an experienced trial attorney, he would know how to mask his emotions.

"Kathy? You're sure?"

Spaulding nodded. "I'm afraid so. Fingerprints."

"I see. That's... unfortunate. What happened?"

"We're still investigating. We were hoping you might help us with a few questions."

"Of course."

"Your relationship with Kathy?"

"Cordial. We've been divorced seven years."

"She still had you listed as her emergency contact."

His brows rose. "I wasn't aware. We haven't spoken in a while."

Janelle had told them Watkins and Kathy shared a son, a freshman in college out of town. But Watkins hadn't mentioned him.

KC spoke up. "When was the last time you saw or talked to her?"

"Around Christmas. We ran into each other at a friend's Christmas gathering."

Still no mention of the son.

"We understand you have a son in college." KC watched his reaction.

"Yes, Joey is a freshman at Clemson, but he's on a semester abroad right now."

His movements were economical, practiced, the gestures of a man accustomed to being watched and judged. But something escaped in the way his fingers drummed once against the desk before he stilled them, something in the micropause before he answered their questions about his son.

"If you'd like us to help notifying him, we have resources for that," Spaulding offered.

"Thank you, but I, er, I can handle it."

They asked a few more procedural questions. Watkins remained polite and cooperative. His phone rang once during that time.

Just as they stood to leave, a knock echoed at the door. A man and a woman stood there. From their bearings and sidearms, KC pegged them as detectives. She didn't recognize them, though.

Her mind went back to the name, Kozlov, as soon as they walked out the door. She'd seen it somewhere recently, but where? Was it significant? The way he snatched it up and pocketed it suggested it was.

"Hello, you spaced out on me again."

She gasped. "Sorry, just thinking."

"You're in your own world a lot. So, what do you think?"

"He's got a great poker face."

"You think he's bringing his son home?"

She shrugged. "I'd think so. At least, for the funeral."

Both their phones dinged with a message as they got into the car.

Body. Edge of Winter Garden.

# CHAPTER 25

## THE CONNECTION

The wedding venue was the kind of place people posted about on social media with hashtags like #BarnWedding and #HappilyEverAfter. Whitewashed wood, twinkling lights still strung between beams, and manicured gardens surrounding the rustic building gave it the look of something out of a magazine spread.

Now, crime scene tape flapped like a warning across the idyllic backdrop.

KC stepped out of the Tahoe, heat pressing down on her like a wet towel. Somewhere inside, faint music played on a forgotten loop, something instrumental and romantic. A discarded bouquet lay wilting near the barn doors, its roses browning in the sun.

She followed Spaulding around the building toward the cordoned-off area, the venue's illusion of joy fading with each crunch of gravel beneath her boots. Behind the barn, a row of hedges bordered the property, and just past it, a patch of disturbed soil bruised the landscape.

A maintenance cart had been parked nearby, abandoned in

the grass. Bags of mulch spilled open like forgotten evidence. A uniform gestured them closer.

"Landscaper's here every Thursday," the officer explained. "He was about to lay fresh mulch when he noticed the ground didn't feel right, said it looked like it had been recently turned. He grabbed a rake, went to smooth it out, and the soil collapsed in a bit. That's when he saw the foot."

Spaulding scanned the crowd. "Where is he now?"

"Over there with Delgado." The officer gestured toward a shaken man in a green polo, face pale, sitting on the back of a golf cart. "The other guy is the manager."

"I'll talk to them. You can check out the body." Spaulding headed toward the landscaper.

She ducked under the tape, heat rolling off the soil in shimmering waves. Luna was kneeling beside the shallow grave, eyes hidden behind tinted goggles, clipboard balanced on one knee.

"She looks like another one." Luna pulled the thermometer out. "Female, early twenties. No ID on the body. No personal effects in the immediate area."

"Time of death?" KC breathed through her mouth.

"About a week. Give or take a day. Which puts her in the same window as the one from yesterday."

KC squatted nearby. The soil was soft and uneven, as if pressed down hastily. No obvious drag marks. Whoever buried her carried her here under cover of darkness.

"Any signs of recent surgery?"

"Ah, right." Luna examined the body again, pointing to the lower abdomen. "This might be it. But can't tell here. The ME will confirm when this one gets on the table. I'll mark this as priority, just in case."

"Thanks."

Footsteps crunched on gravel.

"KC." Travers approached, sleeves rolled to his forearms,

heat-slicked and serious. He moved with intensity, greeted Luna, then focused on KC.

Spaulding returned from his interviews.

She stood. "Commander, Detective Rick Spaulding, my partner. Commander Travers."

The two men nodded to each other.

Travers scanned the scene. "Just came from the town car sighting. No surprise, it's long gone. But I got a witness. A guy making a flower delivery down the block said he saw a young woman get into the back seat voluntarily. No struggle."

KC's heart skipped a beat. "Same MO."

"Description?" Spaulding asked.

"Mid-twenties. Blonde. Green backpack."

Her stomach knotted. "And we don't know where the car went."

"Not yet. But Jack's pulling all the traffic cams in a five-block radius. If we're lucky, we'll find her before it's too late."

"We will find her. We have to." It came out harsher than she intended.

Travers's lips curved up a bit. "I like your determination and optimism. Yes, we'll pull our resources and do our best to find her before she ends up like this." His gaze flicked to the shallow grave. "Jack told me about Chandler. Care to fill me in?"

"He called last night, wanted to talk." KC recounted the phone conversation. "I got the feeling he wanted to confess or propose a deal."

Spaulding picked up. "We were supposed to meet him at his home early this morning. But he wasn't there. I thought he changed his mind."

"Turned out he was silenced." KC wiped sweat off her forehead.

"How'd you know the scene was staged?"

KC explained. The name, Kozlov, popped into her brain while she was talking about Chandler. She had seen the name in

Watkins's office, so why would the former surgeon remind her of the name? There had to be a connection. Had she seen something in Chandler's office?

A touch on her arm brought her back to the present. Travers stared at her, and Spaulding murmured, "Not the time to zone out!"

"Sorry, I just remembered something." She faced Spaulding. "We need to return to Chandler's office. Now."

He lifted his eyebrows. "Now?"

"Go." Travers waved them on. "I'll get my team here. We'll update you."

Spaulding muttered an apology. Then his footsteps and voice followed her. "What's with you? That was the commander."

She didn't slow down. "I know, but there's something in Chandler's office. I know it. Something connecting him with Kozlov."

"What? Who?" His voice was close.

"A card was on Watkins's desk when we walked in. He snatched it, but I caught the name, Kozlov. I'd seen that name before, though. Now, I think I saw it in Chandler's office."

At their car, she went straight to the passenger side. "You drive. Fast."

After pulling onto the county road, Spaulding flexed his grip and frowned at her. "You wanna level with me? What's with you? You on something?"

She tightened her jaw. "Absolutely not." She exhaled, huffing over losing control. "It's… this case. I gotta find the Kozlov connection before we lose the latest girl."

He was quiet for a beat. "You've just seemed off. Zoning out a lot. I need you clearheaded."

"I am."

"Be honest, you must, padawan."

Despite the situation, she chuckled. "Yes, master. I am honest."

They arrived at the office building and proceeded to Apex Surgical Solutions. Flashing their badges, they headed toward Chandler's office.

"Mr. Chandler isn't in yet." The receptionist hurried after them.

"He won't be coming in. Has an appointment with the ME." Spaulding followed KC into the office and blocked the receptionist.

"An appointment with the ME?" She sounded confused.

"I'm sorry, but Mr. Chandler was found dead this morning." The receptionist gasped.

"Now, you mind?" Spaulding shooed her away and closed the door.

KC replayed their last visit in her mind's eye. Her gaze passed the back wall, the shelf, and returned to the plaque there.

She stepped forward and lifted the engraved plaque.

WITH GRATITUDE TO OUR PREMIER DONORS
PRESENTED BY THE SOLACE INITIATIVE

DR. TERRANCE CHANDLER
VIKTOR KOZLOV
BIOCORE MEDICAL GROUP

Her heart kicked.

# CHAPTER 26

## HUNTER AND HUNTED

K C clutched the plaque against her chest like it might somehow save them both, Viktor Kozlov's name burning into her mind like a brand. The drive back to the station blurred past in a haze of traffic lights and half-heard radio chatter. Somewhere in the city, another young woman was running out of time.

Spaulding had called a friendly judge for a verbal warrant to seal off Chandler's office. KC then called CSU to process it and Chandler's townhouse.

Back in the squad room, she placed the engraved plaque onto her desk and sank into her chair. Moments later, Spaulding walked in with two cups of coffee and set one on her desk.

"Thank you." She needed the pick-me-up. The java scent alone perked her up.

"That's a great observation there. I noticed the plaque but paid no attention to the names. Any idea who this Kozlov guy is?" He sat at his desk across from her.

She opened her laptop. "No. But when I saw that name in Watkins's office and he snatched the card up... I guess it jogged my memory. Before that? Nada."

"Let's dig into this guy. So, premier donor. He's got money. I'm gonna call a clerk in the state attorney's office. Maybe there's a pending case involving this guy, and Watkins is the prosecutor."

"You don't believe that, do you?"

"Doesn't matter what I believe." He picked up the office phone and made a call.

KC tuned out his voice, searched the internal database for Viktor Kozlov. No hit, as she expected. She widened the search and found something.

Viktor Kozlov, forty-eight. Investor visa holder, listed address in Miami Beach and another in Bratislava, Slovakia. Russian passport, Florida driver's license. A global presence, and likely hiding something.

Something interesting. Kozlov was the founder and executive director of something called *Hope for Tomorrow*, a pediatric surgical outreach organization. Then there was a list of multiple LLCs registered in a few states and many international holding companies. Financials weren't her forte, but the holding companies sounded like shell companies.

Next, she keyed in Solace Initiative, the outfit that presented the plaque. Their website appeared professional. Mission statement: "Bridging the global health divide by empowering local providers and supporting surgical outreach programs in medically underserved communities."

But when she clicked the *Staff* page, not a single staff member had a photo, and their bios looked generic. Some other pages led her to an *Error 404* page. She called the phone number. After several beeps as the call seemed to forward through multiple numbers, a cheerful voice greeted her. "Solace Initiative, how may I help you?"

She introduced herself and asked to speak with Ms. Lucy Ames, listed as the executive director.

"Ms. Ames? She's traveling overseas right now."

"When will she be back?"

"I don't have her return date."

"How about Dr. Nick Dahl? The website said he was the board chair."

"Oh, Dr. Dahl left the organization. Thanks for the heads-up. I'll get someone to update the website."

The line went dead before she could reply. She frowned at the phone.

"What'd you find?" Spaulding set his phone down. "According to the clerk, Watkins doesn't have any cases that involved Kozlov—at least none she could find."

She put the handset back on the cradle. "So, Chandler donated to this Solace Initiative. I just called them. It's either fake, a scam, or a front." She told him about the beeps and the answers. "Here, take a look."

He walked to stand behind her and bent over her shoulder. "Hmm, this initiative is definitely a fake. And the profile on Kozlov looks superficial. We need a deep dive if we really want to know what this guy is up to."

"Last week, when I asked the White Collar unit to check something, they told me to stand in line."

He sauntered back to his seat. "We can always ask Prime. They'll have someone well-versed in that."

"Fantastic idea!" She pulled out her phone. "Why didn't I think of that?"

"Because you're too focused."

Instead of the commander, KC called Jack, who answered right away.

"I need to do a financial deep dive—"

"You need Quinn for financial stuff." He cut her off. "I'm just the lab guy. Hang on. I'll patch you through."

A couple of beeps later, a female voice answered. "Detective Cassidy? Quinn Sterling. I've heard a lot about you."

"Good things, I hope. And just call me KC."

"All positive. And I'm Quinn. So, you need a financial deep dive on someone?"

"Right." KC then proceeded to explain what she wanted.

"This is the serial case, correct?"

"Yes, we saw a card in Watkins's office and found his name on a plaque in Chandler's office. Chandler and Kozlov were listed as premier donors. Just wanted to find out the connections between them. And if this outfit really exists. I think they could be a front."

"Got you. Will send you what I find when I have it."

She thanked her and ended the call. Leaning back, she reviewed what they knew so far. "We need to find out the connection between Watkins and Kozlov. So, Chandler and Kozlov both donated to this fake charity. That means they knew each other, wouldn't you say? Hey, are you listening?"

Spaulding lifted his head. "I am listening. Given that the initiative is an obvious fake, chances are high they knew each other."

"Okay, Kozlov has to be the link between all of them. Chandler, Kozlov, and Watkins."

"Be careful there. Watkins is an assistant state attorney. We can't go around implicating him in anything without solid evidence."

"I know. But you verified Watkins had no case involving Kozlov, so he has his card for some other reason."

He shrugged. "Kozlov could be seeking donations."

"Hey, we can use that. What if we told Watkins the Solace Initiative was a scam, like we're trying to warn him?"

"Ah, are you gonna tell him you saw Kozlov's name, decided to be nosy, checked out this Kozlov guy, and found this fake charity? Having the guy's card is not a crime."

Her shoulders slumped.

He rolled back his chair, pivoting her way, hands laced across his middle, thumbs tapping. "What we could do is say something like, we've come across Viktor Kozlov's name in connection with a murder investigation. You could mention you remember seeing a card there. We'd like to know what he can tell us about the guy."

She perked up. "Yeah, gauge his reaction. If he denies, we'll know he's lying. Possibly hiding something."

"Or he can tell the truth. He met Kozlov at some events. Happens."

Before she could debate further, her desk phone rang.

She picked up the handle. "Cassidy."

"Hey," Janelle spoke. "Remember that *StreetBeat*'s journalist? The one who livestreamed from Sheri's scene?"

KC sat up. "Yeah?"

"I streamed his news show. Sending two clips now, one from Conners's scene and the other from Bishop's."

A ping hit KC's inbox. Two video files. "Did you see anything?"

"I don't want to spoil it. Besides, it may be nothing."

KC thanked her. "Janelle sent the clips. The *StreetBeat*'s guy's footages."

Spaulding wheeled his chair closer to peer at the monitor. "Well, let's see what TikTok Scooby-Doo got us."

The first video loaded, low-quality resolution, shaky camera. The *StreetBeat*'s guy narrated like a true-crime influencer, zipping past yellow tape and police cruisers.

"Turning the sound off." She reached for the mute key.

The footage unfolded. Officers moved in and out of frame. She spotted herself near the scene perimeter, speaking to the responding sergeant.

Nothing stood out until Spaulding leaned in.

"Pause. Back it up five seconds. Slow it down."

KC reversed and replayed.

"There." He pointed. "Tree line. Right side."

She adjusted the brightness.

A man stood near the sidewalk, maybe twenty feet back. Park maintenance uniform, khaki pants, olive-green polo. Ball cap pulled low. Sunglasses. Expression unreadable. He wasn't recording. Wasn't on the phone.

He was just standing there. Or was he looking at her? No, it was her imagination. The dude was wearing shades.

KC squinted. "That could be anyone. Some guy on a break."

"Maybe." Spaulding's voice dropped a notch. "Play the second clip."

The Celina Bishop scene loaded, another chaotic crowd, another livestream. Different street. Different time of day. She again appeared in the frame, walking from one officer to another, her stride brisk and focused.

"There." He pointed again. Left side of the frame, behind the hedge. Hoodie with the same park maintenance logo. Same sunglasses. Same posture.

Her mouth went dry. "How did we not see that before?"

"Because we were looking at the victims. I can't see his eyes, but I get the feeling he's watching you."

"Nah, just looking in my direction." Still, her stomach clenched.

"Two murder scenes. Same guy. Same day."

"Could be a coincidence."

He drilled her with a hard stare. "I don't believe in coincidences in this business. And neither do you."

"Maybe he's, er, whatchamacallit, a groupie. You know, like paparazzi."

"You mean, like he follows this *StreetBeat*'s channel?"

She shrugged.

He took screen grabs from both videos. "What I think is, we need to identify this guy. If he's just a news junkie, fine. But if he's up to no good or connected to the murders, we're covering our bases. And if he was watching you, we need to know why."

KC swallowed, stared at the guy on screen. Her own frozen

image showed her midstep, head turned toward a detective. Behind her, the man stood still.

*Watching her?*

She hated the idea of going from hunting a killer to being hunted.

# CHAPTER 27

## EYES ON KC

The booth at Vinnie's Deli was tucked in the far back, half hidden behind an old Pepsi machine that hadn't worked in years. Spaulding stirred his coffee, letting the cheap ceramic mug warm his fingers as he stared out the rain-slicked window.

He'd told KC he was grabbing takeout for them both. That wasn't a lie. The bags were sitting beside him. But it was also an excuse to get away. He needed to make a phone call, but first, business.

He tapped his phone, then called Jack.

"Detective Spaulding."

"Hey, I just sent you screen grabs of a guy who was at two crime scenes. You have ways to clean it up and do a facial rec?"

Silence, except for the beeps. "Got them. Yeah, I can clean it up. As for facial rec, unlikely. Dude's wearing shades. But lemme do a few things and see what we get."

"Thanks."

"I'll put this in the queue."

Not what he wanted to hear. "Wait, this guy could be targeting KC—"

"Now, why didn't you say that? Where'd you get the screen-shots, anyway? Do you have the source?"

"Yeah, *StreetBeat News* segments."

"Oh, that outfit! All right. I'll get right on it."

Spaulding thanked him again and hung up. That was the easy call. The next one was a tough one. He started to dial, then stopped. He gulped some coffee, then dialed again.

"Tanner." The FBI agent answered right away.

"Spaulding here."

"Detective, what's up?"

He took a deep breath. "Has KC ever zoned out on you?"

There was a pause. "No, not recently."

Was the agent being truthful? Spaulding frowned. "Not recently?"

"Okay, she's got some quirky traits, but I don't think it affects her at all."

"I agree, but she's zoned out on me a few times now. And she, like, walked out on the commander at a crime scene, drag-ging me to another vic's office."

"Oooh, that doesn't sound good, although I hear the commander is pretty easygoing."

"I'm more concerned about KC. I asked her to level with me. She claimed she wasn't on anything."

"She is not. I guarantee it." Tanner's voice was firm. Then a sigh. "I hear you're working on a serial case. Lots of pressure."

"Are you saying she crashes under pressure?"

"No, no, absolutely not. It's just that that kind of pressure could—how do I say it?—make her peculiar traits more noticeable."

"What does that even mean? She got some kind of illness?"

"Not that I know of."

"Then what? Come on, man. She's my partner. I need to know."

Tanner didn't say anything for a beat. "All right. Let me see what I can do. Meanwhile, just trust me. She's good. And have her back."

"Always." Spaulding checked his watch. He'd been gone too long. "Oh, I gotta get back."

He ended the call and headed back to the station. When he walked into the squad room, the rich scent of deli meat and pickles clung to his jacket. A sharp contrast to the burnt-coffee smell that filled his nostrils at Vinnie's.

KC stood up to stretch, eyeing the deli bags like she'd just remembered she was starving. "About time! CSU called. They didn't find anything useful at Chandler's office. They did take his computer. Queuing up for the IT guys to examine it."

He muttered a curse. Everybody was overworked. "Let's see if Prime can tag it as a priority."

She grabbed the desk phone, dialed, and put it on speaker.

"Prime lab," a female voice answered.

"It's KC—"

"Hey, it's Quinn here."

"CSU took a computer from Chandler's office. Waiting for IT people. Spaulding and I thought you guys could put a rush on it?"

"Sure, I'll get them to send it over. Jack or I will take a crack at it. By the way, Eli revised his profile on our serial. I'll send you guys a copy."

"Who's Eli?"

"Oh, Eli Feldman. Retired BAU profiler. First time he's consulting with us, but I understand he'll do that on cases that interest him from now on."

"Color me impressed. You have a BAU profiler on call?" KC's eyebrows arched. "And thanks. Anything you guys don't do?"

Quinn chuckled. "Autopsy."

KC grinned. "Good to know there's still something."

"Hey," Spaulding called from his desk. "Seeing that you guys do everything, any chance you can get a warrant for Chandler's townhouse?"

More chuckles. "I'm sure you can fill in the blanks on the templates. Now, if you need a friendly judge, we have a list."

Somebody's voice mumbled in the background, then came through louder. "Detectives, Jack here. I cleaned the images. So, facial rec's a no-go. The guy's wearing mirrored sunglasses, and not the cheap kind either. These babies are made to block everything. No iris, no eye shape, not even a decent skin tone sample with the way the light hit. I ran it three different ways. Still nothing—"

"Jack," Quinn interrupted. "Bottom line."

"Oh, right. He's watching KC."

KC gasped. "Are you sure?"

"Yes, I ran a head pose estimation model, basically analyzing how his skull's angled across the frames. And I synced that up with timestamps and movement cues…"

By her eye roll, she regretted doubting the lab tech.

"…based on the way he's standing, where his head's turned, the direction of his torso, this guy wasn't sightseeing. He was looking straight at you. Well, there was no one else. The detective you turned to talk to was standing way to your left. I'd bet— ow. Hey."

"Sorry, guys. Jack likes to ramble on," Quinn broke in. "If there's nothing else, we'll get working on the computer and other things."

Spaulding and KC thanked them and hung up.

KC stared at the phone, her face pale. "So he's been following me. Watching me work crime scenes."

Spaulding cleared his throat to respond, but the phone rang again.

"Jack, again. I kept running the analysis and found something else." His voice was tighter now. "I pulled footage from news coverage of all our crime scenes. This guy shows up at every single one."

KC winced as if her stomach dropped.

"But here's the thing. He's only watching KC at those two scenes. At the other ones, he's watching everyone—cops, lookie-loos. But somehow his focus turned to KC."

Her breath caught. She pressed her palms flat against the desk, but they still shook. Her gaze swung to the door. Easy to imagine, the squad room suddenly felt too small, too exposed.

# CHAPTER 28
## MAKING IT PERSONAL

The squad-room buzz faded to background static, phones ringing, printers humming, keys clacking. At her desk, KC barely heard any of it. Her half-eaten sandwich sat forgotten in the wrapper, the pickles gone but the rest still untouched. Watkins, Kozlov, Chandler—the names circled in a mental loop. There had to be a connection.

She stood. "We should go see Watkins."

Spaulding didn't look up from whatever he was doing. "It's late, KC."

"So?"

"So, unless you've got a badge that says state attorney's office, we're not walking in there after hours. He'll be gone, anyway. Let Quinn do her thing. Maybe she'll find something that gives us leverage when we talk to him." He rubbed his eyes, rolled his chair back, and tipped his head her way. "We'll go first thing tomorrow, okay?"

She huffed and plunked back down. "I hate waiting."

A familiar figure stepped through the glass doors, silhouetted against the twilight.

She smiled at the sight. "Tanner. What are you doing here?"

He shrugged. "Finished up early. Thought I'd stop by." He nodded to Spaulding. "Detective."

"Agent Tanner." He put the papers in a stack. "I'm gonna head home. Tanner, take her home. She needs some sleep."

"Yes, sir." Tanner gave a two-finger salute. Then, he approached her. "You heard the man. Pack up. Let's go. I hear gelato calling your name."

Few things tempted her more than gelato. She turned the screen off, got her bag, and stood. "College Park or the other one?"

Tanner gave a courtly bow, one hand sweeping to the side like a stage actor. "Whatever your heart desires, milady."

She laughed all the way out.

Twenty minutes later, KC stepped inside the shop, letting the sweet chill ease her tension. Tanner followed. Behind the marble counter, the gelato case glowed like a treasure chest overflowing with jewel tubs of pistachio, limone, hazelnut, stracciatella.

"Pistachio. No cone. Small cup."

Tanner ordered the same, but a medium cup.

They took a table outside under a row of hanging lights, the city buzz fading into the background.

"So how was your day?" Tanner settled into his chair.

"Same serial killer, different dead ends." She spooned pistachio gelato. "You? Hmm, this is so good."

"Paperwork. Lots of paperwork." He wiped his mouth. "Speaking of your case, Spaulding is your partner. He needs to be able to trust you."

Her brows rose. "Where'd that come from? Of course, he can trust me. Did he say something to you?"

"Let's just say, he's concerned about you. I hear things, like how you walked out on the commander at a crime scene."

She gasped. That incident had slipped her mind. Travers had to think she was rude, or worse, insubordinate. Well, he wasn't her superior, so it wouldn't be insubordination. But what if he told Coleman?

"...like now. Are you with me?" Tanner snapped his fingers in front of her.

"Oh, sorry. Yeah, I'm here. What were you saying?"

He ducked his head, gripped the back of his neck. "When you focus on something, you lose track of everything else. I noticed in December when you were working that councilman's murder back in Pine Grove. You hid it well—"

"But you noticed," she whispered, searching his face, his eyes. Was there any judgment or condemnation? None, just concern.

"I'm a trained and experienced investigator. I notice things." He touched her hand. "Back then, I didn't know you that well. Figured you were just... quirky. You are, but some things felt off. Like how you'd bring two beers, act like you were drinking yours. Then, when you thought I wasn't looking, you'd switch it out for the nonalcoholic one."

He shrugged. "After your aunt hinted at it, I looked into it. What it meant for babies born to addicts, the possible lingering effects like obsessive behavior and prone to addiction."

She frowned at her glistening gelato. "You talked to Aunt Mae?"

He held up a hand. "In case you were wondering, she volunteered it. I didn't pry. She wanted me to understand. You don't like being labeled, and you don't like the idea of being seen as different or damaged. But you're neither. You are a smart and good detective."

"I used to see a therapist for it. Thought maybe I was... broken." A bitter smile twisted her lips. She dipped the spoon and scooped some sweetness to coat the bad flavor. "Aunt Mae said I just had a mind that needed to make sense of the world. Still do."

"You should let Spaulding know."

Aha. She understood now. She pointed the spoon at him. "Spaulding thought I was on something. He asked you."

"Don't blame him. You zoned out on the guy a few times. And then you walked out of the scene with the commander there. He's a cop. The natural thing for him to consider is you're using. You need to talk to him." He unfolded a napkin and wiped the dollop of gelato she'd dropped onto the tabletop. "You were the only detective at the Pine Grove Sheriff substation. Now, you have a partner."

She plopped the spoon in her mouth, the creamy treasure coating any bitter residue. "I know and I will."

"Don't wait too long." Tanner smirked, reached across, and wiped the side of her mouth.

"Thanks."

His eyes twinkled. "I've got your back—so does he. Make sure he knows you've got his."

By the time she pulled into her driveway, the sky had darkened to a washed-out slate. It had started to rain when they left the gelato shop. Rain clung to the edges of the windshield. Her little bungalow sat quietly, the porch light blinking like it couldn't decide whether to stay on.

She liked the place. Small, modest, tucked into a quiet residential street. The detached garage leaned slightly, but it reminded her of home.

She cut the engine, grabbed her bag, and froze.

Someone moved. Just a flicker, a figure slipping out the side kitchen door.

A jolt shot through her chest. Pure adrenaline.

She shoved the door open. "Orlando PD! Stop!"

The figure didn't stop.

He ran.

KC took off after him, boots slapping wet pavement. He ducked down the alley. She stayed on him.

"Police! Stop right now!"

He vaulted a fence. She followed, barely clearing it. He cut across a yard, sprinted behind a row of bushes, disappeared into the dark.

KC reached the corner, gun in hand. Nothing. He was gone.

Back at the bungalow, her weapon stayed drawn as she approached the side door, still ajar. No damage. Picked?

She swept the house.

Living room—empty.

Bedroom—clear.

Closet—nothing.

Finally, the kitchen.

It appeared untouched. No drawers open. No footprints. No broken glass.

On the counter, perfectly centered, untouched.

A note. One line.

LET CHANDLER TAKE THE FALL.

She stepped back, heart thudding in her ears.

This wasn't a warning.

It was a statement.

Whoever had been watching her…

Had just walked into her house.

And made it personal.

She could smell something else now, cologne, faint but unfamiliar, lingering in her kitchen like a signature.

# CHAPTER 29

## THE WATCHER

The rain had stopped, but the city still steamed, pavement slick with runoff, the streets bathed in the sodium-orange glow of streetlamps flickering to life. Inside the Hub, the air was cool and dry, but tension ran warm beneath the surface.

Frank stood near the front, one hand resting on a reclaimed wood table scarred by years of use, the other wrapped around a mug of black coffee gone lukewarm. Behind him, the bullpen stirred with quiet movement, keyboard taps, and low-voiced updates underscored by the distant whir of centrifuges and the occasional beep of lab monitors from Jack's glass-walled lab beyond the kitchen and courtyard.

No walls here. No doors between desks. Just open sight lines, exposed brick, industrial fixtures spilling pools of light, and the hum of purpose.

This was his watchtower. Ground-level. No glass office, no separation. If something was coming, he'd see it face-on.

And something *was* coming. He could feel it in his bones.

Damon stepped into view with Claire close behind, tablet in hand.

Frank turned from the window and took the coffee mug from his desk, cold now, bitter as old ash. "What've we got?"

Claire pulled up a profile on her screen, her glossy brown hair skimming her shoulders. "Brian Shipley. Twenty-one. Junior at UF. Premed. Clean record. GPA's strong. Tutors other students. Works at Shands Hospital. Volunteers at Orlando Family Wellness Clinic every Saturday."

Damon ran a hand over his bald head, the shave clean, brown eyes alert. "Kid's a saint, according to everyone we talked to. Early bird, stays late, does the work. Staff loves him."

Frank raised an eyebrow. "Sounds like a good kid."

"Here's the relevant detail. Six weeks ago, minor laceration case. Shipley attempted his first suture under supervision. He botched it. Made the cut worse."

"He panicked?" Frank asked.

Damon shook his head. "No, froze, but didn't run. The doc took over. No real harm done."

"But it's in the file." Claire tucked her hair behind her ears.

Frank paced a few feet. His boots echoed on the concrete floor, the sound grounding him. "That's not a mistake you forget, especially if you're ambitious. And Foley's autopsy showed sloppier stitching than the other victims. Not just poor technique. Hesitation marks. Repositioning."

From the wall-mounted screen, Jack's lab-pale face popped into view, his dark hair in its typical mess. Then another window opened, a video feed of Eli in what looked like a well-lit home office lined with bookshelves.

"Eli is writing his great American novel, but I got him looped in. Actually, he's writing—"

"Thank you, Jack," Frank cut him off. "We know he's writing a book."

Eli adjusted his glasses and leaned toward the camera. "Sorry, I missed the discussion. Run that by me again."

Claire summarized what they had discussed.

"Shipley might've done that one, yes. Those sutures read like someone still learning or pretending to know more than they do. But the others?" Eli raised one index finger. "Different caliber. Those were done by someone with legitimate experience. A trained surgeon."

"So what does that make Shipley?" Frank stepped closer to the screen.

Eli's left index finger tapped the right first. "Possibly a copy-cat." He held up another finger and tapped too. "Possibly a pawn. But not the architect."

Frank let the silence stretch. The fluorescent lights buzzed overhead. Someone's cell vibrated across a desk. "All right. Let's not write him off yet."

Across the room, Quinn rolled her chair toward the main cluster of desks. "Boss? KC and Spaulding asked us to comb through Chandler's laptop. CSU dropped it off an hour ago. They want it done ASAP."

Frank gestured toward her. "Do it." A surgeon. He turned back to the screen. "Eli, Terry Chandler used to be a successful surgeon. Any chance he could be the one? KC did say he wanted to talk to her before he got silenced."

Eli lowered his hands to his desk. "Any specialty?"

"Organ transplant," Quinn answered right away.

"Then that's your surgeon. Transplant work requires preci-sion under pressure, exactly what we're seeing in the quality victims. He lost his license for what reason? Send me his file, but I'm confident we've found our killer's skill set."

"I'll take care of it now." Claire went back to her desk.

"Wait, there's more." Quinn raised her hand. "KC wants me to dig into some guy named Viktor Kozlov's finances. Said he's connected to Chandler through a group called the Solace Initiative."

Frank squinted. "Kozlov?"

"No further details. Just that she found something at Chandler's office and thinks Kozlov might be a lead. I already started compiling financials. Nothing illegal yet, but weird movement. Foreign transfers. Real estate purchases through cutouts."

Frank rubbed his jaw. "Share whatever you find with them. If Chandler's post-suspension behavior links to Kozlov, it's relevant. Keep digging."

Quinn swiveled back to her screens, her head poised over them, her blonde hair in a loose twist.

From the screen on the wall, Jack waved. "Detective Spaulding told me about some guy lurking at the crime scenes. Turned out he was watching KC. So, I—"

"Watching KC?" Frank looked at the plasma.

"Yes, that's not all. He was at all the scenes. I got the footage from—"

"Put them up." He cut off Jack's inevitable ramble.

The screen split into several sections, each displaying a different image from different crime scenes.

"Yeah, I see him here." Damon pointed. "And here."

Frank spotted all of them. "Jack, you said he was watching KC?"

"Yes." Jack enlarged the two images and shrank the others. "You see the sight line." He drew a red line with a digital pen. "I did it with—"

"I trust you." Frank frowned.

"Jack, the other scenes are the ones before the detectives got involved, correct?" Eli asked from his feed.

"Correct. These two are the scenes of Sheri Conners and Celina Bishop."

"You have a theory." Frank watched Eli's expression, narrowed eyes, lips pressed together.

Eli brought a cup to his mouth, took a sip, and put it down. "I doubt he's your killer. Maybe a watcher. But he sees KC as a threat. Probably because of her intense focus."

Frank's gut clenched. "Facial rec?"

"No hits. The sunglasses block the scan. But—" Jack clicked again. "In one clip, he turns just as a passing car rolls by. I got a partial reflection. I'm enhancing it, but don't hold your breath."

"Keep on it."

Frank turned back to his team.

"Here's what I want. Damon, Claire, keep digging into Brian Shipley. School records, volunteer logs, roommate. I want to know what he's been doing since Chandler was suspended. Who he's been talking to. Who's been talking to him."

Quinn pushed her chair back, tilting his way. "And Kozlov?"

"You don't stop until you hit the bottom. If this Solace Initiative's a shell, find out who's laundering through it and who they're paying."

"Don't mind me. I'll just keep doing what I do," Jack called from the screen.

"Right." Frank paused, listening to the Hub's low hum again. "Somewhere out there is our guy. Maybe two."

Everyone started moving at once.

Then Damon's phone buzzed. One ring. Two. He swiped to answer. "Cruz."

Frank went back to his desk and sat. They had a few threads going. Something would pop. And KC. Her odd, even rude, behavior at the crime scene had him thinking. Her Orlando PD file was thin, given how new she was, but he dug into her background in the Sheriff's Office. Her file there was full of commendations. No red flag.

"That was Louis Shipley. His cousin, Brian, is missing. Evidently, Brian had a med school appointment this morning, but missed it. Louis said he wouldn't miss it for anything. Phone's off. Louis called to see how the appointment went, but got no answer. Brian's roommate said he hadn't seen him since he left for work yesterday. The roommate stayed at his girlfriend's last night, so he doesn't know if and when Brian got home."

Frank stood up again. "Now he's not just a suspect. He's a missing person."

# CHAPTER 30

## THE MESSAGE

K C stood in the kitchen, motionless, the refrigerator's hum the only sound in the small bungalow. Her bare feet were cold against the tile, but she didn't move.

The note remained in the center of the counter, beside a clear evidence bag from her home kit. It wasn't handwritten or typed. Instead, each letter had been clipped from cereal boxes, magazines, maybe even shipping labels, cut and glued to a thick white note card.

LET CHANDLER TAKE THE FALL.

The ransom-style letters gave the message a childish aesthetic, but there was nothing playful about it. The edges were crisp, the spacing perfect. Whoever made it had taken their time, lined up the typography like it mattered. Like it was art.

The card itself remained untouched. She hadn't even flipped it over. After staring at the message, she'd slid it into the evidence bag with gloved hands.

Now the glued-on words stared back at her from behind the plastic, taunting her.

Whoever had broken into her home hadn't come to steal anything. They came to send a message.

The smell of coffee from the half-empty mug beside the sink had gone stale. Her fingers drummed against the counter, a restless rhythm that made the silence heavier.

This wasn't about the victims anymore. Someone had crossed the line. This was about her.

Headlights swept across the front windows, followed by the muted rumble of an engine shutting off. A car door. Footsteps on the walk. She straightened, pulling her arms in tight, the automatic instinct to keep control of her body language. She wouldn't give the intruder, whoever he was, the satisfaction of imagining her rattled.

She had debated, then called her partner. As Tanner reminded her, Spaulding needed her trust.

He filled the doorway when it opened, big shoulders, jacket unbuttoned, eyes already scanning every corner. He didn't say anything at first. Just stepped inside and let the door close with a soft click.

"Where's the note?"

A jut of her jaw directed him toward the kitchen counter, where his gaze found the evidence bag.

KC stepped aside, letting him get a closer look. "No forced entry. Nothing broken. Nothing missing. Just the note."

Pulling on gloves from his pocket, he picked up the bag and turned it over. The back of the note was blank. Then he slid his phone out.

"No, we can't call this in."

He frowned at her. "What do you mean? CSU needs to process the scene. Prints, fibers, boot treads, anything we can get."

Before she could answer, hurried footsteps pounded outside, getting closer. Her hand went to her weapon.

"Relax. It's your boyfriend."

She scowled. "You called Tanner?"

Tanner appeared in the doorway, then stepped inside. "Thank goodness he did." His gaze swept over her, checking for signs of harm. "Are you all right?"

"I'm fine." Annoyed he was here? Maybe. But also... relieved. She hated that it showed.

Spaulding looked up from the note. "Guess what? She doesn't want me to call it in."

Not to state the obvious, but... "If the loo finds out, I'm benched. I become a witness, not a cop."

Spaulding gave Tanner a look. "The lab won't even process the note without a case number. And if we find this guy later, this thing becomes inadmissible."

"I'd bet there's no usable prints." She let her arms relax, tried for friendly. "No DNA. He was in and out, gloves, fast, surgical." The word *surgical* rolled out before she could stop it, conjuring the memory of Chandler's death, staged with the same kind of control.

"I might have a way to have it tested." Tanner moved in for a closer look. "And KC is probably right. Whoever made this went through the trouble of clipping and pasting. Chances aren't good, but you never know."

Spaulding raised a brow. "I don't know if I should just hand it to you."

Tanner smirked. "I know. Chain of evidence is kind of drilled into us. Let me make a quick call." He moved into the living room.

While Tanner was gone, Spaulding clattered out a stool and sat. "So, did you see him?"

"Not clearly." She braced a hip against the counter. "Not the face. Lean build, maybe five ten. Athletic. Blue hoodie with the hood up. Could've been white or light-skinned, but it was too dark to say for sure."

Her partner fiddled with his phone, then tilted it to face her. "Could it be the guy from the scenes?"

She leaned closer. The still was from the Sheri Conners footage, but the image was sharper and clearer. Jack said he cleaned it up, but he didn't send her a copy. "Jack sent it to you?"

"I asked."

She closed her eyes, mentally replaying the incident frame by frame. Was there a time he turned toward her? Did he carry himself the same way as the guy in the footage? The clothing, yes, the clothing! Her eyelids popped open. "The hoodie! I believe he was wearing that same hoodie in the Celina Bishop scene."

"Okay," Tanner called from the other room, reentering. "We're good. Deanna will test it for prints, trace evidence, all the good stuff. It's loosely tied to Kozlov, right? She'll use that case number."

That'd do. Her shoulders relaxed.

Spaulding opened his mouth, then closed it.

"All right, then." Tanner poured out her old coffee, rinsed the cup, then dried his hands. "Man, that stuff stinks. So, what'd I miss?"

Spaulding passed over his phone. "She thinks it's the same guy who's been watching her. At least at two crime scenes that we know of."

Tanner studied the image. "Can't do a facial rec with the sunglasses. How can you be sure he was watching KC?"

"I'm not, but Jack, the Prime lab guy, is. Something about head pose, some tool or program he was running. I wasn't listening."

Tanner crossed to her, gripped her upper arms, and bent to eye level. "Are you sure you don't want to call this in? Seems like you've rattled somebody's cage. You're a target."

Her heart pounded. "I can't. If the loo knows, he'll bench me."

"That's protocol." He rubbed his hands up and down her arms. "You know, for your safety."

Maybe he thought he could chase off the chills. She eased away and shook her head. "There's no guarantee they won't come after me even after I'm off the case. They must think I know something. Otherwise, why me? And not Spaulding?"

"Maybe because I wasn't at those scenes?" Spaulding tucked his phone into his back pocket. "Remember, I was tied up in recert? You walked the scenes by yourself."

"With the commander at the Celina Bishop scene. Regardless, I can take care of myself. It only means we're getting close, even when I don't know it."

Tanner groaned. "So… does Jack have some tricks to find out who this guy is?"

"Beats me." Spaulding shrugged. "He said he was still combing through the footage. Who knows? Maybe he'll find something."

"We need to ID this guy." Tanner grabbed the evidence bag. "I'm gonna take this to the lab. Will you stay with her? I'll be back."

*Hold up.* "I don't need—"

"No argument. You just got yourself a shadow." Tanner raised the bag. "Either that or you report it." Then he took off.

Spaulding had the nerve to grin.

She dropped onto the nearest stool. "Enjoying yourself?"

He pinched two fingers together. "Little bit."

Before he could add a quip, both their phones chimed. She unlocked hers before he managed to retrieve his from his pocket.

"Jack texted. 'Town car just resurfaced. Stationary. Parking garage off Colonial. Sending location now.'"

Keys in hand, she hopped up and checked her firearm.

Someone wanted to rattle her, to make her back down. Instead, they'd given her another reason to catch him. "Let's go before it disappears again."

# CHAPTER 31

## ASHES AND CLUES

The garage was a concrete cavern, lit by buzzing sodium lamps that painted everything in a jaundiced glow. KC's boots echoed as she stepped out of the Tahoe, the sound swallowed by the low hum of air vents pushing stale, exhaust-tainted air through the levels.

On the way there, she texted Tanner and got a thumbs-up emoji back.

The black town car sat in the far corner like it had been waiting for them, centered in its space, chrome trim catching the light in thin, sharp glints.

Spaulding scanned the shadows, his voice low. "Feels like a trap."

KC kept her tone even. "Let's make it quick."

With their guns out at the low ready, they approached the vehicle. Spaulding gestured he was going to the driver's side, so she angled toward the passenger side, gaze sweeping the undercarriage out of habit.

Something caught her eye, a flash of silver and black just beyond the front wheel. Not the neat, factory-tight lines of brake cables or exhaust tubing, but a sloppy twist of electrical tape and exposed wire dangling low. Her stomach dipped.

"Spaulding—"

She never finished. A sharp pop cracked through the stillness, followed by a bloom of orange fire licking out from beneath the chassis. Heat rolled at them in a wave.

"Back!" Spaulding yanked her hard toward the nearest concrete pillar as the flare roared into a hungry fire, sprinklers stuttering to life overhead.

A rolling *whump* followed, not the shattering punch of a bomb, but the roar of an accelerant-fed fire. Heat slammed into her face, searing the air in her lungs. Black smoke boiled upward, thick with the stench of burning plastic and gasoline.

Shards of headlight glass and melted trim clinked and skittered across the concrete. The sprinklers spat water in jittery bursts, hissing as it hit the fire and flashed to steam. The glow reflected off the wet concrete and the chrome of the cars parked nearby, throwing restless orange across the walls.

KC coughed, wiping water from her eyes. "Evidence just went up in smoke."

Spaulding tapped on his phone. "Calling this in. Whoever lit it wanted us to see it."

They stayed back until the fire crew rolled in, letting the firefighters finish before stepping closer. What was left of the town car was a warped shell, blackened and dripping. Thank goodness, it was a small, targeted explosion.

"We'll need CSU to process what's left." KC's thumbs typed.

After the paramedics cleared her and Spaulding, she brushed off the soot and dirt from her clothing as best she could.

"What happened?"

She turned to the voice and answered the wiry man in a security guard outfit with a faded ball cap. "A small car bomb."

"Do we need to evacuate?"

Spaulding shook his head. "The fire captain doesn't think so. You work here?"

The guard nodded. "I was in the management office and heard this boom. Came running. Been standing here a while waiting to talk to someone."

"Good. Have you seen this car?" She showed him the photo of the town car before the fire.

"Yeah, I've seen it. Comes through now and then. Same guy? Different guys? Don't know. Don't pay much attention unless they block the ramp."

"You have footage?"

"Just the entrance and exit."

Spaulding pointed to the orb facing the office's sliding door. "What about that?"

The guy glanced toward it. "Oh, that. Yeah, that too."

"We need to see it," Spaulding prompted.

"Follow me." The guard took them to the management office, sat, and tapped some keys to bring up the footage. She and Spaulding went behind the counter to watch the grainy videos.

The town car went in at 3:54 p.m., never left. They switched to the sliding-door camera. At 4:01 p.m., a man in a suit walked in from the garage. Two minutes later, three teenagers came through. Another three minutes passed before a group of high schoolers entered.

In between, a few office workers walked into the garage.

What happened to the car's occupants? They brought the girl here. Where'd they go? KC frowned.

"Let's see the exit," Spaulding suggested. "Maybe they walked out of here."

She didn't think so, but she watched, anyway. Nobody walked out. "Wait. Go back a bit and play at half speed."

The guard rewound and struggled to slow down the playback.

"May I?" Her impatience won out, and she reached forward.

"Please." The guard stood up, stepped aside. "Help yourself."

KC got it to the right place, pointed for Spaulding. "You see this sedan? Three minutes after the town car went in. I think I see two people inside." She tried to zoom in, but the outdated equipment lacked the capability.

"Yeah." He braced a hand on the desk. "It looks like a Toyota Camry. Too bad no angle on the rear plate."

"We'll send the footage to Jack. Maybe he'll find something."

"So, what are you thinking? They swapped cars?"

She straightened. "Only thing that makes sense."

"You know, the town car went silent and only pinged several minutes ago." Spaulding watched the last of the flames sputter out.

Right. She pushed away from the desk. "Like you said, they wanted to lure us here. Wanted us to watch the evidence burn."

Speaking of Jack and the town car... KC scrolled down her phone messages. "I forgot Jack found the plate and the registered owner. Here it is."

"Right!" Spaulding hit his forehead. "I must be getting old. Whose car is it?"

"Registered to Evergreen Assets Inc."

"We'll head back and check it out."

Before they left, she studied the tenant directory mounted beside the elevators. A blur of law offices, consultants, and finance companies with names bland enough to mean anything. She didn't recognize a single one, but she took a picture, anyway.

Twenty minutes later, she plopped down at her desk chair with a fresh cup of coffee. The squad room was quiet, but not dead. Two other detectives hunched at their desks, one murmuring into a phone, the other bathed in the glow of a desk lamp. Burnt coffee and copier toner still tinted the air.

She ran the name, Evergreen Assets Inc. through every database they could. Empty shell.

"Let Prime take the first swing in the morning." Spaulding rocked back in his chair, rubbing the bridge of his nose.

"Fine. I'll work the tenants."

The door swung open, letting in a gust of cold air and the faint scent of street rain. Tanner walked in, hair damp, jacket unzipped. "Deanna's working on it."

She flashed a smile. "You didn't have to come."

"But I do. I'm taking you home."

"Let me finish this." She scrolled down the list of tenants. Halfway down, a name snagged her attention: Elite Prep Solutions. Her head popped up. "Have we come across Elite Prep Solutions?"

"Think I've seen that before." Spaulding rummaged through the case files.

Tanner looked over her shoulder, scanning the list. "Horizon Aid Society. That's familiar. Came up in a case we kicked to White Collar, tax evasion, offshore transfers. Not violent, but shady."

She starred it and pulled up their website. The homepage was squeaky clean, smiling volunteers, stock-photo handshakes, charity buzzwords. She clicked the *About* page.

Her pulse ticked up. "Affiliated with Hope for Tomorrow," she read aloud.

"Mean anything to you guys?" Tanner's gaze traveled from her to Spaulding.

"Yeah." The word came out flat, tight in her throat. "Kozlov's nonprofit."

Before the weight of it could settle, Spaulding tapped a page in the file. "Found it, Kathy Foley. She tutored at Elite Prep Solutions. Twice a week."

KC stared at the laptop screen, the image of the burning town car still vivid in her mind. Kozlov. Kathy. Same building.

# CHAPTER 32

## PAWN OR PREDATOR

The Hub was quieter than usual this morning, no rapid-fire keyboard clicks, just the low hum of monitors and the distant gurgle of the coffee maker. Frank stood at the mezzanine window, the glass cold against his palm as the city woke beneath the pale morning. Last night, he reviewed everything about Brian Shipley. How was the kid involved in this whole mess?

Thanks to KC's efforts, the team learned about Brian. If he were involved in any way, why would he allow his ex-girlfriend to be a victim? According to KC's interview with Sheri Conners's mom, Brian was surprised to hear of Sheri's disappearance. KC was under the impression he hadn't known about her death until she told him.

But he fit the profile of the inexperienced practitioner who had sutured Kathy Foley's wounds. And now, he was missing. So, was he a suspect? A pawn? Or an innocent caught up in this mess?

Damon and Claire had spent the better part of the night tracking down leads, but nothing concrete had come from it. Frank drummed his fingers against the windowsill. They entered without their usual morning banter, shoulders slumped. He hurried down to the bullpen to join them.

"A coworker spotted a cut on Brian's hand a few days ago." Damon dropped his bag on the floor by his desk. Stubble poked through in a ring around his baldpate. His eyelids drooped.

Claire sat and pushed her brown hair away from her face. "No other updates. Everything matches what Louis told us. We talked to his coworkers."

Frank braced against her desk. "No hint as to where he might have gone? Or if he was abducted?"

Damon shook his head. "Nada."

"From what the cousin said, it doesn't sound like Brian disappeared voluntarily. He wanted to go to med school, and he wouldn't have missed his appointment. However," Claire added, "we have Brian's laptop."

Damon dropped it off on Quinn's desk.

"I see you have a present for me." Quinn walked in.

"With love, from Brian Shipley," Damon quipped.

"It's password protected," Claire called out.

No worries on that. Quinn or Jack would crack it.

"I didn't realize you guys had such a great setup back there." Eli sauntered in from the kitchen, steam rising from his mug, the rich scent of fresh coffee trailing him. "Jack gave me a tour of his lab."

"You're in early." Frank moved to his own desk.

"Yeah, I was intrigued by the disgraced doc. And then, the missing student. I read up on their files." He settled at a desk by Frank, reserved for visiting detectives or agents. "Don't let me interrupt you. Please, carry on."

"Found something!" Quinn's fingers flew across her keyboard, the rapid clicking punctuating her announcement.

Brian's laptop screen glowed against the dim morning light filtering through the blinds. She'd cracked it in minutes.

"Yes?" Frank prompted.

She pointed to the plasma on the wall. Seconds later, what looked like Brian's search engine history appeared there.

"He was searching for organ transplant and surgical diagrams."

"Given that he's a premed, it shouldn't be that unusual." Frank scanned the list. A lot of searches regarding the disappearance of Sheri Conners. Some online prayer requests. Then an odd one—successful interview tips.

"Here's his emails." Quinn rolled her chair to face the main screen, stylus in one hand.

"Can you open the one from Deacon Mark?" Eli asked.

The cursor blinked. The email showed up.

"Okay, asking the deacon to request the congregation to pray for the safe return of Sheri Conners. I assume this was sent before the discovery of the body?" Eli looked in Frank's direction.

"Correct."

"His search history shows online prayer requests. I believe he submitted the same prayer request to those sites."

It would prove he cared about Sheri. Instead of bolstering Brian as a suspect, it just got more puzzling. "What are you thinking?"

"Let's see what else they find?"

Jack's face popped up on the screen. "Morning, folks. So, my trusty program combed through the twenty-mile radius of campus. No sign of Shipley's car. I went back a few days, set the parameters to—"

"What'd you find?" Frank needed Jack to focus.

"Right. Coming up." Jack's face now occupied a small square in a corner of the screen. "See here? He was at a gas station ten miles from campus two days ago, wearing a baseball cap."

"So?" Damon frowned.

"Patience."

While the gas was pumping, Brian dumped a filled-up shopping bag in the dumpster. While that in itself didn't mean anything, the location wasn't near his apartment, the campus, or the hospital where he worked. He had gone out of his way to get rid of whatever was in the bag.

"Anything else?" Frank asked.

"Yes." Quinn poked the stylus into her updo and wiggled it as if chasing an itch. "Brian's bank account shows a sudden influx of cash. Ten grand. Direct deposit. I'm tracing it now."

"Sounds like he's running," Claire said.

Frank crossed his arms. Where did the guy get the money? Was it payment for Foley's suture job? The email to the deacon asking for prayers. Could that be code for something?

"Damon, Claire, go back and talk to his professors, the deacon. Quinn, find the source of the money. Eli, anything you want to add?"

The profiler straightened from behind Quinn. Frank hadn't noticed he'd gone to stand behind her. "Not now. But I would urge you not to rush to judgment. I see some inconsistencies."

When Frank waited for him to elaborate, Eli just returned to his desk. Frank nodded to Jack on the screen. "Expand your search area. Whether he's a suspect or just a missing kid, he's a person of interest. I want him found now."

The sharp electronic chime cut through the room's murmur, drawing all eyes to the main screen. Claire, closest to the remote, hit to accept. KC and Spaulding appeared on screen.

"A bit of an update. You might have heard of an exploding car. That's the town car." Spaulding updated them on the office building tenants, as well as their theory of car swaps. "We got the surveillance footage from the office. KC is sending the file to Jack. Maybe he can find something useful."

Frank, in turn, briefed them on Brian Shipley. "We'll stay with Brian Shipley. You guys follow up with the office tenants."

"Will do." Spaulding signed off.

"All right, go find Brian!" Frank ordered.

Damon grabbed his jacket. "Leaving."

Claire headed for the door. "Going."

"Searching," Jack called from the screen.

"Frank, after hearing the updates, it's looking like the one in charge is tying up loose ends. We need to find this network before it closes shop and moves on."

Pulling up a chair, Frank sat across from Eli. "You're suggesting Brian is a pawn? And this is a network?"

Since Prime started this case, it appeared to be more than a serial killer. How gratifying to hear Eli thought the same.

Eli finished his coffee. "You're being modest. I'm sure you deduced as much. True, Brian has the skill set to be the one to suture Kathy Foley's wounds. If he did that, he was coerced, lied to, or used. He wouldn't have knowingly participated in this." He shuffled the files on his desk. "Terry Chandler was an interesting study."

"What's your take on him?"

"Chandler wasn't a monster by design. He had the skill set they needed, a serious vulnerability in his addiction history, and a fall from grace that left him broke and isolated. Once he lost his license, his identity as a surgeon went with it. People in that position are desperate to matter again."

"So whoever is behind this lured him in?"

Eli nodded. "I'm sure they pitched it as giving people a second chance, filling a gap in a broken system. They made him believe he was still saving lives. And once he realized what they were really doing, he was already in too deep, financially, legally, morally."

"He called KC the night before he died. They set up an appointment to meet the next morning. She got the impression he was going to turn himself in, make some kind of deal. He never made it."

"That fits. They were monitoring him. And when they realized he was going to the cops, they had to silence him."

"Boss," Quinn called from her desk, then pointed at the screen. "Found something in Brian's gallery."

A few photos populated the plasma. Surveillance photos? But Brian wasn't a PI. "What am I looking at?"

"Not sure, but one is the office building where Chandler worked. And another is his townhouse. Then there are several of Chandler and Viktor Kozlov."

"Zoom in on those." Frank stood up, walked closer to the screen.

One showed them in a garage talking. Another one showed Chandler following Kozlov into a warehouse. "You know the locations?"

"Not yet. Working on it."

"Now this is interesting." Eli shook his head. "Brian may be playing with fire and got burned."

"Hey, boss." Jack's face popped up on the screen. "You need to see this surveillance footage from the student center." The plasma screen flickered to black-and-white security camera footage. Brian Shipley looked into the camera before shoving something bulky into a locker and walking away fast. "Time-stamp shows this was four days after Sheri Conners was reported missing."

# CHAPTER 33

## THE LIE

While Spaulding disconnected the video call to Prime, KC finished her second cup of java. It wasn't even 9 a.m. yet. *Going to be one of those days.* The ancient radiator clanked to life, adding its metallic wheeze to the morning sounds of ringing phones and shuffling papers.

"Seems the kid has some explaining to do. Ten grand." Spaulding's stern face creased into tighter lines. "Kind of like that kid."

"I still don't think he's involved." She stood up. "Let's hit the morgue. Have they called about the latest victim?"

"No, they're probably just doing the autopsy." He finished the last bite of his breakfast burrito and tossed the wrapper in the trash. "Wait. Let's find out if they did the post first. No sense going there if they don't have anything to tell us yet."

"Prime would have flagged it as priority."

"Yes, but it still takes time." He picked up the office phone and dialed.

She blew out a sharp breath and dropped into her chair hard enough to make it squeak. Her gaze traveled to the board, four victim photos pinned under harsh fluorescent lights that made their pale skin look almost blue. Sheri Conners, Celina Bishop, Kathy Foley, and the latest body. Foley had to be the outlier, the key, to unravel this.

He hung up. "They just started—"

"We got nothing."

"Patience, padawan. We have a name. Chantille Deters."

She searched the database for Chantille Deters. Reported missing two months ago by her foster sister. She would have been twenty-one in a week. So young!

Before KC got any further, her phone buzzed. Deanna's name flashed across the screen.

KC swiped to answer. "Morning, Deanna."

"Good morning. The note's clean. No prints, no usable trace. But that word 'Chandler' is from a legal document."

"How'd you know?"

"I'm sure you don't want a lecture in forensic science. So, basically, the font and the faint impression of a page number stamp gave it away. Wish I could tell you more."

"Can you tell what kind of legal document?"

"Given time, I can tell you a lot more. But for now, it's from a legal transcript."

"You mean, like a deposition?"

"Yeah, or trial, hearing, grand jury, even witness statements. Any court filings."

"So, it wouldn't be readily available anywhere else outside of a courthouse or an attorney's office, correct?"

"Correct."

Spaulding was now watching her with interest.

"Thanks, Deanna." She hung up and leaned back in her chair. "Legal transcript. Who do you think has access to these documents?"

He shrugged. "Oh, lawyers, court reporters, lots of people."

"But who is also connected, no matter how tangentially, to these cases? And especially one particular victim?"

"I bet that would be your favorite ASA."

"What do you say we pay him a visit? Weren't we gonna do that anyway?"

"Yes." He got up. "I was hoping Quinn would find something in Chandler's electronics linking him to Watkins, but I haven't heard anything yet."

She grabbed her bag and hurried after him. "I get the feeling they're casual over there."

"Where? Prime?"

"Yeah."

"I've heard the commander doesn't like formality and treats his team like family."

"That's nice."

Twenty-two minutes later, they were in Watkins's cramped office, the air thick with the smell of instant coffee and stress sweat. The attorney's jaw tightened when he saw them, his welcoming smile never quite reaching his eyes. New lines creased the corners of his eyes, and his shoulders sagged as if he were carrying extra weight.

"Detectives, what can I do for you now?"

Spaulding settled into a guest chair. "We ran into Viktor Kozlov's name in an investigation. Detective Cassidy thought she'd seen his card here before. We thought we could get some background information on Kozlov."

"Kozlov." Watkins flicked his gaze toward KC. "Yes, I met him at an event a while ago. He was asking for a donation to his nonprofit. A children's medical group, I believe. I must have dropped his card in the office."

"Has he reached out since?"

"No."

Even though Spaulding was asking the question, Watkins's sight kept turning to KC.

"So, no communication."

"Detectives, I'm not sure if I can help at all. Met the guy

once. Don't really know him."

"I see." Spaulding stood up. "We're just crossing the *T*'s and dotting the *I*'s. You know how it is." He extended his hand. "Thank you for your time."

KC got up, nodded to the attorney, and followed Spaulding out the door.

The elevator's cables groaned as it descended, and the floor numbers flickered in the dim light.

Spaulding's chuckle echoed off the metal walls. "The way his voice cracked on 'detectives' and how he kept fidgeting with his pen, your intense stare had him on edge."

"I didn't stare." She stepped out of the elevator, and he followed.

"You did."

"He's hiding something." She got into the passenger seat. "He didn't just drop the card in the office. The way he snatched it up said he didn't want us to see it." A beat. "I wish we could monitor his phone. If he's calling Kozlov—"

"We don't have probable cause for a warrant to tap his phone."

"Do you think Prime could do it?"

"I doubt it. They'd need the same warrant."

"I wonder if his son is back now. We should talk to him."

Back at the squad room, KC found the notes from Janelle about Watkins's son. Joseph Watkins, a freshman at Clemson. She looked up the registrar's office on the school website and dialed.

Three transfers later, she got the right person and explained the purpose of her call yet again. Why couldn't they just relay the information instead of making her repeat it every time?

"I suppose you don't have his student ID?" The registrar's voice crackled through the phone's cheap speaker, barely audible over the squad-room chaos.

"No, but I have his name, date of birth, social." She could

add his driver's license, address, and his parents' information too, but best not to sound too condescending.

Keyboard clicks came through. Then the woman asked for the date of birth and social to confirm it was the right student. And it was. "You said he was in a semester abroad?"

"Yes, that's my understanding. Can you tell me where he is? Or if he's back in the States?"

"Hmm, it's the right student, but it's not showing anything about study abroad. And he's not in any class or program that offers that."

KC hung up.

Spaulding waited with anticipation.

"You're not gonna believe this. He's not in a semester-abroad program."

His frown deepened. "So, he lied to our faces."

"He did. The question is why."

# CHAPTER 34

## THE DUFFEL

KC had just pulled up Joseph Watkins's information on her computer when hers and Spaulding's phones chimed with an alert from Prime. "What is it?"

"Update on Brian Shipley. Jack is sending footage from the student center cam."

After Spaulding relayed the news, another ding signified the arrival of the video. She tapped the icon on her phone to watch the video. Black-and-white footage of a bright hallway lined with storage lockers, a vending machine humming in the corner.

Brian Shipley crossed into frame, cap low, glancing up. Then he muscled a duffel into a middle-row locker and spun the dial. He walked out fast, shoulders tight.

"Looks a bit suspicious." He read the caption. "Said it was four days after Sheri went missing."

She rewound it and played it again. Other than his demeanor, nothing screamed criminal. "Doesn't prove anything."

"He could be hiding something. Besides, he's missing. He could be running."

"Or he could have been abducted. If it were incriminating evidence, wouldn't he have destroyed it or tossed it?"

"You just don't want to believe he's got anything to do with it." He crossed his arms and out came his Jedi voice. "Well, here's lesson one. Put your feelings aside when you're investigating."

It wasn't so much her feeling, but she interviewed the guy. Everything about him told her he cared about Sheri. "I say we find out what's in the bag."

"Let's." He stretched. "Warrant is gonna take time. Call the cousin. Maybe he knows something about it."

She did just that. A minute later, Louis answered the phone. "Dr. Shipley."

"Doctor, this is Detective Cassi—"

"Did you find Brian?"

"Um, not yet. We're working on it. Do you know if Brian has a locker at the student center?"

"Yes, no, I mean, it's nothing official. He just puts a lock on one. That's it. Other students do that too. He lets me use it."

"We've got footage of Brian putting a bag in the locker. Maybe nothing, but we need to see what's inside. Do we have your permission to take a look?"

"Sure. It's probably just his clothes, books, or other junk. But, yeah, go ahead."

"You have the combo? Can you text it to me?" And she gave him her number.

She ended the call and stood up. "We're on."

Spaulding grabbed the keys. "Let's go."

Two hours later, they walked into the campus student center. The murmur of students talking, squeak of sneakers on tile, and hiss from a nearby espresso machine in the food court brought back memories of her college days. They approached the bank of lockers along the hallway to the bus and rideshare entrance/exit and found locker 492.

KC held her phone up and hit Record. She gave her name,

badge number, time, and location. "We're opening locker 492 with permission from Louis Shipley."

Spaulding tapped the combination, the metal dial ticking under his fingers. The latch gave with a tired clank. He looked to KC. When she nodded, he swung the door wide.

A gray duffel sat on the shelf along with some books. She kept filming. With gloved hands, Spaulding pulled the bag closer to the front and tugged the zipper open. As Louis predicted, gym shorts, a clean change of clothes, and toiletries. Under that, a white box with a ribbon, crushed slightly at one corner.

Spaulding's eyebrow lifted. "Well now."

"Keep going," KC murmured. Her pulse beat in her throat.

He eased the box out. She moved the camera closer as he cracked it open. Satin spilled like liquid light. A pale blue set—delicate, pretty, meant to be seen. Tucked beneath it, a folded card and a thin bracelet on a foam pad, tiny heart charm, cheap but earnest. A receipt curled at the bottom, date-stamped for the morning after Sheri went missing.

Spaulding set the lingerie back. "He's a Romeo, all right."

Footsteps scuffed at the end of the row. "Excuse us!"

KC paused the recording. She recognized them from their video calls with Prime.

"Hi, KC." The bald man, on the shorter side, only an inch or so taller than his partner, approached first. "We haven't formally introduced ourselves. Damon Cruz and Claire Santos."

"Detective Cruz—"

"It's Damon and Claire." Damon shifted to see the locker's contents. "I see you beat us here."

KC hit play again. "Detectives Cruz and Santos present."

Claire stepped beside Damon, dark-eyed gaze cutting to the open locker. "That the bag?"

"Yep." Spaulding showed the box, the bracelet. "Gift, card, gym gear. No blood, no cash, no lockpicks."

Damon frowned. "Could be nothing. We still haven't traced the ten grand."

She hit the Stop icon. "If you were hoping to find anything incriminating, it's not here."

"No," Claire chimed in. "Not sure if you heard. We found some photos. Brian may have been playing detective."

"I was hoping maybe he had stashed some evidence here." Damon's fingers rasped over the stubble ringing his head.

"Really? What kind of pictures?" Spaulding asked.

"I haven't seen them. Sounds like they're photos of Chandler and Kozlov."

*Why didn't Brian mention that?* "If he'd done that, he could've been abducted. Someone might've found out."

"Exactly. That's why the commander wants him found pronto." Claire examined the rest of the locker's contents.

KC captured her rummaging through the locker, then ended the video with the announcement of the time. "I think we all agree we don't need to take any of his stuff into evidence."

When nobody objected, Spaulding shut the locker and spun the dial.

"We're heading back to the Hub." Claire waved goodbye.

"We're going back to the station." Spaulding gestured KC on ahead. "Let's go."

They drove back into Orlando under low clouds that scudded like bruises. Afternoon rain had rinsed the streets clean. Puddles held pale versions of the skyline and the slow crawl of traffic lights. Spaulding cracked his window, and the city's wet-oak smell pushed in.

KC couldn't stop thinking about what Prime said. It would be stupid and dangerous for Brian to investigate on his own. And how did he know about Kozlov? Chandler did approach Louis, so perhaps he mentioned it to his cousin. Then Brian watched Chandler and saw him and Kozlov?

"Hey, zoning out on me again?"

Spaulding's voice jolted her.

"Sorry, just thinking." A tiny voice in her head, Tanner's voice, reminded her to talk to Spaulding. She looked out the window, turned back to him in the driver's seat, opened her mouth, and closed it. *How?*

"What's the matter? You okay?"

"My mom was an addict when she had me," she blurted out. "I'm a crack baby."

He blew out a breath. "Okay."

"Okay? That's all you're gonna say?"

"What am I supposed to say? You are not an addict, correct?"

"Absolutely not! I don't even drink, and I avoid narcotic painkillers because I'm at a greater risk of getting addicted."

"Well, there you go." His lips pursed. "Is your zoning out like, uh, residual effect or something?"

"I guess you could say that. My therapist didn't quite put it that way. I just have this focus issue. I'm hyperfocused, obsessed sometimes."

"You can say that again."

Was he uncomfortable with her as a partner, or judging her, or doubting her? She studied him. "So, are you cool with it?"

"Why wouldn't I be? You're a good detective and a good partner. Well, except when you walked out on the commander."

"You see, when I was in Pine Grove, I was the only detective there. And there were hardly any hard crimes."

He nodded. "Okay, I'll make you a deal. When something like that situation with the commander on scene happens again, you let me know and let me take the lead. I promise you, whatever inspiration you have, we will follow up. But we do not walk out on higher-ups or crime scenes."

"Deal." A weight lifted from her shoulders. "I'll check on Jill Conners, see what she has to say about Brian's snooping around or if she even knows."

"Go ahead."

She scrolled to Jill's number and hit *Call*.

"Hello." Jill's voice was thinner today, stretched by sleeplessness.

"Jill, it's KC. How are you doing?"

The woman sighed. "Better, thank you. Your aunt Mae has been such a blessing."

It brought a smile to her face. "Yeah, she's good that way. Do you know if Brian was trying to find Sheri?"

"Let me think."

A television murmured somewhere. A fork clinked on a plate. "I don't think so." Jill's voice warmed. "The last time he came by was a week ago during that long weekend. He told me not to give up hope, said he was still distributing the flyers. I saw him at church too."

"A week ago? And he stayed in town that whole weekend?"

"Yes. You can ask his folks. I think it was Miriam's birthday. His mom."

"Okay, thanks."

After another round of take cares, call me anytimes, she ended the call. "Did you hear that? Brian was in Pine Grove a week ago. That's the time frame of Kathy Foley's murder. He couldn't have been involved in that."

"Need a third-party confirmation."

"I know." She speed-dialed her aunt. After a brief conversation, she ended the call. "Aunt Mae was at Brian's mom's birthday party. She saw him. He was also at church, and she spotted him around town."

"We need to update Prime. Now, I'm curious where he got the ten grand. You know I don't like loose ends."

"Quinn or Jack will find out. Maybe it's a loan."

She stared through the windshield as a cyclist shivered past in a poncho, rain beads like glass on the plastic.

# CHAPTER 35

## MISSING PIECES

Ten thousand dollars. Still unexplained.

Frank stood in front of the main case board, cold coffee in hand, gaze traveling from Kathy Foley's picture to the circled name *Kozlov*, then down to the wire transfer record pinned dead center.

The Hub sat quiet around him, save for the steady whir of ceiling fans and the faint hum of electronics. Coffee scent drifted from his cup, mixing with the sharper tang of warming monitors.

The glass doors sighed open. Damon and Claire strode in from the rain, shedding the outside like two currents pushing into the room. Damon's jacket was damp at the shoulders. He ran a hand over his bald head, flicking off any droplets. Claire shook out her umbrella before leaning it against her desk.

"Locker's a bust." Damon dropped his bag on the floor by his desk.

Frank set his mug on the ledge beneath the board. "What do you mean?"

Claire unlocked her tablet with a swipe, the light flaring across her face and glossing her brown hair, before she offered it to him. "Here's the video KC sent. She and Spaulding beat us there. Bag had gym clothes, toiletries, and a gift box, lingerie, card. Date-stamped receipt for the morning after Sheri went missing. Romantic, not criminal."

"And no surveillance photos or logs," Damon added.

Claire picked up the thread. "We also tried the deacon, but he was unavailable. We left a card for him at the campus ministry. The receptionist said to call." She checked the time on her phone. "About now."

"Call him." Frank stood in front of the plasma.

Moments later, Deacon Mark Moore was on screen. Fiftyish, with salt-and-pepper hair, calling from what looked like a modest office with a wooden cross mounted on the pale wall behind him.

After a brief introduction, Moore started by apologizing for missing the detectives. "I was meeting with an engaged couple. So, how can I help you?"

Frank began. "We appreciate you making time, Deacon. We're looking into Brian Shipley's recent activities. Anything you can tell us would help."

Moore folded his hands. "Brian's not heavily involved in the campus ministry, but he attends Mass regularly. He's premed, works, stays busy. I've never known him to cause trouble."

Claire rolled her chair to better face the screen. "Has he mentioned going to Orlando often?"

The deacon hesitated, gaze flicking off-screen before returning. "I... did put Brian in touch with my brother-in-law, Linc Huff. He's a private investigator. I'm not sure what became of it."

"Any idea what it was about? Why would Brian need a PI?" Damon asked while Claire started working on her laptop.

"No." Moore shook his head. "Linc hasn't said anything about it. But then, he would never divulge any confidential information. That is, if Brian did engage his service."

"He emailed you asking for prayers, do you recall?" Frank prompted.

"Yes, a friend of his went missing, I believe. The prayer chain is aware of it. Have you found her?"

"I'm afraid it's not good news. When was the last time you had any contact with Brian?"

"I saw him by the library the other day. Monday, maybe. We didn't talk. He was in a hurry to go to class."

"Has he mentioned Terry Chandler? Or Viktor Kozlov?"

His head tilted. Recognition flickered. "I've heard of Terry Chandler, not in any connection with Brian, though. I was in the insurance business in my previous life. There was a big scandal some years ago. As for the other guy, I can't say it rings any bell." A beat. "What's this all about? Is Brian in any trouble?"

So, the deacon had no idea Brian was missing. "His cousin is concerned since he missed his medical school appointment."

Now, the man's mouth formed an *O*. "That's not good. He has his heart set on following the family tradition. I'll add that to our prayers."

"Thank you, Deacon." Frank glanced at Claire and made a slashing motion across his neck. The screen went dark. "Damon, the PI."

"On it." Damon stood up.

Claire tapped at her phone. "Sending you his info."

Before Frank could turn back to the board, the plasma lit again, this time with KC and Spaulding in frame.

"Thought you should know that Brian couldn't have had anything to do with Foley's murder." Spaulding began, then signaled for KC to continue.

"I talked to Jill Conners. Brian was in Pine Grove the weekend Foley was killed. He was seen at church and other events with family. Multiple witnesses. My aunt saw him around town all weekend. No way he was in Orlando. Would have taken too much time traveling back and forth."

"You guys making any headway on the ten grand?" Spaulding asked.

"Not—"

"We traced the ten grand." Quinn popped her head into a bubble on the screen.

"Looks like we just did." Frank crossed his arms and waited for Quinn to continue.

Jack leaned into the frame beside her. "We traced the source of the deposit. An escrow account, which belongs to Edna Morrows. It took me a while to find the connection, but—"

Quinn took over. "His grandmother had a modest trust fund for the grandkids. They get the funds when they turn twenty-one. Brian just had his twenty-first birthday. End of story."

A presence came up beside him. Eli spoke in a soft voice. "You find him fast before something happens."

The main line at the Hub rang, sharp and insistent. Quinn answered. Then her head snapped up so fast that a twist of blonde hair slipped loose from her updo. "Boss, Brian Shipley just walked into a police station."

# CHAPTER 36

## GROOMED

Frank frowned. What was Brian Shipley playing at?

"Are they still on the line?" Eli asked, eyebrows raised.

Quinn nodded.

"How does he look? Did he say anything?"

She relayed his questions. "He has minor injuries, nothing serious, and looks like he's been sleeping rough. Stubbled, disheveled." Her gaze flickered between them. "And he asked for Detective Cassidy."

"Tell KC I'll meet her there." Frank grabbed his keys, the metal jangling as he started toward the exit.

Before he could leave, Quinn called, "Boss—"

He turned back. "Yes?"

"Thought I should tell you that I got into Chandler's phone records. There's a lot of calls and texts between him and Kozlov."

Frank went rigid. "A lot?"

"Daily. Sometimes multiple times a day. But the texts are coded."

"Work with Jack to decipher them."

"On it." She got up and headed to the lab.

He pivoted to Eli, who went back to his desk. "Eli, I think you're right about Chandler."

"Maybe the texts will give us more clues." Eli looked up from his computer screen. "Actually, before you leave, can I see those records? Sometimes patterns jump out that data analysis misses."

Frank hesitated, keys clicking in his palm. The drive to I-4 would take fifteen minutes, but KC and Spaulding could handle an initial interview. He tapped the intercom. "Quinn, can you put the call logs and texts on the screen?"

"Sure."

A moment later, the plasma screen hummed to life, displaying the call logs and message threads.

"Communications went back years. Started about nine months after Chandler lost his medical license."

Eli walked closer to the screen, studying the frequency chart. "Look at this escalation. Classic manipulation timeline. Kozlov didn't recruit Chandler overnight."

"How so?" Frank set his keys down with a sharp click, standing beside Eli.

"Early contacts are short, professional. 'Thanks for consulting on the cardiac case.' 'Appreciate your expertise.'" Eli touched the screen, scrolled down with a smile. "I've seen you guys do this. Didn't think it'd be this easy. Here, see how the tone shifts? A few months passed, and Kozlov's making requests, not just expressing gratitude. 'Could use your skills on a special case.' 'This patient needs someone with your precision.'"

Frank leaned closer to the screen, his neck muscles tightening. "Grooming him."

"Exactly. Appeal to professional pride first, then create dependency." Eli's finger traced the message timeline. "Spacing the requests isn't random. It's reinforcement. Makes Chandler feel chosen, indispensable. Classic psychological manipulation."

Jack's lab-pale face popped into a small circle on the screen. "I've cracked about thirty percent of their system. They're using medical terminology disguised as construction and business language. It took me a while to figure it out. I tried—"

"What did you find?" Frank cut him off.

"Right. Foundation work would be surgical prep. Installing new systems would be organ extraction. Quality materials are viable organs. And I believe client deliveries mean transplant recipients."

"But these coded messages appear much later," Eli indicated. "This is when Chandler knew what he was getting involved in."

"And willingly participated?" Frank frowned.

"He would justify it as helping people."

"But why did he want to turn himself in? At least, that's what KC thought he was planning to do."

"A trigger. An event. Until then, the lie was enough, telling himself he was saving lives while Kozlov used him."

"And something happened that jolted him to face reality?"

"Or someone."

Frank studied the message threads. Now that he knew what the codes were, the messages made sense. He scrolled down, scanning the content until the end.

"Is this another code?" Frank pointed to one message a couple of days before Chandler died.

"'Warehouse inspection at 847 Industrial Drive.'," Jack read it aloud. "Nah, it's an actual address. Pulling up aerial images."

It showed a warehouse.

"Storage facility?" Eli suggested.

"Or operating location. Quinn, find out everything you can about this location."

"Yeah, boss." Her face was gone from the plasma, but her voice carried.

"Boss." Jack waved his arm. "The coded messages reference specific medical equipment. Portable surgical units, anesthesia machines, cold storage systems. This isn't back-alley surgery. This is a sophisticated medical operation."

"Which explains why they needed Chandler." Eli nodded. "Underground organ harvesting requires legitimate surgical expertise."

"They recruited him gradually, convinced him he was helping patients, then trapped him in something he couldn't escape from."

"I think so." Eli returned to the guest desk.

"Boss, are you still going to the station?" Quinn popped back onto the screen.

"Yes." As Frank left, Eli's words echoed in his head: *Classic manipulation timeline.* If Chandler had been groomed, who else was already on Kozlov's hook?

# CHAPTER 37

## ESCAPE

Now that they'd cleared Brian of any involvement in Kathy Foley's murder, Jill's confirmation putting him out of town during the critical timeframe, KC went back to picking apart Watkins's smooth lies about his son when her office phone rang. The caller ID showed only a four-digit extension, no name attached.

"Cassidy."

"Detective, this is Sergeant Gibson, I-4 substation. We've got a walk-in here asking for you. Says his name is Brian Shipley. Kid looks roughed up pretty good. Claims he escaped from somewhere. Won't talk to anyone but you two."

Her pulse quickened. She caught Spaulding's eye and mouthed, *Brian* while pointing at the phone.

"On my way." She stood, grabbing her bag. "Don't let him leave. And, Sergeant? Keep him comfortable, but don't let him use a phone."

"Copy that."

The line went dead. "Let's go!" She tapped Spaulding on the shoulder. "I-4."

He pushed his chair back, the legs scraping against the floor, and hurried after her.

The I-4 Substation sat in the middle of an industrial corridor a few miles outside downtown, a fifteen-minute drive from the main station on South Street.

"I wonder what happened." KC adjusted her seat belt, fingers twitching to disconnect it, whole body eager to be out of the car and on the case.

"We'll know soon enough." Spaulding pulled into the small parking lot between a tire shop and a strip mall. A faded OPD emblem hung barely visible above glass doors that had seen better decades. The building looked tired, the kind of place where coffee went cold in forgotten mugs and paperwork accumulated like sediment.

Inside, the air carried the particular law enforcement cocktail of burnt coffee, industrial disinfectant, and the faint musk of nervous sweat that clung to every precinct KC had ever entered. Fluorescent lights hummed overhead, casting everything in an unflattering institutional glow.

Sergeant Gibson emerged from behind the desk, a stocky man with graying temples and the weathered look of someone who'd seen enough to stop being surprised by anything. His uniform was still crisp despite the hour, but his eyes held the fatigue from too many years of responding to other people's emergencies.

"Detectives." He shook their hands with the firm grip of someone who'd learned first impressions mattered. "Kid's been here about twenty minutes. Wouldn't even take water until I mentioned you were coming."

"How's he look?" Spaulding scanned the hallway to the interview rooms.

"Shaken. Split lip, bruising on his face and arms. Nothing that needs immediate medical attention, but he's been through something." Gibson gestured toward the back of the building.

"Interview 3. We've got him set up with a bottle of water and some crackers from the vending machine."

KC followed Gibson down a narrow hallway lined with scuffed walls and decades-old motivational posters. The fluorescent lights flickered until the corridor felt longer than it was.

"Prime put out a BOLO on this guy. I called it in. Commander Travers got back to me a few minutes later. Said he'd be here shortly." Gibson glanced at them as they walked. Then he pointed at the door. "Kid's inside."

Beyond the one-way glass, Brian sat with his shoulders hunched forward, both hands wrapped around a plastic water bottle like it was the only solid thing in his world. His volunteer hospital polo shirt was wrinkled and torn at the shoulder seam. His dark hair stuck up in irregular tufts, and even from this angle, the purple bruising stood out along his left cheekbone.

"Ready?" Spaulding gripped the door handle.

"Let's do it." She stepped inside the standard-issue interview room—beige walls, metal table bolted to the floor, three mismatched chairs that had seen better decades. The air-conditioning unit wheezed like an old man climbing stairs, and the overhead light cast harsh shadows that made everyone look either guilty or dying.

Brian's head snapped up when the door clicked shut. His eyes were wide, pupils dilated, and telltale signs of someone running on pure adrenaline stood out in the tremor of his hands and the way his gaze darted between their faces like he was calculating escape routes.

"Brian." KC kept her voice soft as she pulled out the chair across from him. The metal legs scraped against the linoleum floor, and he flinched. "It's Detective Cassidy. You remember Detective Spaulding?"

He swallowed hard. Up close, the damage was more extensive, the split in his lower lip looked fresh, maybe a few hours old, and the darker bruise along his temple suggested he'd taken a solid hit to the head.

"You're safe now," she continued. "No one's going to hurt you. Just tell us what happened."

Brian's gaze flicked to the one-way mirror, then back to her. "Someone is watching behind the mirror?"

"I don't think so. It's just us talking, okay? Take your time." No reason to tell him their conversation would be recorded.

Brian took a shaky sip of water, then set the bottle down with both hands, like he needed the stability. "I left my hospital volunteer shift around nine Tuesday night. Everything was normal. Went home, packed for my morning med school interview." His voice cracked on the word *interview* as if he'd just realized what he'd missed. "I was asleep by midnight. I know because I set three alarms."

"Then what?"

"Next thing I remember, I'm waking up somewhere else. Felt like—you know when you wake up from anesthesia? That floating feeling, like your brain's swimming through molasses?" He touched the bruise on his temple. "But I could smell everything—bleach, that sharp medical smell. Like a clinic, but not any clinic I'd ever been in."

"No windows?" Spaulding asked.

Brian shook his head. "Just walls and a locked door. I tried the handle first, then started pounding on it. Yelling. I don't know how long, maybe ten minutes, before someone came."

KC leaned forward. "Who?"

"Go back a minute." Spaulding put his hand up. "You were out cold the whole time?"

Brian frowned. "I don't know. Hard to tell. If I came to earlier, they must have dozed me again 'cause I don't remember."

"All right, you were saying, someone came in. Who?" KC prompted.

"Two guys. One in scrubs and a white coat had a syringe in his hand. Doctor, I guess. The other guy..." Brian rubbed his arms, maybe trying to warm himself. "Big guy, bald, all in black. Military bearing, you know? The way he stood, the way he moved. Like security, but more."

"What happened then?"

Brian's breathing quickened. "They tried to grab me. Hold me down so the doctor could use the syringe. I fought back. I mean, wouldn't you? I'm not just going to let some stranger inject me with who knows what."

He looked at his hands, flexing his fingers like he were testing them. "The syringe ended up in the big guy's arm instead. The doctor freaked out, started yelling something I couldn't understand. That's when I ran."

"Through the door they came in?"

"Yeah, no, I'm not sure. Let me think... No, they came in from a connecting door, I think. I just went out the closest door, and that took me to this hallway. But it wasn't a hospital hallway, maybe a warehouse someone converted. Concrete floors, exposed pipes overhead, but with medical equipment scattered around. I just kept running until I found a side exit."

A converted warehouse with medical equipment suggested resources, planning, permanence. Not some fly-by-night operation.

"Do you remember anything about the location? Street signs, landmarks?"

Brian closed his eyes. "I ran for maybe six blocks before I found a main road. South of downtown. I think there was this mural on the side of a building, something about 'hearts of the city,' and a corner store called... Sam's Quick Mart? Or Sonny's? The letters were faded."

Spaulding made a note. That should be enough to narrow down the area. Before that, she needed to ask about the latest victim.

"Let's back up a bit. Did you see or hear anybody else? A young woman?"

He frowned. "I don't think... Wait." His eyes narrowed. "I heard something. Like a groan, maybe a moan. Not sure. But I didn't see anyone but those two guys."

She ground her teeth, then forced them to unclench. It was something. A thread. The latest victim could have been there.

"All right." She laced her hands on the cool desk. "The men who held you, any other details you remember?"

"The big guy had a scar running from his left temple down to his ear. Fresh-looking, maybe a few months old. No name tag, no uniform markings." Brian's voice grew steadier as he focused on the concrete details. "The doctor never said a word to me. Just worked with his hands, blue nitrile gloves, the kind we use at the hospital. But his eyes..." He shuddered. "Like I wasn't even human. Just something on his to-do list."

A chill having nothing to do with the overworked air-conditioning skittered over her. Brian shuddered, probably reliving the ordeal.

"Brian, is there anything else? Anything at all that might help us find this place?"

He started to shake his head, then stopped. His eyes went wide, and she could imagine the memory surfacing like a bubble rising through dark water.

"There were monitors. Security feeds, like a surveillance setup. I saw them when I was running down the hallway."

"What did they show?"

His hands began to tremble again, and he gripped the water bottle tighter. "Multiple locations, I think. Different rooms, maybe different buildings, I couldn't tell. But on one of the screens..." He paused, swallowing hard. "Someone was tied to a chair. Young guy, maybe my age. Dark hair, pale skin, could have been Latino or mixed race, maybe white. Hard to tell because his head was slumped forward, but he had an IV line in his arm."

KC's heartbeat picked up.

"Was he…" She had to clear her throat. "Could you tell if he was alive?"

"His chest was moving. Breathing, but slow. Real slow. Like he was heavily sedated." His words thinned to silence, eyelids fluttering as if sleep was dragging him under while the fight drained out of him, likely leaving only exhaustion and pain.

Spaulding got to his feet, ran around to catch Brian before he fell. "Let's get you to a hospital."

KC opened the door, ready to call for an ambulance. Then she noticed Travers.

"Paramedics on the way." The commander pocketed his phone. "I caught most of the interview. Quinn and Jack are working on identifying the location based on his description."

Before she could respond, all their phones dinged with an alert.

# CHAPTER 38

## THE WAREHOUSE

KC pulled out her phone. A chill settled in her chest before she even read the screen: *Explosion reported at 847 Industrial Drive.*

Spaulding waved two uniforms over to watch Brian, whom Spaulding had lowered to the floor.

"We've got him." The first officer gave a firm nod.

"That's the address from Chandler and Kozlov's messages." Travers held his phone and headed toward the exit, KC and her partner on his heels.

Her pulse kicked up. "Commander, you got into Chandler's systems?"

"Quinn cracked them." His pace was measured as they pushed through the substation's side exit. "Eli believes Chandler was their surgeon. The one who harvested the organs. Kozlov had been grooming him for months."

The substation's controlled chaos faded as they stepped into the parking lot. The late afternoon air hit KC's face, but couldn't touch the chill spreading through her chest.

"But that address?" Travers gestured toward the horizon. "It could be their operation center."

Spaulding swore under his breath. "They're torching the evidence."

"I'll meet you there." Travers veered off to his vehicle.

KC slid into Spaulding's passenger seat, slamming the door as he gunned the engine. Through the windshield, that glow was getting brighter.

"Drive faster," she said.

Twenty minutes later, Spaulding parked the Tahoe beside a cruiser. KC hopped out before the car fully stopped.

It wasn't the chaos of a bomb scene. No craters, no shrapnel sprayed across the lot. The warehouse had folded inward on itself like someone had cut its legs out. Smoke bled from the gaps, curling over exposed steel ribs and collapsed roofing. The acrid tang of scorched metal and chemical dust clung to the back of her throat as she picked her way past shards of glass and bent rebar.

Travers was already there, talking with a fire chief in sooty turnout gear, floodlights cutting through the haze of smoke and falling ash. KC and Spaulding ducked under the tape, the air thick with scorched chemicals and wet ash.

"What do we know?" Spaulding asked.

The fire chief, C. French stenciled on his turnout coat, blew out a tired breath. "Not an accident. Controlled demo. Charges placed to bring the building down clean. Whoever did it knew what they were doing."

"You were telling me a guy who called it in?" Travers prompted Chief French.

"Yeah, well, actually, I believe we got several calls about that. They heard the loud bang or saw the smoke, but this guy was actually here. An officer took his statement. He's still around somewhere with his shepherd."

Survivors were paramount. While Chief French scanned the wreckage for the officer and the witness, KC raised her phone and snapped shots of the scorched surroundings.

"We need to confirm this is where Brian was kept." Her throat tightened. "And if it is…" She swallowed the lump rising in her chest. "He thought he heard someone. The latest victim could have been here."

Travers and Spaulding both swore under their breath.

"So far, my crews haven't found any survivors or remains," Chief French said.

For one suspended heartbeat, no one breathed. Then the air left them in collective relief.

Travers turned to KC, his gaze sharp. "Let's confirm with Brian. If he was held here and escaped, they torched the place to wipe out evidence, knowing he might talk."

Spaulding muttered, "Let's hope they're not already setting up shop somewhere else."

"There he is!" Chief French pointed to an SUV.

KC followed the chief's finger to a figure with a German shepherd standing by the vehicle.

*You've got to be kidding me.*

"I can't believe this. What are the chances?" She strode toward the guy.

"You know him?" Spaulding hurried after her, Travers close behind.

"Cyrus Jagers. He was at Sheri Conners's scene. His dog found the body."

"Not the kind of place to be walking your dog," Travers said.

"Let's ask him." KC stopped in front of the man. "Mr. Jagers."

Jagers smiled. "Detective Cassidy. Twice in one week."

She introduced Spaulding and Travers. "You called in the explosion."

"That's right. I was here for a meeting. Orion Global Logistics. Office right there." He motioned to a modest suite still standing beside the wreckage. "Import/export consulting."

Spaulding cocked his head. "Funny spot for a meet and greet."

Jagers didn't blink. "Their line of work is freight. Warehouses make sense."

Travers eyed the German shepherd, muscles coiled under a thick coat, amber eyes sharp. "And you brought your dog?"

"Eeyore goes everywhere with me." A faint smile ghosted his lips. "They know him. He's part of the package."

"Tell us what happened." Travers held his phone.

Jagers glanced down at Eeyore. "We parked. I let him stretch his legs before going inside. I should say that he's a retired military dog, trained to detect explosives. As soon as he started barking, I didn't hesitate. Turned us back just in time." He gestured at the ruin. "Called 911."

His account sounded real enough, but KC wouldn't write him off yet. Two crime scenes, just too convenient. "Can you tell us who you were meeting with?"

"Of course. The fire crew evacuated the block just in case. Seamus lingered for a while and went back inside when they said it was okay. And that's Seamus Devers."

"Thank you. We'll be in touch." Spaulding nodded, pulling KC away. When they were some distance away, he whispered. "I checked him out. Upstanding citizen. No record. Nothing. A war hero for the Brits, but still."

"You never know. Kozlov has no record either."

"True, but look at the commander. He moved on already. He's more interested in what can be salvaged inside the warehouse."

She scanned the wreckage. Indeed, Travers was directing CSU to search the scene. "At the very least, we should talk to this Devers guy. Just to cross the *T*'s and dot the *I*'s."

"Absolutely." Spaulding led the way to Orion Global Logistics.

KC's gaze shifted to the office building beside the wreckage.

Would Devers's story hold up as neatly as Jagers's had? It was remarkable that this outfit sat a stone's throw from the destroyed warehouse, untouched except for a dusting of soot across its windows.

KC pushed through the glass door into the lobby with Spaulding at her back. The word *lobby* was generous. The space was little more than a box with beige walls, a fake ficus, and a desk from some office supply clearance aisle.

A woman in her thirties looked up from behind the desk, her expression guarded. KC flashed her badge. "Detectives Cassidy and Spaulding. We'd like a word with Seamus Devers."

"Of course. One moment." The woman rose and slipped through a door at the rear.

The stale air carried the smell of old carpet and industrial cleaner. No company logo. No posters. Just generic art prints. The kind of space designed to look professional while saying nothing.

The woman reappeared with a man in his forties, trim, business casual. His handshake was firm. "Detectives. Seamus Devers."

"May we talk somewhere?" KC asked.

"Certainly. This way."

They followed him down a narrow hall, more like a corridor, into a cramped office barely large enough for its contents. A desk with a closed laptop, a filing cabinet wedged against one wall, two chairs that left little room to maneuver. The walls bare except for water stains near the ceiling. No windows. Nothing lived-in, nothing personal.

Devers gestured for them to sit. "Please."

They asked about Orion Global Logistics. He slid a glossy brochure across the desk, featuring clip art ships and cargo crates, generic copy about freight solutions. His voice was smooth, his answer bland. Import, export, freight management. Nothing KC could pin to anything real.

She leaned in. "I understand Cyrus Jagers had a meeting with you."

Devers nodded. "We had one scheduled, but the explosion next door canceled it. We've rescheduled for next week."

Spaulding tilted his head. "Irish?"

Devers chuckled, the sound warm. "Almost four years here, and I still can't lose the brogue."

KC cut in. "He brings his dog here often? Seems unusual for business meetings."

"Oh yes, we all know Eeyore. He's part of the furniture by now. And thank goodness too. From what I hear, his alert saved Cyrus's life."

KC sat back, hiding her frustration. Everything lined up—the meeting, the dog. Still, it irked her. Before she could press further, both her phone and Spaulding's chimed in unison.

TRAVERS

CSU pulled a drive. Salvageable.

# CHAPTER 39

## HOPE FOR TOMORROW

K C couldn't shake the image. The latest victim sliding into that town car, trusting and unsuspecting. The warehouse was ash now, but the girl had been alive when she'd gotten into that car. Where had they taken her?

"The drive is tagged and on the way to Jack. Let's hope we get something." Travers scanned the scene, shaking his head. "I'll have Jack check IRIS and Orlando Connect. A camera had to have captured something."

Being from Pine Grove, KC wasn't well-versed in the Orlando street camera system, although she knew IRIS was the acronym for city-owned street cameras. She elbowed Spaulding and whispered, "What's Orlando Connect?"

"Big Brother on a budget. The city borrows everyone's security cameras—businesses, homeowners. It's voluntary registration, but it integrates with IRIS."

"With that many cameras, we'd better get something."

Travers did another sweep of the area, then returned to them. "I'm heading back to the Hub. I'll get word to you the second Jack pulls something from that drive."

Spaulding tilted his head toward KC. "She took pictures of the site. We'll go to the hospital and hope to get confirmation this is their base of operation."

"And hopefully, Brian will remember more things," KC added.

Travers nodded. "Keep me posted."

Half an hour later, KC and Spaulding walked into the ER of Orlando Hospital, fluorescent lights casting everything in harsh white. The familiar cocktail of antiseptic and floor wax hit her as she approached the counter, badge already out. "Brian Shipley was brought in here a couple of hours ago. Where is he?"

The nurse consulted her screen. "He's in room 4, down the hall."

KC thanked the nurse and hurried after Spaulding down the polished corridor. Through the drawn curtain, she heard Brian's voice, stronger than she'd expected, with none of the earlier shakiness.

"Sounds like he's feeling better." Spaulding stopped KC from barging in. "Let's wait for the doc."

Moments later, the curtain parted with a sharp scrape of metal rings, and a harried doctor stepped out.

Spaulding flashed his badge. "Doc, a word? How's the patient?"

The doctor's gaze traveled from Spaulding to KC, then back to Spaulding. "He was a bit dehydrated. Had a few lacerations. Tests don't show anything of note. Given the circumstances, I'd like to keep him overnight, just for observation. But he's not having it."

"I saw the test results. I'm fine." Brian's voice carried through the thin curtain, no longer the frightened whisper from the substation.

The doctor rolled his eyes. "Premed!" As if that explained everything. "Anyway, he'll be discharged later."

"Good. So we can talk to him." KC stepped inside.

With a dismissive wave, the doctor walked away.

"Detectives." Brian sat up on the bed. "Did I hear him say he'll let me go?"

KC smiled. "Why don't you want to stay overnight for observation? You could have a concussion."

"No, I don't. And my tests all came back okay."

Spaulding stood on the other side of the bed where the machine was. "Do you need us to call your folks? Your cousin?"

"Nah, I'm getting out of here."

"Are you sure? You were taken from your bed, remember that?" Spaulding asked.

"My student insurance isn't the best."

Hospital stay was costly. She didn't want it to turn into a drawn-out debate. So, before Spaulding could say anything else, she pulled out her phone and opened the gallery. "I need you to look at something."

She swiped open the first photo, an exterior wide shot of the warehouse skeleton, caution tape fluttering. "Does this look familiar?"

Brian frowned, studying the jagged remains. "Hard to tell… Like I said, I woke up inside."

Spaulding gripped the bed rail. "What about the inside? We found bolts in the floor. Something heavy anchored there."

Brian's hands twitched against the blanket. "Yeah. A gurney. At least one. Maybe more. I could hear metal when they moved it. There was this smell too—chemical, sharp. Like hospitals but stronger."

KC thumbed to the last shot, the street view. "Does this street look familiar? Is this where you escaped from?"

"Yes, that's it." He pointed to the umbrella logo. "I remember seeing this."

She exchanged a glance with Spaulding. Confirmation. The warehouse had to be their base of operations.

"Thank you, Brian. That helps." She tucked her phone back

into her pocket. "Earlier, you said you thought you heard a groan. Do you remember that clearly? Did you see—"

Spaulding held up a hand. "Do you remember anything else?"

Brian's brows knitted together. His eyes had a distant look. "Did I tell you this? The two guys came in from a connecting door to the other room. I don't know what's in the other room."

"You did." She smiled. "You said you went out the closest door to the hallway."

"Well, more like a hall or a room with a bank of monitors."

"And you saw a young man on one of the monitors?"

"Oh, right, yeah. But that's it. Wait." He sat up straighter. "Why did the photos look like that? Like the building was burned?"

Spaulding exhaled. "There was an explosion. The warehouse was destroyed."

Brian's eyes widened, voice dropping to barely above a whisper. "They blew it up?"

When he looked like he might be sick, KC steadied him with a hand on his shoulder. "Don't worry! You focus on getting better and returning to your life."

"Was I...? Were they going to...?"

"No, son." Spaulding looked him in the eye. "They destroyed that after you escaped. The explosion wasn't meant for you."

Brian took a few deep breaths. "Okay."

"We'll be in touch." She squeezed his shoulder.

"There you are!" A familiar voice sounded behind her.

"Dr. Shipley." Spaulding nodded.

KC shifted.

The young doctor strode beside her to address his cousin. "I talked to the attending. You should stay here overnight, just to be safe."

"I'm fine."

While the cousins argued, Brian's voice rising with frustration, his cousin's measured and professional, KC and Spaulding slipped out. The corridor smelled of antiseptic, punctuated by the squeak of sneakers on linoleum. Machines beeped in staggered rhythms, a counterpoint to the tension between Brian and his cousin.

Once out of earshot, she elbowed Spaulding. "They weren't going to spare him."

"Yeah, but you don't want the kid to think that."

"I wonder if Jack got anything from the drive yet?"

"They'll let us know. Let's head back to the station. Maybe we got a name for the latest victim. And I'll have another run at the tenants at that building."

Their Tahoe was right where they left it in a *Law Enforcement Only* spot. Good thing Spaulding was driving so she could mentally replay the conversation with Brian. Back in the squad room, she'd double down on Kozlov. But first, she needed to dig into Elite Prep Solutions where Foley had tutored.

The air was heavy with late-day humidity the AC couldn't quite beat back. After updating the lieutenant and Travers, KC settled at her desk, the metal chair creaking under her weight. Around her, the day shift was winding down, muffled phone conversations, the tap of keyboards, someone's radio crackling with dispatch calls.

An email from Elite Prep Solutions waited for her. The list of students Foley tutored. No name jumped out.

Her gaze kept darting back to the list, scanning and rescanning. Still nothing. But when she expanded the list to show all columns and looked again, one name stood out. Not so much the student's name, but the billing information. She clicked the student's name, Jesse Bell, to view the intake form.

"Spaulding!"

"What?" He looked up from across her desk.

"Come see. Guess who's paying for this kid's tutoring session?"

He came around to read over her shoulder. "Hope for Tomorrow. Why does that sound familiar?"

"Because its founder is none other than Viktor Kozlov."

# CHAPTER 40

## PERFECT PATSY

The warehouse confirmation settled one question but raised another. What had Brian stumbled onto that made them grab him? His escape had spooked them enough to torch their base of operations.

Frank stepped inside the Hub, the familiar hum of servers and cooling systems greeting him in the dimmed lighting. He'd have Damon and Claire dig deeper with Brian, but the place felt hollow. Most workstations sat dark, screensavers casting shifting patterns across empty desks. Eli had gone home hours ago, Quinn was buried somewhere in the lab with Jack, and his detectives were still running down leads in the field.

The building's air-conditioning cycled on with a mechanical wheeze, stirring papers on abandoned desks. Even at this hour, the Hub never truly slept, red and green status lights blinked across server racks, and the soft glow of emergency lighting traced pathways through the maze of cubicles. But without his team's voices, the space felt more like a mausoleum than a command center.

He unlocked his phone, thumb hovering over Damon's number, when footsteps echoed from the main entrance. His two detectives appeared through the doorway, their clothes damp with Orlando's humidity. The scent of rain and exhaust drifted in with them.

Claire dropped into her chair with a tired exhale, the leather squeaking under her weight. Damon made it to his desk but remained standing, rolling his shoulders like he was working out kinks from a long day.

"Talked to Huff?" Frank pocketed his phone.

Damon loosened his tie. "Kid hired him."

"He took the pictures on Brian's laptop." Claire pulled off her blazer and draped it over her chairback. She smoothed her sleek hair as she spoke. "He was only watching Chandler. Huff didn't even know Kozlov existed. Chandler happened to be meeting with Kozlov on one occasion Huff was following him."

"Doesn't sound like Brian knew anything about Kozlov." Frank began his familiar pace across the polished concrete floor, his footsteps echoing in the quiet space. Movement helped him think, helped him see patterns that stayed hidden when he sat still.

"No, he never mentioned that name to Huff." Damon's chair rattled as he slid it out to sit.

"But he had to have uncovered something to spook them enough to grab him." Frank paused midstep, turning to face them. "Right?"

Claire shrugged, fatigue evident in the gesture. "Could be they needed someone to replace Chandler. They already tried Brian's cousin."

"But the kid isn't a doctor. Not even in med school yet." Frank stopped pacing, a new possibility taking shape. "He was a person of interest in our investigation. Then we thought he had disappeared. What if—"

"They took him and made him disappear." Her eyes sharpened as she finished his thought. "That way, we'd think he was running."

"A perfect patsy." Damon scooted to the edge of his chair.

The wall screen flickered to life without warning, bathing the dim room in harsh blue light. Jack's face filled the display, his headset askew, hair wild, the lab behind him alive with the glow of multiple monitors and blinking equipment.

"Hey, boss. Got something. Actually, got a couple things." His voice crackled through the speakers, excitement cutting into the late-hour fatigue. "First, I've been scrubbing the camera feeds around where that town car burned up." His fingers moved across unseen keys, and the view shifted to grainy street footage that made Frank squint.

"Roll it back." Frank strode closer to the screen.

Jack complied, rewinding the feed with practiced ease. "So, first pass, nada. Second pass, I widen the search parameters and bingo." He froze the frame on a dark SUV sliding through the pixelated blur. "License plate matches Kozlov's registered vehicle. Drives through there twice in the same week before the car got torched."

A low curse traveled through the room, though Frank couldn't tell which detective muttered it.

"Wait, wait." Jack held up one finger, grinning despite the late hour. "It gets better. Or worse, depending on how you look at it." Another frame froze on screen, this time catching the chrome edge of a sedan that reflected the streetlights. "Assistant State Attorney Gavin Watkins's car. Same area, same timeframe. Different direction."

The room went dead quiet except for the persistent hum of electronics. Frank stared at the frozen image. Kozlov and Watkins in the same area, twice, around the time of a murder. Too much coincidence for his liking.

"Quinn?" he called out. "You there?"

Her face appeared next to Jack's on the split screen, blonde hair pulled back, lab coat visible over her shoulder. "Right here, boss."

"What do you have on Kozlov?"

"Still digging. Shell companies all the way down." She rubbed her eyes, the strain of staring at screens evident. "His financials look clean on the surface, but I'd bet money he's got offshore accounts we can't touch without international warrants."

"And Chandler?"

"Nothing new yet, but I'm working through his digital footprint piece by piece."

Frank nodded. The puzzle pieces were scattered, but patterns were emerging. "You two go back to Brian. We need to know if something specific he uncovered triggered his abduction. Our theory about them needing a patsy sounds good, but we cover all bases."

He turned back to the screen. "Quinn, Jack, do a deep dive on Watkins. Financial records, travel patterns, known associates. But keep it quiet. If he's involved, we can't afford to spook him. Jack, recover anything from the drive from the blast site yet?"

The chatty tech was subdued. "Nah, I'm not giving up yet. The drive isn't toast, but it'll take a lot of TLC to coax something out of it."

"All right. Keep at it."

The implications hung in the air like smoke from the destroyed warehouse. A state prosecutor potentially connected to an organ trafficking ring. If true, it explained how they'd stayed ahead of law enforcement for so long.

# CHAPTER 41

## UNDERGROUND

Two hours later, KC was still digging into Jesse Bell's background. The deeper she went, the more questions emerged. The kid was solid, honor roll, planning prelaw, clean record. His parents seemed ordinary enough: Thomas Bell, IT professional; Nancy Bell, bookkeeper. Middle-class professionals in a suburban neighborhood.

She clicked through the intake form again, then pulled up a basic background search. A family photo from Jesse's social media made her pause. The kid had olive skin, dark hair, Middle Eastern features. His parents were pale, blond and light-brown hair, Caucasian.

"Spaulding."

He looked up from his computer. "Yeah?"

"Come look at this." She turned her monitor toward him. "Does something seem off to you?"

He squinted at the photo, then at the intake form. "Kid's adopted."

"That's what I'm thinking. But here's the thing. If he's adopted and Kozlov's foundation is paying for his tutoring, then the parents know about the connection. Could this be Kozlov's son?"

"Wow, that's a leap. Or he could have placed the kid with them. Either way, the parents might be in on something. Or it's a sponsored kid, and they're totally innocent."

She shivered. "If Kozlov is strategically placing children, grooming them through their adoptive families, it suggests an operation far more sophisticated than we think."

"We'd have to dig through adoption records," Spaulding said. "Private versus agency, sealed files. Could take days."

"Add it to the list." She saved the information to her case file. Something to revisit when they had more resources. "But right now, I want to know who else Hope for Tomorrow is sponsoring."

"You're gonna burn a hole in that monitor." Spaulding shut down his computer. "It's almost nine. Time to call it."

"There's something here. I can feel it." She rubbed her eyes, the fluorescent lights making them water. Around them, the squad room had emptied out, leaving only the night shift and the persistent hum of electronics.

"Fresh eyes tomorrow." Spaulding stood and put his jacket on. "When's the last time you ate something that didn't come from a vending machine?"

She couldn't remember. Her stomach chose that moment to growl, answering for her.

"Come on. I'm driving you home, and we're stopping for food on the way."

"I can drive myself—"

"KC." His voice carried years of watching a partner's back. "Remember the mysterious note left in your home? Tanner texted he was tied up, asked me to make sure you got home safe."

She wanted to argue, but the exhaustion was catching up. The adrenaline from the explosion, Brian's confirmation, the

Kozlov connection, all felt like a weight pressing on her shoulders.

Twenty minutes later, he pulled into a burger joint's drive-through, the smell of grease and salt proving how hungry she was. They ate in comfortable silence as he drove toward her house, the radio crackling occasionally with calls from other units.

"You should consider staying somewhere else." He parked in her driveway. "At least until we wrap this up."

KC shook her head, already reaching for the door handle. "I'm not running scared. Besides, Tanner's coming by tomorrow night."

"That's tomorrow. What about tonight?"

She gestured toward the doorbell camera. "There's a camera in the back too. I'll be fine. Call me if anything breaks on the case."

Spaulding waited until she'd unlocked her door and waved from the window before driving away. She double-checked the dead bolt and engaged the chain lock, habits from her early days in patrol more necessary tonight.

Her bungalow seemed different somehow. Not unsafe, but charged with the day's tension. She checked the windows, made sure the blinds were drawn, then settled on the couch with her laptop. Sleep seemed impossible with her mind still churning over Jesse Bell and Kozlov's foundation.

But exhaustion won. She woke on the couch at dawn, her laptop dead on her chest, neck stiff from sleeping at an odd angle. Nothing had happened overnight, no mysterious calls, no sounds that didn't belong.

## FRIDAY

KC arrived in the squad room at seven thirty, earlier than usual but needing the familiar routine to shake off the previous day's weight. The coffee was fresh, and she claimed a cup before settling at her desk to review the Jesse Bell file again.

Spaulding appeared at eight fifteen, looking like he'd slept better than she had. "Anything new from our mystery student?"

"Still digging." She reopened the tutoring records. "What if there's a pattern to when Hope for Tomorrow pays for students? Maybe it's not random."

"Good angle." He powered up his computer, then grabbed his phone. "Let me check in with Jack, see if they got anything from that drive."

KC half-listened to his conversation while scrolling through financial records. Hope for Tomorrow funded tutoring for twelve students this year, all through Elite Prep Solutions. All high achievers.

"Nothing yet." Spaulding hung up. "Drive's damaged worse than they thought. Jack's working some kind of digital magic, but it'll take some time."

"What about the camera footage around the warehouse?"

"Still processing. Orlando's got thousands of cameras, but most of the feeds near Industrial Drive are from private businesses. Takes time to get cooperation."

A uniformed officer approached KC's desk. "Detective Cassidy?" He held up a padded envelope. "This came for you. Hand-delivered to the front desk about ten minutes ago."

She eyed the package. "Who brought it?"

"Courier service, but no company markings. Guy was already gone by the time I got down there." The officer set the package on her desk. "Went through the usual screening. No explosives, no hazardous materials."

No return address, no postmark. Just her name and the precinct address in block letters across the front.

She turned the envelope in her hands. "Feels like a thumb drive."

With a letter opener from her drawer, she slit the top. She then removed a flash drive wrapped in tissue paper, nothing else. No note, no explanation.

"I'll let you look first." A smirking Spaulding smacked her arm, then rolled back to his desk. "Who knows? Could be Tanner playing tricks to cheer you up."

She scowled. "Gimme a break. The guy may have a class-clown vibe, but he wouldn't do this." *Would he?*

She held the drive up to the light to look for any identifying marks, with a tissue to preserve prints, if any. Standard black plastic, the kind you bought at any electronics store. "I could text him and ask."

"And you think he'd tell you?"

She plugged the drive into her computer. Two video files appeared in the directory, each time-stamped from the previous night. "This isn't a practical joke. Come look."

He went around to her side.

Her heart rate kicked up. She double-clicked the first one.

Grainy surveillance footage filled the screen, black and white, the angle off-center. The same parking area where they'd stood yesterday looking at the wreckage.

"That's our warehouse." Spaulding tapped the corner of the frame where part of the building was visible.

The timestamp showed 10:47 a.m., three hours before the explosion. A dark sedan pulled into view, disappearing into an underground parking entrance. She squinted at the license plate, but the resolution was too poor to make out the numbers.

"There." She paused the video. "Underground parking. I didn't see that."

"Hidden entrance. Smart."

She opened the second file. Different angle, different building, but the same block. This camera was positioned to catch an exit, and the timestamp was 12:23 p.m.

The same dark sedan emerged from a loading dock, moving quickly but not recklessly. Professional. Planned.

Spaulding muttered a curse. "I bet you a tunnel connects these buildings."

KC rewound both clips, replayed them again. The vehicle was identical, but the timing told the story. Someone had entered the warehouse complex through a hidden garage, then exited through a different building.

"How is it that we don't know about the tunnel? We should have checked the blueprint." She clicked the mouse with more force than necessary.

"Well, we don't usually check that. Now we know how they got the girl out before the explosion." He gestured toward the drive. "But who sent this?"

"No clue."

"And why?"

She played them a third time, went back, and paused at the beginning. "The angle is off, though. The camera isn't directed at the entrance."

"You're right. It's set to watch the back of a building. Fast-forward. Let's see the exit."

She did. "This one too. The angle is worse than the other one."

"That begs the question. Whose camera? Wait, the envelope was addressed to you, correct?"

She nodded, but checked to be sure. "See for yourself."

"So, whoever sent this knows you." He narrowed his eyes. "Can it be Tanner? Maybe his team is investigating something in that area?"

"I don't know. Wouldn't he give me a heads-up?"

"Well, unless it's not quite official. I mean, like maybe he wasn't supposed to let you see?"

In December, when she was still in Pine Grove, he'd helped her, but he got his boss's nod. Or so he'd told her. Could it be? "I don't know. I'll ask."

She ejected the flash drive and sealed it in an evidence bag. The mysterious sender had given them a crucial piece of the puzzle, but every answer generated two new questions.

Outside the squad room windows, Orlando was waking up to another day, traffic building on the highways, people heading to work with no idea that somewhere in their city, killers were moving through hidden passages beneath their feet.

The flash drive was a breadcrumb, but was it leading them toward the truth or deeper into the forest?

# CHAPTER 42

## COMPLICIT OR COMPROMISED

The Hub came alive with the kind of low buzz Frank liked best, not frantic, not idle, just the hum of work in motion. Morning light spilled through the high windows, catching dust motes above the bullpen. He stood near the mezzanine railing with his first coffee of the day, his mind on the smoldering warehouse and this complex case.

The string of murders initially appeared to be a serial case before evolving into an organ harvesting operation. Except for the anomaly of Foley. Was it a pure organ harvesting operation? Was it something else? And if Foley was a crime of opportunity, why mask her death like the others?

Stepping back from the railing, he went down the stairs toward the kitchen. In the early days after his wife's passing, he'd basically lived in the office, turning the attic into his room. While he worked past his grief and moved home, he still cooked at the office sometimes.

Now, he pulled eggs, bacon, chopped onions, and frozen hash browns from the fridge, freezer, and cupboards. He set about making bacon and egg skillet hash.

"Yes! I knew I wasn't imagining the smell," Jack exaggerated, inhaling as he came from the lab. "Something smells delicious. Is that you making breakfast, boss?"

Quinn's footsteps padded along with a heavier set. Sure enough, Damon showed up, followed by Claire.

Frank turned off the stove. "Gather around. Grab a plate if you want some."

His team didn't need to be told twice. Damon and Jack lined up with plates. Quinn got their coffee cups.

"If I'd known you were back to making breakfast, I'd have eaten here." Claire sat at the farmhouse table.

Frank shrugged. "Sorry, guys. I know it's been a while. This case…" He shook his head. "Thought this would bring our spirits back up. I gather you're not having any of this." He scooped the rest of the hash to his plate.

"No thanks."

After they sat down, Damon said grace, and the others were respectful of him. Then they started eating, the familiar comfort of shared breakfast settling over the team.

Jack kept glancing up from his plate, clearly bursting with something.

Frank pointed his fork at the kid. "Go ahead, Jack. What's on your mind?"

"I cracked it." Jack gulped down his bite. "Well, didn't get a whole lot, but something you might find interesting.… Hmm, you gonna start cooking here again?"

"Maybe. Now, what did you find?"

"A poor footage of a young man tied in a chair. I tried, did my best, but it was the best without sacrificing resolution. I'll beam it over to the plasma after breakfast."

Claire tapped Damon's arm. "Isn't that what Brian said when we talked to him?"

He nodded, his mouth full.

Frank scooped a bite of eggs. During the interview at the station, Brian mentioned the same thing. It'd be interesting to see that. "What else did you find out from Brian?"

Claire finished her coffee. "He did hire the PI, uh, Linc Huff, to check on Chandler. His cousin, Louis, told him about the doc's proposition. And since being a resident, Louis has been super busy. So, Brian took it upon himself to find out about Chandler. I think the picture with Kozlov is by chance."

"Sounds like it. So, the PI didn't find anything useful?"

She stirred her coffee. "You always make the best coffee, by the way. Anyway, his budget was too small for a deep dig. When we caught up with Huff, he told us he did the basics. Surveillance for a few days. Social media scans, public records search, talked to the people at his office. Said he didn't find anything without digging deeper."

Frank wiped his mouth, stood up, and put his plate in the dishwasher. The others knew the drill.

A short while later, the team was back in the bullpen. Jack grabbed the remote. With a click, the screen flickered, resolving into a distorted frame, grainy, monochrome, the kind of image defense attorneys shredded in seconds.

A young man. Tied to a chair. Head bowed, wrists bound.

"Just like Brian described." Damon stared at the screen.

Jack clicked again. This time, they were watching a clip. "Sorry, can't do much about the snow." He pointed to the blurry footage with the remote. "Best I can do. This is the same dude. They must have a camera watching him."

"I think he's white. Late teens, early twenties." Claire rubbed her eyes, then refocused on the screen. "Beyond that, I can't tell much."

Frank stepped closer, forcing himself to study the pixels. At one point, when the guy looked up, Frank stiffened. "Freeze it!"

Jack did.

The blurred jawline, the grainy features. *Could it be?* Frank wouldn't voice his suspicion just yet. "Any better resolution?"

Jack grimaced, tugged at a fistful of his hair. "This is the ceiling unless NASA loans us their toys. Sorry."

"Fair enough." But Frank's mind was replaying Watkins's visit. The attorney looked off, blamed it on his son being in and out of the hospital.

"Did you find anything useful from the cameras in the vicinity?" Damon asked.

"Not yet." Jack released his hair, tufts sticking up now. "There aren't many cameras around the area. And it takes time to screen all the feeds from Orlando Connect and IRIS."

"Keep at it," Frank ordered.

Leaving them to their work, he went upstairs to the glass-walled conference room, the one place in the Hub that still offered privacy. He keyed the secure line. Seconds later, Eli's face appeared, calm as ever, coffee mug in hand.

"You look like a man with something on your chest." The profiler braced his elbows on his armrests, hands locked around the mug over his lap.

Frank sank into a chair. "Need your opinion." He updated him on the image and clips from the drive, the young man's resemblance to Joey Watkins. "If that's Joey, Watkins is either complicit or compromised. I don't like either option."

Eli leaned back, sipped his drink, and lowered the cup back to his lap. "And your gut?"

"In my line of work, coincidences don't exist."

The profiler tapped his index fingers against the cup, eyes narrowing. "If Joey's been taken, Watkins would be under pressure most people can't imagine. Men like him cling harder to control when they're cornered. How did he seem to you?"

"He was sweating and nervous. Definitely off. But he put it down to his son being in and out of the hospital. When Damon and Claire talked to him, they said he was all professional."

"That's armor. Without studying this more, I can't tell you if he's a pawn or a player. But if he's being blackmailed, confronting him might backfire. And if he's complicit, you'd drive him and the whole organization deeper underground."

A knock brushed the door. Quinn poked her head in, her blonde hair in a low knot at her nape today. "KC and Spaulding on video for you. Something about a flash drive."

Frank ended the call with Eli and went back downstairs.

KC's face filled the main screen, Spaulding at her side. She held up a clear evidence bag with a black thumb drive. "This showed up at the precinct this morning. Courier. No markings, no note. Just my name."

Frank's jaw tightened. First, the corrupted image and footage. Now this. Too many breadcrumbs, too much deliberate timing. "Send it over. Jack will examine it."

She gave a curt nod. "Understood."

The screen went dark.

He pursed his lips, flexed his tight jaw, the teeth hurting from his clamping them together. His wife used to tell him he had to stop that. Was the attorney blackmailed? If so, why didn't he reach out for help? If he were in on it, what would entice the attorney to turn?

# CHAPTER 43

## GIFT HORSE

K C sat in the squad room, her screen glowing before her. She'd sent the flash drive to Prime. But she'd also done the practical thing. Janelle had made her a copy, and KC wasn't about to let go of it, not when something about the video prodded her like a splinter under skin.

She replayed the footage, her trained eye catching details she'd missed before. She traced her finger along the screen, following the path of the vehicles. Two cars, both dark sedans, entering from the east side. The camera captured them head-on before they disappeared around the warehouse. Professional setup, not some random security cam aimed at a dumpster.

She closed her eyes, visualizing the warehouse and its surroundings. Where could the camera be mounted to capture the vehicle entering? She inspected both clips. Considering the angles of the footage, she had a suspicion of which office owned the surveillance.

"Spaulding." *Huh. He's not at his desk. Did he go somewhere?* "There you are!"

He walked back with a pizza box and a carton of coffees. "I took the liberty of ordering lunch."

He plopped the box on his desk and handed her a cup.

"Thanks." Aunt Mae had raised her to eat healthy. The life of a detective didn't accommodate that habit. She pried free a cheesy piece. "Hey, I want to show you something."

"Okay." He circled to her side, balancing two slices on a paper plate. "What've you got?"

"Before you ask, I checked with Tanner. He didn't send the flash drive."

"So, you have another admirer."

She rolled her eyes and hit *Play*. "Look at the footage again. Picture the scene. Where do you think the cameras would be mounted?"

"Wait. Stop there." He circled something in the frame. "I saw that sign before."

"Which sign?" She paused the video.

"That painter's sign behind the fire hydrant. The yellow one." He tapped the screen. "I noticed it when we were at Orion Global. It's in their back lot area, near their rear loading dock."

The pieces started clicking. "So this camera angle would be from…"

"Their building. Has to be. That sign is practically in their backyard. Now, why would *they* send it to you? What did the guy say they do?"

"Import, export."

"Why would they need this kind of surveillance?"

She wrapped cheese around the tip of her piece, one finger keeping the front from wobbling as she brought it to her mouth. *Man, that smells good.* "No idea. Why didn't they tell us when we were there? And why not include a note?"

"Let's make sure. Pull up Google Maps."

She sampled a bite as her greasy fingers smeared the keyboard. The satellite view showed Orion Global Logistics' building, a gray rectangle against the industrial landscape. She switched to Street View, the familiar Google interface loading the 360-degree perspective.

"There." He pointed at the screen. "That's where I saw the sign."

She navigated the virtual street, using the arrow keys to move toward the back of the building. "The sign isn't here, but Google doesn't update frequently."

Spaulding set down his plate. One hand on the back of her chair, the other on the desk, he crowded in by the screen. "Pan the view. See? Doesn't this look like the first footage?"

"Let's see." She minimized the windows and put them side by side. "Yes. There must be a hidden door. Like a garage door."

"Let's go talk to the Irishman again." He made quick work of the pizza, wiped his fingers, and grabbed his jacket.

By the time they parked in Orion's lot, the sun was high, baking the asphalt. The building looked the same as yesterday. Next door, the warehouse ruins smoldered under yellow tape. KC wrinkled her nose at the acrid reek of smoke and melted plastic.

Ash cushioned their steps as they waved to a fire investigator and a CSU tech combing through debris. She thanked God no one had been killed and Brian had made it out.

"You coming?"

"Yeah, coming." She hurried after Spaulding.

The acrid smell followed them into the air-conditioned building. The same woman sat behind the desk.

Spaulding held his badge up. "We're here to see Mr. Devers. We know the way."

Without waiting for her response, they headed straight to the back office. The door opened before they could knock. Maybe the woman texted Devers.

"Detectives, come in." He gestured toward the chairs.

Not wasting time, she didn't bother to sit. She displayed the still frame on her phone, laid it on the desk between them. "This footage. Did it come from one of your cameras?"

Devers studied it, then lifted his gaze with a practiced smile. "Detective, I've never seen this before. Are you certain it came from us?"

Spaulding sat back. "Do you have cameras?"

"We do, but the system's handled by corporate. I don't have access to the raw footage. And most of it gets overwritten every couple of weeks. If something was pulled, it didn't come from here."

She braced a hand on the desk. "So you're saying this isn't your building?"

"I'm saying I can't confirm the origin of an image I've never handled. If you'd like, I can put in a request with our compliance office. They'll verify what we have on file."

"Okay, thank you for your time." Spaulding got up.

She pushed away from the desk, biting her lip.

"Of course, always trying to be helpful."

Such platitudes!

Devers hadn't answered their questions, just deflected. The footage came from this building, but the footage helped their investigation. Whoever it was wasn't the enemy, so why the secrecy?

Back in the passenger seat, she just sat there, staring through the windshield at the soot-streaked warehouse ruins. The smell of char still clung to the air, a bitter reminder.

Spaulding buckled in. "Are you thinking what I'm thinking?"

"We should talk to Cyrus Jagers."

"See? We're in sync. Mr. Dog Whisperer with a front-row seat at two crime scenes in one week."

"He said he had a meeting here. Might as well see if he stands by that story."

While he drove, she called Janelle for Jagers's address. She plugged it into the GPS. "Our next stop."

Twenty-six minutes later, they were cruising in an upscale community. "I wouldn't have pegged Jagers living in such a nice neighborhood."

"What does he do now? When I checked, the only profession listed was security consultant." Spaulding parked.

She looked at her phone. "Retired. Didn't say what he did before. Now, he does part-time consulting gigs."

He gestured at the manicured lawn and sleek modern façade. "Part-time consulting? Guess we're in the wrong business."

"Or he made big bucks before he retired as a security consultant."

A deep bark thundered from behind the door as they approached. Eeyore's silhouette loomed in the frosted glass. The lock turned, and the door swung open. Jagers stood there, relaxed in a button-down shirt, Eeyore by his side.

"Detectives." His smile was warm. "My new friends. Please, come in."

The house was as polished as the exterior. High ceilings, cool tile floors, furniture that might've been chosen from a catalog. In the absence of family—no framed pictures, no signs of children, no wedding photos—a few paintings hung on the wall.

On the mantel above a sleek electric fireplace, a delicately carved music box, the lid etched with the unmistakable profile of Princess Diana, drew her eye.

Her mouth fell open. Aunt Mae had one just like it. She lifted the lid, and soft music came out. She closed it quickly.

When KC was about nine, Aunt Mae had bought a new house and displayed that music box. Entranced by the tinkling melody spilling from the open box, KC had reached for it, tracing Diana's likeness with a curious finger. But Aunt Mae had hollered at her not to touch it, and the box slipped from her grip. Aunt Mae caught it before it hit the floor. Her words echoed even now: *"It's not a toy. It's very special."*

KC shook off the memory, eyes narrowing further at its twin gleaming in Jagers's immaculate house.

He smiled. "It's a memento from a special time in my life."

They settled into a sitting area where Eeyore lay at Jagers's feet, watchful eyes tracking them.

"So"—she kept her tone neutral—"we understand you've done work with Orion Global Logistics."

"That's right." Jagers crossed his legs and smoothed his slacks. "Occasional projects. Advising on compliance, helping navigate international shipping regulations. Nothing exciting."

Spaulding tilted his head. "And you were scheduled to meet them the day the warehouse exploded."

"Yes, unfortunate timing."

KC pulled out her phone and set it on the table, showing the paused frame from the flash drive. "Have you ever seen this footage?"

"I don't think so. Where's it?"

Spaulding arched a brow. "You don't recognize it?"

Jagers scanned the footage again. "Should I?"

"We believe these footages were taken from cameras mounted behind Orion Global Logistics. Someone sent the flash drive to me."

Jagers bent to scratch Eeyore's alert ears. "I assume this helps your investigation? If so, then I'd say, 'Don't look the gift horse in the mouth.'"

He had a point, but shouldn't she uncover the sender? Maybe there was a connection to the case? Before she could think of a good comeback, Spaulding stood. "Thank you for your time, Mr. Jagers."

"Always glad to be of assistance."

She pursed her lips and took their leave. Back in the car, she buckled her seat belt. "Maybe I should listen to him."

Spaulding didn't answer right away, just sat staring at the house.

"What?" KC asked.

His thumbs tapped the steering wheel, the thud jarring. "Just… getting strange vibes. Him, Devers. They're Brits living in the States."

"So? You don't think they're illegal, do you?"

"No, no. This guy is retired. Now, he's consulting part-time. Look at his house. We've got lots of retirees in our state. Most have pictures of their grandkids. Or talk about their old jobs. How glad they don't need to get up early anymore, etc. The ones who miss work will let you know that too. But this guy…" His thumbs tapped faster. "Then the Irishman. That outfit is a typical front."

"Front for what?"

The taps stopped. He started the car, backed down the drive, and veered onto the street. "I don't know. But maybe Ron knows, or he knows someone who knows."

He must mean SAC Ron Peters, Tanner's boss. Which meant Spaulding was thinking Jagers and Devers might be spies.

KC's stomach dropped. *Spies.* The word lodged in her head like a stone. She'd signed up to catch killers, not navigate international espionage. Jagers's pristine house receded in the side mirror. And a shiver slipped over her.

Did these murders just get messier and more complicated?

# CHAPTER 44

## BACK OFF

The music box wouldn't leave KC alone. Diana's carved profile, identical to Aunt Mae's treasured keepsake. *What are the odds?* Her pulse quickened. *Does Aunt Mae know Jagers?*

"What's going on in that head of yours now? Not zoning out again, are you?" Spaulding parked the Tahoe in the station lot, gravel crunching under the tires.

"Just thinking about Jagers." She climbed out, but her mind stayed fixed on that pristine mantel.

"What's next?"

The music box would have to wait. She had a case to solve. "I'm gonna dig into Watkins's son. Watkins lied, remember? His son isn't in any semester-abroad program."

"You do that. I'll look into Jagers and Devers."

The fluorescent lights hummed overhead as KC settled at her desk, the familiar blend of stale coffee and industrial disinfectant filling her nostrils. Her keyboard clicked steadily as she scrolled through university databases, cross-referenced student directories, made phone call after phone call. Each dead end tightened the knot in her stomach.

Finally, buried in a dormitory roster from last semester, she found it. Joseph Watkins's college roommate, Ethan Laird. More searching yielded a cell number. KC wiped sweaty palms on her jeans before dialing.

Two rings. "Hello?"

"Hi. Is this Ethan Laird?"

A pause. The silence stretched long enough that KC checked her phone screen. Still connected.

"Yes? Who's this?"

"This is Detective Cassidy, Orlando PD. I'd like to ask you a few questions. Would this be a good time?"

Dead air. Then the sound of silverware clinking, a TV murmuring in the background.

"Uh, yeah. Sure."

KC hunched over her desk, pen poised. "I understand you used to room with Joseph Watkins."

"Joey, yeah. Last semester. But he's taking a medical break now."

Her pen stopped moving. "A medical break?"

"That's what I heard, what he said anyway. He had some kidney disease. Always tired, drank tons of water. He'd disappear for half days at some clinic for treatments. After the holidays, he just… quit school."

"So he's not enrolled this semester at all?"

"No way. He's on the transplant list. You know that, right? Anyway, last time we talked, he said he was up next. I figured that means he's getting his kidney."

The pen slipped from her fingers, clattering onto her desk. "Transplant? Kidney transplant?"

"Yeah, poor guy's been waiting forever. I sure hope he's okay. Did something happen to him?"

Her throat felt dry. "I hope not. Thanks for all your help. If you happen to hear from him, call me immediately." She rattled off her number, ended the call, and put the phone down.

"Hey, Spaulding!"

"What?" He looked up from his screen, eyebrows raised.

"Watkins's son was having dialysis and is on the transplant list. He told his roommate he was up next for a new kidney."

"If it's true, why wouldn't his father just say that?"

She shrugged, reaching for her phone. "I guess we need to verify it."

"You'd need a subpoena for hospital records. Better try Brian's cousin. Maybe he can check if the Watkins kid is on the wait list."

"Right." She scrolled through her contacts, found Louis's number, and hit *Call*. Her leg bounced under the desk.

Louis picked up on the first ring, the familiar clatter of a hospital break room echoing behind him—voices murmuring, vending machines humming, chairs scraping linoleum. "Detective Cassidy?"

"Louis, I need a favor." She explained while Spaulding pretended not to eavesdrop.

"Er, Detective, I'm not sure this is... kosher."

"We can get a subpoena, but time is critical here. Remember what happened to your cousin? I just need to know if Joseph Watkins is on the kidney wait list."

A pause. Ice clinking in a cup. "For a kidney transplant, right?"

"Yeah."

"Okay. I'll see what I can find out."

"Thank you." Something Brian mentioned nagged at her. "Before you go, quick question. If someone's on dialysis, what happens if they stop treatment?"

"And they don't get a new kidney?" Louis's voice grew serious. "Depends on their residual kidney function, but it's dangerous. Really dangerous. Fluid overload, potassium levels spike. The patient could get critically ill within days."

"Okay, thanks." She hung up and turned to Spaulding.

"Remember what Brian said about seeing a young man tied up, hooked to some kind of monitor?"

"Yeah?"

"I know it sounds crazy, but what if that's Watkins's son? Louis just said stopping dialysis could be life-threatening."

Spaulding's pen tapped against his desk, tap, tap, tap. "You're thinking the attorney's being blackmailed?"

She lifted her shoulders. "Just throwing out ideas."

His brow furrowed. "It's weird that he didn't mention his son's condition and lied about him being overseas. But he's still an assistant state attorney. We can't go in guns blazing on pure speculation. Find the son first. If we locate him safe and sound, this whole theory's shot down."

"And if we can't find him? That gives us grounds to press Watkins for his son's contact information."

"Sounds like a plan."

KC dove back into her search. Joey's last known address before college was with his deceased mother. Court records showed his father had visitation every other weekend, bare minimum involvement. She pulled up social media next.

Unlike most kids his age, Joey's online presence had gone dark. His TikTok account hadn't been updated in almost two years. Same with Instagram. In the last post, he looked gaunt and pale at some college party, fake smile. KC frowned at her screen. For a twenty-year-old, complete social media silence was like digital death.

Her phone buzzed. Louis.

She swiped to answer. "What did you find?"

"Got lucky. Renee, the transplant coordinator, took a peek at the list for me. I just need to… never mind." Louis didn't waste time with pleasantries. "Joseph Watkins is on the kidney wait list. In our region, he's number 2,487. He wouldn't be getting a kidney anytime soon through normal channels."

Her stomach dropped. "He's not next in line?"

"Not even close on the official list. Unless…" Louis paused. "Unless you're talking about transplant tourism."

"Transplant tourism?"

"Patients with financial resources sometimes go abroad, like India, Mexico, Philippines, to buy an organ. But, Detective, I have to warn you. Most of those operations aren't… legitimate."

She rubbed her thrumming temples. Watkins claimed his son was studying abroad. Now she knew his son desperately needed a kidney. If Watkins arranged something overseas, wouldn't he be with his son for major surgery? Or was this elaborate lie covering something darker?

"Detective? You still there?"

"Yes, sorry. Thanks, Louis. This helps more than you know."

She disconnected and dialed Quinn Sterling at Prime.

"Sterling."

"Can you guys check international flight records without the paperwork? I need to find out if someone left the country in the last month."

"Sure thing. If I have the full name and details, I can have it within the hour. Is this the serial case?"

"Yes, it's related." KC gave her Joseph Watkins's information. Quinn promised to call back soon.

Spaulding returned with a fresh cup of coffee, the bitter aroma cutting through the station's stale air. KC hadn't even noticed him leave.

"You should get your prostate checked," she said without looking up from her screen.

"And you should stop obsessing over cases. Wake up and smell the roses once in a while." But his tone was fond, not annoyed.

"While you were taking a bathroom break, here's what I learned." She filled him in on the transplant tourism angle, his expression growing more serious with each detail.

Spaulding sat on the edge of her desk. "Smart thinking.

While you were playing phone tag, I dove into financial records. Nothing jumped out. The kid drives a car registered to Daddy. He's on Daddy's insurance. Uses Mom and Dad's credit cards for everything. If he's ever paid for anything himself, there's no paper trail."

"What about work history? Summer jobs?"

"Tax records would tell us, but those require more paperwork than we have time for." Spaulding sipped his coffee, made a face. "Ugh, this tastes like motor oil. Oh, and we need to update Prime and the lieutenant on where we stand."

"Did you find anything connecting Jagers and Devers?"

He drained his cup and plunked it beside her keyboard. "Still digging."

An hour later, they finished updating Lieutenant Coleman and wrapped up a video conference with Travers. The commander's questions came rapid-fire, his interest piqued by the Jagers connection and the flash drive. He promised to look into Jagers and Devers and asked them to keep on finding the boy.

After finishing her paperwork, KC glanced at the wall clock. Six already. Despite her protests, Spaulding and Tanner had insisted on escort duty, citing the obvious threat against her.

The drive home felt longer with Tanner's headlights in her rearview mirror. When she parked in her driveway, he pulled to the curb, engine idling, dashboard lights casting blue shadows across his face.

The porch light glowed yellow against her front steps, moths spinning lazy circles in the humid air. Somewhere down the block, a dog barked twice and went quiet.

She walked to his window. "I'm fine."

He got out and wrapped her in his arms. "I just need to be sure you're gonna stay put."

She put her hands on his chest. "I thought you had a case. Your team needs you."

"Be careful." He leaned in and kissed her. Then he scanned

the area one more time, got back in his car, and backed out with a wave.

After his taillights disappeared around the corner, she returned to her car. Her refrigerator held condiments and questionable takeout. She needed real food. But if Tanner knew she was going out again, he'd insist on escort duty, and the man had his own cases to work.

The grocery store's parking lot shimmered with heat even after sunset, the smell of hot asphalt mixing with the chemical tang of air-conditioning units. She grabbed eggs, coffee, and vegetables that would wilt before she ate them. Then she checked out quickly.

A block from her home, the sedan came out of nowhere.

Metal shrieked against metal. Her steering wheel jerked hard right. The seat belt locked across her chest, driving the breath from her lungs. Her head snapped back against the headrest, stars exploding at the edges of her vision. The car rocked to a stop with a sickening, rubbery lurch.

"Argh!" Her hands gripped the wheel, knuckles white.

Car doors slammed. Footsteps on asphalt. A man's voice, artificially loud and concerned. "Ma'am? You okay in there? Don't try to move. You might be hurt."

He bent toward her open window. Sunglasses reflected the streetlight's glare, a black mask covering everything from nose to chin. When he spoke again, his voice dropped to barely above a whisper for her ears alone.

"Detective Cassidy." Her name crawled down her spine like ice water. "Back off your investigation."

Her heart slammed once, hard enough to hurt. His lenses distorted her reflection, and her every instinct screamed to reach for her weapon, trapped beneath the locked seat belt.

The man straightened, voice rising again for any potential witnesses. "I'm really sorry about this, ma'am. My insurance will cover everything."

"KC? KC, are you okay?" Leyla called from across the street. The neighborhood watch couple rushed over. The husband, Don, pulled out his phone. "I'm calling 911."

KC forced air into her lungs, arranged her face into something resembling calm. "I'm fine. Just shaken up."

She couldn't ask the elderly couple to detain the man, couldn't risk them getting hurt. By the time she managed to fumble for her phone to take a photo, he was gone.

"Did you see which way he went?" KC asked.

"That's the strangest thing." Leyla shook her head. "He stopped to check on you, seemed all concerned. But as soon as he saw us coming, he took off on foot."

"His car…"

"Still here. Probably drunk or high. That's why he ran." Don pocketed his phone. "Paramedics are on their way. I can hear the sirens already."

KC frowned at the abandoned sedan, memorizing the license plate. This was no accident. Someone wanted her to know they could reach her anytime, anywhere.

# CHAPTER 45

## OFF THE CASE

Spaulding's phone rang as he was circling Lake Avenue. KC's name lit the screen. He reached for the turn signal. "Heard it on the scanner. I'm on my way. You okay?"

"Yeah." Her voice came back, tight and breathless. "You don't need to come. I just want to tell—"

"I'm close." He hung up before she could argue.

When he stopped behind her car, a patrol unit sat crooked, doors open. KC's sedan idled with its flashers on. Paramedics packed up, his partner still in her driver's seat. An older couple lingered nearby.

He hopped out and went to her. "You hit your head?"

She gave him that too-dry smile. "Just my pride."

"You saw his face?"

"Sunglasses. Mask. But he knew my name. It was a warning. Told me to back off."

That landed heavier than anything she could've said about bruises. Spaulding scowled. "Witnesses?"

She jerked her chin toward the couple. "Don and Leyla are the neighborhood watch. I don't know if they saw it happen, but they came out soon after. I asked, and they didn't see the guy."

"Stay. I'll go talk to them." He jogged over and introduced himself.

Don Richards, maybe seventy with arthritic hands that shook when he gestured, braced against his front gate. Nice white-picket fence. "Heard the bang, looked out the window. Some guy in a hoodie was talking to KC. As soon as we came out, he ran toward the main road."

"Get a look at his build? Height?"

"Average, I guess. Maybe five nine? Hard to tell from our window."

Leyla, thin and sharp-eyed behind wire glasses, looped an arm around her husband's waist. "He moved fast. Like he knew where he was going."

A few more questions yielded nothing useful. Spaulding thanked them and walked back to the car. He rapped a hand against the roof and bent to the driver's door. "I'm calling Coleman."

"No." She sprang from her seat, got right in his face, bit out hard words. "I'm. Fine."

"This wasn't a note left on your kitchen counter. This was an aggravated assault. I'm calling this in. CSU is coming to process the car and the site. Since you refused medical care, you're well enough to come with me to the station and tell him yourself. Or I'm calling him now."

"It's late. I'm sure he left for the day."

"Wrong. He's got a mountain of reports to review. There are cases other than our serial. Let's go."

A half hour later, they stepped into the squad room. The fluorescent lights felt too sharp after the parking lot's sodium haze, and the familiar burnt-coffee and industrial-disinfectant odor hit him like a wall. But Coleman was in his office, jacket off, tie askew.

"Thought you guys left." Coleman looked up from the papers.

"We did." Spaulding nodded to KC to talk. And she did.

"He bumped you and told you to back off," Coleman repeated once she finished. "Oh, and someone left a note on your kitchen counter. You didn't see fit to let me know?"

"I didn't think it was a big deal." She glared at Spaulding, who had filled the lieutenant in about the earlier threat.

"Loo, we get threats all the time." Spaulding tried to mitigate the damage.

Coleman drilled him with an angry look. "And you are the senior detective. You're supposed to have more sense." He pinched the bridge of his nose. When he dropped his hand, his tone had cooled but not softened. "All right, KC. You're off the case."

"But—"

Coleman cut her off with a raised hand. "We have other cases for you to work. You are a target. I'd like you not to be a dead one. Spaulding, arrange a patrol unit to sit on her house. And have one take her home now."

"Yes, sir."

Outside the office, they walked in silence past empty desks and abandoned coffee cups. At her desk, KC collapsed into her chair, the glow of her monitor adding to the sallow cast of her skin, the darkness under her hazel eyes. Her hands lay flat on the desk, fingers spread like she was trying to anchor herself.

"You okay?" he asked.

"No." She didn't look at him, but fixed her gaze on a fresh-faced uniform heading toward them.

"Detective Cassidy?" The officer, who didn't look old enough to shave, approached with the careful deference of someone new to the job.

"Yes?"

"I, uh, I'm supposed to drive you home."

KC grunted, grabbed her jacket from her chairback, and followed him out without a word. Her spine rigid, she kept her distance from the young officer like she might bite if he got too close.

Breath rushed from Spaulding. A short laugh followed. He wouldn't want to be that kid right now. Once they were out of the room, he took out his phone and called Tanner.

The guy picked up on the first ring. "She texted me, but she made it sound like it was just a tap on her bumper."

"More or less, physically speaking. She's not hurt. But that's not why I called. Coleman pulled her off the case. Problem is, you know her. That obsessive streak she inherited won't let this go."

"I agree. This case… she won't quit."

"Exactly. We need to keep an eye on her. Unofficially."

A groan, then papers rustled on Tanner's end. "What are you thinking?"

"Take turns. Make sure she doesn't do anything stupid while she's angry and sidelined."

"Let's make a plan."

# CHAPTER 46

## PRESSURE

The house was quiet. Frank sat at the scarred oak table in his kitchen. Yellow lamplight spilled across a scatter of folders and his battered leather notebook. The papers curled in the damp Florida air, though the AC unit hummed in the background. He'd been staring at the same image for half an hour, a still frame frozen on his laptop.

A young man. Tied to a chair. Eyes closed, head lolled to the side, wrists bound. Grainy resolution. Frank leaned in, fingertips pressed against his temples, and whispered to no one. "Joey Watkins?"

He didn't want to say it out loud. Saying it gave it weight.

He flipped back through his notes, neat block letters in his heavy hand:

- WATKINS: EVASIVE. SWEATING. NERVOUS.
- JOEY: HOSPITAL VISITS? KIDNEY?
- BLACKMAIL ANGLE?

His pen hovered over the margin, but he didn't add anything

new. The written words pulsed with implications he couldn't yet face.

The refrigerator kicked on with a low grumble, startling him more than it should have. He rubbed his eyes, groaned, and shoved back from the table. Maybe he needed air. Maybe he needed a drink.

The crunch of tires on gravel froze him midstep.

He glanced toward the window, heart ticking harder in his chest. He lived in a quiet cul-de-sac. At this hour, past 9 p.m., nobody just "dropped by."

He moved to the front room, the old floorboards creaking under his weight. He pulled the curtain with two fingers. A sedan parked crooked in his drive, headlights off. A man's silhouette lingered behind the wheel, motionless.

He didn't need to see the face to know.

He opened the front door. "Gavin."

The attorney stepped out, shoulders hunched, suit jacket rumpled, tie askew, like he'd yanked it loose hours ago. The porch light caught his face, drawn, gray, eyes ringed with shadows. "I… I didn't know where else to go."

Frank opened the door wide. "Come on in."

"I don't—" Watkins raked both hands through his hair, fingers trembling. "I don't know what to do anymore."

Thick and humid, the night air carried the faint scent of cut grass and someone's charcoal grill. A dog barked, then went silent. Every detail struck more sharply than it should.

Watkins strode forward but lingered in the doorway.

"What's going on?" Frank stepped aside, opening the door wider. "Why don't you come in?"

Watkins's gaze darted toward the dark yard, then back. "I'm in too deep." His breathing quickened, the words spilling out as if he couldn't dam them. "Every move I make, it gets worse. I tried—I thought I could steer it, but now—" He paced two steps forward, then back, palms out as if pleading with someone only he could see.

Frank watched. Listened. Took in the sweat streaking Watkins's temple, the restless flick of his eyes. The stubble he never would have allowed in court. "You're not making much sense. Why don't you come in and start from the beginning?"

Watkins shook his head hard. "If I tell you, it's over. For me. For him."

*For him.* "Joey? You came here for a reason." Frank crossed his arms, cocked a hip against the doorjamb. "You need help. I'm here. Just tell me."

Watkins froze, hands braced against his knees, breath sawing in and out. For one raw second, Frank thought he might break, might spill everything.

Instead, Watkins straightened, shoulders snapping back like he'd remembered the rules of the game. "I shouldn't have come. Forget this."

"Gavin—"

But the attorney was moving, fumbling toward his car. His shoes scuffed the gravel. His ragged breathing cut through the humid night. He yanked the door open, slid inside, and the engine coughed to life.

Frank didn't chase him. He stood on the porch, arms folded, while the taillights bled red down the street until they vanished.

Only then did he let the curse slip between his teeth.

Back inside, he shut the door with a quiet click. The house swallowed him again, still too quiet. The lamp still burned over his notes. The frozen image of the tied-up young man still waited on the laptop screen.

But Watkins's words now echoed in the silence.

*I don't know what to do. I'm in too deep.*

The house felt different now. Too hollow, like the walls had heard something they weren't supposed to and were holding their breath. He sat back down at the kitchen table, lamp buzzing faintly overhead, his notes stood in silent accusation.

The still frame on his laptop hadn't changed, but it carried more weight now. The bowed head, the tied wrists, the blurred jawline. He didn't need Eli's instincts to tell him what his gut already screamed. Joey Watkins.

He rubbed the back of his neck, then reached for his phone. He eyed the screen for a long beat before scrolling to the contact. Midnight calls weren't his habit. But tonight wasn't routine.

The line clicked. "You sound like a man who can't sleep," Eli said.

"Watkins showed up at my house."

A pause. "And?"

"And nothing." Frank shuffled through his inked notes. "He didn't say much. Just circled the drain. 'I don't know what to do. I'm in too deep.' Then bolted like he realized he'd broken the rules by coming."

"Body language?"

"Frayed, like a man coming apart at the seams. Couldn't stay still. Sweating. Wouldn't meet my eyes for more than a second." He tapped the photo on his desk. "And he mentioned *him.* Without saying his name. I'd bet a year's salary it's Joey."

Another pause. "So he's cracking."

Frank leaned back, the chair creaking under his weight. "That's what it looked like. Like the pressure's eating him alive."

"And men under pressure do two things." Eli's voice lowered. "They break, or they double down."

"Yeah." Frank closed his eyes, seeing Watkins's hunched figure lit by his porch light. "Not sure which way he'll fall."

"Keep watching him. Don't force it. If he came to you once, he'll come again. Sooner than later."

Frank nodded, though Eli couldn't see it. "Appreciate it."

"Get some rest, Commander. You'll need it."

The line went dead.

Frank sat in the silence, then reached for his notebook. He underlined the word he'd written earlier.

**PRESSURE.**

He circled it twice, drew a line to Joey's name. Then he shut the folder, closed the laptop, and pushed it all away.

The house was still too quiet. But somewhere in that silence, he felt the shape of the storm gathering, waiting for the crack.

# CHAPTER 47

## SHELL GAME

F rank read Coleman's text twice. He set his coffee mug down, ready to call the lieutenant when the follow-up arrived.

> Cassidy off the case.
>
> Someone hit her car last night. She's okay but got a warning.

Standard protocol. Protect your people. He'd have done the same. Problem was, in the short time he'd worked with KC, she'd struck him as someone who didn't follow orders when she disagreed with them.

The team usually took turns showing up on Saturdays to keep the fire burning, but they had this big case. Everyone was in.

He tapped the control to call Jack at the lab.

"Boss, you called?" The tech walked in from the kitchen with a tablet.

"Oh, yeah. I didn't know you were in there. KC's car was hit last night."

"Is she okay?" Quinn's voice rose above the chorus.

"Yes. Jack, find out about the vehicle that hit her and, better yet, locate the driver."

"Found the report." Quinn again. "She got hit close to her house. Two witnesses, but they can't identify the driver."

"Well, then, let me go hunting." Jack pivoted toward the lab, one hand already knotting up his shower-fresh hair.

Frank stood up. "Updates?"

Quinn rocked her chair side to side. "KC asked me to run Joseph Watkins against outbound manifests."

He raised his eyebrows. What prompted the detective to search for Joey's flight activities? "What'd you find?"

"No flights, domestic or international, in the last two months. Nothing out of MCO, Sanford, Tampa, or Miami."

Now, his brows furrowed. "Did she say why?"

"Nope, but she did say to flag destinations like Mexico, India, the Philippines, and a couple other ones."

"They're popular places for illegal organ procurement," Claire chimed in.

"Is his kid sick?" Damon asked.

Watkins did mention his son was in and out of the hospital. Frank's shoulders slumped. "I'm not sure. What about you guys? Found out anything?"

Damon and Claire came to stand near the plasma by him.

Damon spoke first. "Yes, something flimsy."

Claire picked it up. "Kozlov and Watkins both belong to Willow Bend Country Club. Not exactly secret-society material, but we talked to staff. Bartender remembered seeing them together, laughing like old friends."

"Anything beyond that?" Frank asked.

Damon shook his head. "Nope. No deals in the parking lot, no money exchanging hands. Just two guys in golf shirts sharing scotch."

A familiar ringtone blasted from Frank's phone. "It's the mayor. Gotta take it." He stepped away to the kitchen to answer.

"Mayor Porter," he greeted.

"Frank, we've known each other long enough. You need to stop calling me Mayor Porter."

"Okay, Elaine, if you're calling about the case—"

"Yes, and no. I heard you were looking into Cyrus Jagers and Seamus Devers."

Why would she be interested in those two characters? "Yes?"

"I just got word from the governor, who likely heard from someone higher up. Anyway, stop digging into them. If I had to guess, they're either CIA assets or who knows what. They're not suspects, are they?"

"No. That's fine. Thanks."

"Now, about this serial?"

"We're getting close."

"Suspect?"

"Yes, but we're not ready for any arrest yet."

"All right, keep me posted."

"Of course." He hung up. When he went back to the main room, Jack's pale face was on the screen, dark hair sticking up on one side.

That was fast, even for Jack. Frank stopped in the screen's glow. "Did you locate the guy who hit KC?"

"Oh, not yet. I mean, I got the footage from the neighborhood watch couple's door cam. Covid mask, sunglasses, no facial rec point. The vehicle was reported stolen yesterday. CSU is still processing, but I doubt they'll turn up anything. The guy is careful. He wore gloves. It was planned all right. I found him getting into a truck a block away. No visible plate." A pause. "But remember the flash drive someone sent to KC?"

A chorus of yeses.

Jack continued. "One of those sedans? Thought it was a ghost at first, bad angles, glare, you name it. But I caught a partial plate. Ran it, cross-checked with toll records, and boom, got a hit. The vehicle tracked to a residence in Windermere. Big house. Gated neighborhood. The kind of place where mailboxes cost more than my first car."

"Owner?" Frank sat against the nearby guest desk.

"Registered to a shell LLC. Of course. But the neighbors? Totally the type who peek from behind curtains. If that car's been coming and going, someone saw."

"Damon, Claire, go." Frank crossed his arms. "Listen, I want you all to focus on locating the latest victim and the guy who was tied up. They're likely being held at the same place. Quinn, check all the medical supply stores. The equipment Brian mentioned seeing in the warehouse. Check for any recent orders of the same type of equipment."

"On it."

"And have—"

"Backup is ready for them, boss."

He nodded.

Damon and Claire took off, leaving Quinn busy on the computer and Jack doing his thing in the lab.

Frank retreated to the kitchen, made a fresh pot of coffee, then poured himself a cup. Sipping it, he stared out the window, Watkins's visit fresh in his mind.

*I don't know what to do. I'm in too deep.*

Another sip went down smooth, the bitter heat doing nothing to clear his thoughts. Kozlov and Watkins belonged to the same country club, but so did many other people.

He moved to the window overlooking the parking lot. All the victims, except for Foley, were young. Even Eli agreed Foley was the outlier. Assuming the young women were victims of an organ harvesting network, how did Foley fit in?

She was the weak link. Though they had no concrete evidence, Kozlov must be behind the organ harvesting network. There were enough murmurs in the various agencies. But how would Frank go about proving it?

And KC was warned off. She had to be close to something.

What was she working on? Joseph Watkins. She had to be on Watkins's scent too.

He pulled his phone out and scrolled through his contacts until he stopped at what he was looking for. His jaw tightened as he tapped *Call*.

# CHAPTER 48

## THE MUSIC BOX

### PINE GROVE, FL

K C paced her living room, phone pressed to her ear. "I'm telling you, Watkins is the key. Either he's being black-mailed, or he's complicit. We just need to find a way to break him."

"Not we." Spaulding's voice came through the speaker. "*I'll* handle it. *You'll* relax."

She stomped to the window. "We have a case to solve, and Coleman benched me."

"So take a break and go see your aunt. I'll let you know if something comes up. I mean, you can't be involved, but you'll know."

The patrol unit remained parked across the street. She resisted the urge to wave. "What about my shadow out there? Does Officer Baby Face get to follow me to Pine Grove too?"

"I'll call him off, as long as you're going to see your aunt. Promise me you won't do anything stupid."

"Yeah, sure." She hung up.

Having gotten her shadow out of the way, she could start planning. But first, she needed to see Aunt Mae, in case anyone was watching.

Traffic was tolerable this Saturday morning. KC pulled into Aunt Mae's driveway in good time. Sir Nick ran up to her as soon as she opened the car door.

"Good boy." She bent down to hug the Doberman.

"He misses you." Aunt Mae stood on the front porch.

"I miss him too." KC straightened up and walked to the house with Sir Nick in tow.

The smell hit her first, cinnamon and butter, something sweet still cooling in the kitchen. Inside, the house was a mix of cozy clutter and polished order. Lace curtains filtered soft light, and framed photos gleamed on every wall, while the old mantel clock ticked its life away. KC's shoulders sagged, and her jaw unclenched as the familiar surrounded her, though tension still coiled in her stomach.

They hugged, Aunt Mae's embrace warm and familiar. "You look tired." Aunt Mae guided KC toward the kitchen.

"Occupational hazard." KC sank into a chair at the table, running her hand along the scarred wood surface.

Aunt Mae poured tea into delicate china cups and slid a plate of oatmeal cookies KC's way. They caught up over tea, Aunt Mae updating her on neighborhood news and saying Jill Conners was doing better.

"People are still bringing casseroles, stopping in to keep her company. She's not alone."

"That's good. She needs that." And yet, Sheri'd always leave a ripple of grief behind.

Two hands around her mug, Aunt Mae peered over the brim. "And how are *you*? And Tanner?"

KC shrugged. "I'm okay. We're busy as usual. Once this big case wraps up, we'll come by for dinner." A beat. "By the way, his promotion is official. He's now a supervisory special agent."

"That's fantastic! I'll cook him something special to celebrate." Aunt Mae's smile faded. "Are they sending him somewhere?"

"No, he's not going anywhere. His boss, Ron, is now the SAC. Tanner fills Ron's position."

"Oh, that's good." Aunt Mae's hand strayed to her chest, and she blew a breath.

KC's gaze drifted toward the living room shelf. To the music box there, porcelain gleaming under a shaft of light. She remembered the faint melody spilling from its twin at Cyrus Jagers's house. "Funny thing. I saw a music box just like that the other day."

Aunt Mae waved it off. "Nah. Probably just similar. This one's custom-made."

KC leaned forward. "No. It was the same. Down to Princess Diana on the lid."

Her aunt's hand stilled on the teacup. A shadow flickered across her face. For a long moment, she said nothing. The only sound was the mantel clock ticking in the silence.

Then she murmured, almost to herself. "I didn't know he was in town."

KC's hand froze halfway to her teacup. "You know him?"

"Yes, Cyrus Jagers." Aunt Mae's gaze drifted, as though she were looking backward in time. "A lifetime ago."

"How'd you know him? I don't remember you mentioning him."

"I met him when I was in England. He was... an associate of a client."

"Back when you were a lawyer?"

"Yes, I worked out of the London office for a while."

"He said he was retired, doing some consulting work now. You know anything about it?"

She scoffed. "Retired? Oh, I doubt it very much. But then again, who would've guessed I'd quit the rat race and be enjoying life here?"

Aunt Mae dropped everything to raise KC when she lost her parents. "Thank you. I don't say that enough."

Aunt Mae waved in dismissal. "You're the best thing that happened to me. So, tell me how you happened to be in his house."

"Long story. He's a witness in a case. Do you know anything about Orion Global Logistics?"

"Hmm, it doesn't ring a bell. He's a witness. So, he knows your name?"

"Of course."

She nodded to herself. "Then he knows who you are." She took KC's hand. "If you ever need help or are in danger, call him."

KC narrowed her eyes. "Why would I do that? Who's he?"

Aunt Mae released her hand. "Oh, never mind. Just… he's a good guy. Keep his number handy." She gave a small headshake and reached for her cookie. "So, chasing any bad guys?"

"I was taken off the case I'm working on." KC hadn't wanted to dump that on her aunt, but the words had pushed out, anyway.

Aunt Mae's brow furrowed. "Why on earth?"

"Because someone threatened me. Hit my car last night." Though KC kept her voice calm, the memory of the impact still rattled in her bones.

"Kylie…" The one word carried all the worry KC had expected, but whatever Aunt Mae planned to say was cut off by KC's phone buzzing hard against the tabletop. The vibration rattled the china saucer.

The caller ID flashed, and her eyes widened. *Did they change their mind? Is she back on the case?*

# CHAPTER 49

## UNDERGROUND

### ORLANDO, FL

F rank paced the main room, waiting for Damon and Claire to report in.

"Got something." Quinn pointed to the plasma.

He directed his gaze toward the screen and walked closer. It showed a purchase order list with one line item highlighted.

"See that Affordable Medical Supply? And the orders placed by a Conrad Duncan?"

"Yeah, zoom in."

She did. The zoomed view showed Conrad Duncan's recent orders. Multiple hospital beds and various medical supplies. All placed within the last month.

"Find this guy."

She shook her head. "An alias. But the thing is… the shipping address is the same one Damon and Claire are checking out now."

Frank punched a fist in the air. The familiar surge of a case breaking open rushed through him. He slung on his jacket before Quinn finished talking. "Monitor the situation from here. Tell Damon I'm heading there."

"Yeah, boss."

Twelve minutes later, he pulled up behind a SWAT van.

Palm trees swayed in the breeze, their shadows dancing across the asphalt where SWAT officers checked their gear.

He got out and stopped the first guy in SWAT gear. "Who's in charge?"

The guy tilted his head toward someone conferring with Damon. "Lieutenant Wolf."

Frank approached the SWAT commander, whom he had worked with before. "Status?"

"We're all set." Wolf led Frank back to the van.

SWAT staged two doors down, black-clad and restless under the bright Orlando sun. The upscale manicured lawns made an odd backdrop for tactical vehicles, while evacuated residents watched from behind curtains three blocks away.

The street hummed with contained energy, radio chatter crackling in short bursts, the metallic click of weapons being checked, boots shifting on hot asphalt.

The surveillance officer reported. "Thermal shows at least half a dozen inside. Two heat signatures in the basement, smaller bodies. Could be your packages. Could be staff. No external cameras active, but that doesn't mean they're not watching."

Frank yielded the incident command to Wolf, who got here earlier and was familiar with the setup. While he put on his earpiece, Wolf ordered, "All units, green light. Go."

The front gate buckled under the breaching ram, hinges shrieking as SWAT poured through. Doors slammed. Footsteps pounded. Shouts rang in unison. "Police! Don't move!"

Frank followed the stack inside, Glock raised. Hardwood echoed under boots, crystal chandeliers trembling with each concussion charge upstairs.

Then he caught a blur, Joey Watkins, face pale, darting through a hallway.

"Joey!" Frank surged forward.

Gunfire answered.

A figure stepped from the stairwell, dragging Louis Shipley tight against his chest, pistol jammed against the boy's temple. Louis's eyes were wide, terror and defiance tangled together.

"They wanted me to—"

"Shut up!" The figure pivoted on his heel to Frank. "Back off! He dies if you don't!"

Damon froze in the doorway, weapon trained but steady. Claire shifted to flank. Frank raised a hand, stopping them cold. And then Claire signaled left. Damon followed her lead.

"Easy," Frank called, voice low. "Nobody wants the doctor hurt."

Louis flinched as the gun dug deeper.

Frank measured the angle. No clean shot.

"Package 1"—the voice crackled in his earpiece—"with another subject. Back door. White van waiting."

His jaw clenched. They were seconds away from losing him.

"Package 2, secured." Claire's voice rang out. She emerged from a side room with a trembling young woman wrapped in a blanket, eyes hollow but alive.

The gunman shifted with Louis, edging away from the stairs toward the rear.

Frank caught Damon's glance.

Damon fired first. One sharp shot, shoulder hit. The man cried out, grip loosening just long enough for Louis to dive forward.

Frank lunged and slammed the man against the wall. The pistol clattered to the floor.

Louis hit the ground hard. Blood streaked his sleeve. He clutched at it. "I'm fine."

"Stay there." Frank pressed him down. "You're okay."

Shouts from the rear. A van engine revved. Tires screeched.

"Package 1 and the second subject…both heat signatures are gone."

He bit off a curse. "How's that possible?"

"Not sure, sir. Possibly went underground."

SWAT dragged the wounded gunman upright. A hard face, shaved head, hate-filled eyes.

Frank stepped close, voice steel. "Where are they taking him?"

The man spat blood and laughed. "You'll never get close. He's already gone."

Frank slammed him against the wall again. "Then you can start talking in interrogation." He intercepted an officer. "Cuff him and take him back to the station. Have Detective Spaulding question him."

"Yes, sir."

"The girl is with the paramedics. She's gonna be okay." Damon jutted his chin toward the ambulance. "We need to search this place."

"Get Claire. You guys take the house. I'll take the outside."

Damon gave a curt nod and disappeared into the house with Claire.

Left alone, Frank surveyed the property. The inside would reveal more, but he always wanted to check the outside. Once, down in the dry throat of an abandoned well, he and his team unearthed a cache of stolen arms. That had been then. There was no well on this property, but there was a shed.

He headed there. The door creaked when he opened it. Just the usual garden tools, lawn equipment, grass seeds. Nothing out of the ordinary. Did the sound seem different? He stepped back and walked forward again. Yes, there was a slight echo.

He turned on the flashlight and examined the floor. On his second run, he found it. He keyed in his mic. "Shed now."

A couple of minutes later, Damon and Claire hurried in.

Frank put a finger on his lips and pointed at the trapdoor. The two detectives stood at opposite sides with weapons out. Frank grabbed the ring and pulled. No shots were fired.

Damon shone a flashlight down the steps. "I don't think

anybody is down there." And he started down. Claire followed, and Frank brought up the rear.

The air was damp, metallic. Frank flicked his flashlight, the beam catching stainless steel tables, portable monitors, IV poles still threaded with empty bags.

"Wow," Claire muttered. "It's a clinic."

Not makeshift, professional. Outfitted like an outpatient surgery ward.

"This must be the replacement for the warehouse they burned down." Damon found a light switch. Light flared on.

Frank shut off his flashlight. "That's why they nabbed the doc. I should have had someone guard him."

"You couldn't have known." Claire opened drawers with her gloved hands.

"Secure everything. Photos, samples, the works. This is our proof."

At the far wall, Damon called out. "Boss!"

Frank hurried over. Damon stood by an open door. A narrow tunnel sloped upward, concrete giving way to raw dirt. They jogged forward, light bouncing. The passage stretched long, twisting, the stink of fresh earth filling his lungs.

They emerged two blocks away through a disguised storm drain. Empty. Just tire tracks gouged into mud, still wet.

Frank stood in the afternoon glare, chest heaving, Glock still tight in his hand, the victory slipping through his fingers. "This is how they disappeared."

They had a rescued girl. A captured soldier. An exposed clinic.

But Joey was gone.

And Kozlov was still out there.

# CHAPTER 50

## THE CALL

### PINE GROVE, FL

K C didn't want to be hopeful when she swiped to answer. "Am I back on the case?"

"You wish. I promised to update you. So, sit down and listen." Spaulding's voice had that taut, post-adrenaline edge.

"Why? What's going on?"

"We got the latest abducted girl out alive. And guess what? Watkins's boy was there."

KC's stomach dropped, adrenaline flooding her veins. "Is he okay, though? Louis said it could be life-threatening if he missed a dialysis."

"That's another thing. They grabbed Louis. I haven't talked to him yet, but I bet they needed him to work the machine to keep the kid alive. The doc got injured in the confrontation, but it's just a flesh wound. He's fine."

She heard wind blowing. "Are you driving?"

"Yeah, the commander wanted me to question the guy they bagged. I thought you'd like to know."

"Thanks. You said Watkins's son was there, not that you got him. Now that they don't have Louis anymore, what will happen to Joey Watkins? Who's gonna take care of him?"

"I'm guessing they'll grab another doc, or who knows? Does he need dialysis daily? I don't like to say this, but he could be a liability soon. Unless they're keeping him alive for a reason."

"Well, then, you guys better find him."

"You know it. Gotta go. You stay safe."

Dust drifted in the shaft of light cutting across Aunt Mae's china. Sir Nick's nails ticked on the hardwood in the next room. "Yeah, I'll be good."

"You don't even know what that means." Affection roughened the grumble. "I'll ping you."

The line clicked off. KC set the phone down, screen still glowing like an accusation.

Aunt Mae studied her over the rim of her teacup. "Bad?"

"Mixed." KC rolled her shoulders to shake the hum under her skin. "They found a girl alive but couldn't get the other hostage."

Aunt Mae reached to refill her cup. "You are vibrating, Kylie."

KC tried to smile and failed. Her gaze snagged again on the music box, porcelain gleaming like a secret. The melody in her head felt colder now.

Aunt Mae set the pot down and covered KC's hand with hers, warm and steady. "You've got that look."

"You know, sometimes I really wish you were still a lawyer."

Her aunt raised an eyebrow. "Oh?"

"Then I could retain you as my attorney. Strategize with you. Tell you all about my cases. And it'd all be privileged."

Aunt Mae laughed. "You can still talk to me, although you can't discuss ongoing cases."

Dating Tanner had its benefits. She could always bounce ideas off him. And he was a great investigator.

KC stared into her teacup, so many possibilities she couldn't voice. She needed space to think this through. Sir Nick's nudging gave her an idea. "I'll take him for a walk."

Sir Nick heard the word *walk*. He trotted to the door, waiting. KC followed him, claimed the leash hanging by the door, clipped it to his collar, and went out.

The neighborhood stayed the same. Nothing changed much in Pine Grove. Lawns steamed faintly, sprinklers ticking. A dragonfly stitched the air above Aunt Mae's roses. Sir Nick set an easy pace down the sidewalk, muscles moving under his coat like coiled silk. She let him lead and let her brain run.

"Okay, you're gonna be my sounding board." She waved to Mrs. Parrish, who was watering her plants. "I know Watkins is involved somehow. Even the commander agrees. Really strange to get a call from their profiler. Why didn't the commander call me directly? Anyway, I need to come up with a plan. Not easy when I'm on the bench. What do you suggest?"

Sir Nick's ears flicked back at her voice. They passed the little free library on the corner, paint sun-faded, a paperback with a cracked spine staring out from behind the glass. Two kids on scooters shot past, laughter ricocheting down the block. Normal life, loud and oblivious.

"That's not a suggestion. I suppose I just need to confront him."

Instead of giving her any help, he hauled her toward a dog coming their way. She nodded toward the owner, a young man she didn't recognize. It hadn't even been a couple of months. Was he new to the area or just a visitor? Late twenties, casually dressed, on the phone. Harmless.

"Where were we? Yes, a plan."

They reached the end of the block and crossed to the greenbelt. The path cut under a canopy of live oaks, the air a few degrees cooler, damp with leaf scent and the mineral tickle of lake water somewhere nearby. Cicadas wound up in the branches like a power line about to blow.

"What excuse can I use to see him now that I'm off the case?"

Sir Nick huffed.

"Now I can't use you as an excuse. If I weren't off the case, I could use his son." Her phone chimed. A glance at the screen made her pause. An unknown number. She held tight to the leash and swiped with her other hand to answer. "Cassidy."

"Detective, I'd like to meet. Somewhere private and safe."

"May I ask what this is about?"

"I think you know. It's time we talked. I'll text you. Just you."

"Wait!"

Watkins already hung up.

What to do? She didn't get to tell him she was off the case.

Sir Nick started pulling on the leash, so they walked in silence for a stretch, the rhythm of footfalls and paws lining up with her breath. Somewhere behind a fence, a dog barked twice, then thought better of it. A car door thunked shut three houses over.

Watkins had just handed her the opportunity she needed. She wouldn't have to devise some excuse to see him. He'd made the first move.

Sir Nick sniffed along a hedge, then flicked his gaze back to her, waiting. Watkins's text came through. He wanted to meet at four. That gave her two hours to prepare.

They looped back toward Aunt Mae's. The sky had shifted to the high-gloss Florida blue that always looked manufactured, clouds stacked like ships on the horizon.

KC paused at the gate and crouched to unclip the leash. Sir Nick pressed his head into her shoulder, heavy and warm.

Inside, Aunt Mae looked up and read KC the way she always had. "You have that look again."

"I have to go."

"Of course. Remember what I said about Cyrus. Keep his number handy."

"I will." She hugged her aunt and then walked out, patting Sir Nick on her way.

KC started the car and AC, but didn't move yet. She unlocked her phone and sent a text. She was determined but not reckless. This could be a trap. Someone needed to have her back.

# CHAPTER 51

## LEVERAGE

### ORLANDO, FL

F rank surveyed the empty roadway. Nothing, no witnesses, no trail to follow. When he and Damon climbed up from the storm drain, Joey and his captor were long gone. The roadway offered nothing. Several pairs of tire tracks all led to the highway. They made their way back.

The house was still hot with gunpowder and sweat. CSU moved in waves through the wreckage, cameras flashing, bags crackling. He stood in the foyer, his shirt clinging, absorbing the bustle without really seeing it. The place smelled of bleach and copper, the aftertaste of violence that never washed out.

"Commander." A CSU officer approached, latex gloves powdered white. In his hand, a portable fingerprint scanner blinked. "Got a hit on the prints."

Frank shifted. "From one of the dead guys?"

The officer turned the screen. A mugshot filled the display. "Yeah, Raul Mendoza, small-time crew associate. But here's the thing. He's the brother of the guy you captured alive."

Frank's jaw tightened. Brothers. He could use that. "Thank you."

His phone buzzed against his thigh. He pulled it out and

scanned the text. His lips curved up. Time to make the necessary preparations.

He pocketed the phone. "Tag and bag everything, Claire. Damon, with me."

He explained the plan as they drove to the station.

"Claire and Quinn don't know? Jack?" Damon asked.

"No, not yet. But Jack needs to get the tech ready, so he knows." Frank scanned the texts and alerts.

Damon made a face. "You trust that chatterbox to keep it quiet?"

"No choice, but he can keep a secret if necessary."

"Okay. But how'd you know Watkins would approach her?"

"I didn't. I thought he'd come to me again. But Eli studied the note left for KC and the hit with the warning and thought he might reach out to her."

"She's off the case."

"Exactly. That's why I didn't call her."

After Damon dropped him off at the station and took off to secure the rendezvous point, Frank pushed through the glass doors. The air-conditioning hit like ice, raising gooseflesh on his arms after the Florida heat.

Down the hall, Spaulding put his jacket on and picked up a thin folder. "Commander, anything I need to know before I go in?"

"Yes, his brother Raul's dead. But he doesn't need to know that."

The detective nodded. "If he asks about his brother, I say he's injured. If he wants to see him, he'll need to cooperate."

"Yes, but if he doesn't ask, tell him his brother is spilling his guts in the next room. They know the drill. Early bird gets the worm."

"Will do." Spaulding led the way to the interrogation room.

Beyond the one-way mirror, Diego Mendoza, the suspect, sat

cuffed to the table, head down. When Spaulding stepped inside and closed the door, Mendoza raised his head.

Spaulding read him his rights and asked if he understood.

This wasn't Mendoza's first rodeo. He acknowledged right away.

"If it's all right with you, we'll chat a bit," Spaulding started.

"Did you kill my brother?" Mendoza snarled.

"Your brother?" Spaulding flipped some papers in the folder. "Ah, Raul Mendoza. No, he's injured, being treated at the hospital."

Mendoza eyed Spaulding. "I wanna see him."

"That can be arranged, but only if you'll tell me who you work for."

It'd be nice to stay and watch, but a glance at his phone told Frank he needed to get back to the Hub and check on Jack's progress.

Fifteen minutes later, he walked into the lab.

"They are ready." Jack jerked a thumb toward the gadgets on the counter. "That watch looks just like any smartwatch, but it also records audio. I could have juiced it up more to add more functions, but you didn't give me a lot of time."

"I know. This is good. You can monitor the conversation in real time?"

"Right here." The tech tapped the screen. "I'll hear everything, and it'll be recorded. And the sunglasses there. They have cameras. I'll see the footage right here on the screen. Of course, they'll be recording as well. We can use a necklace, a brooch, or other jewelry, but—"

"Sunglasses will do. It's outdoors, so they'll work. Remember, zip your lips."

Jack mimed zipping his lips. "You sure you don't want Quinn to go?"

"No, you'll do fine. Just drop them off at the location. You'll be back in fifteen minutes."

The flippant tech stayed quiet. He shed the lab coat, picked up the gadgets, and headed out, hair sticking up where his right hand had been clawing at it.

Quinn, who was field-certified, might've made a better choice. Nah, Jack would do.

With Jack off doing the drop-off, Frank hurried back to the station to catch the end of the interrogation. When he entered, Spaulding just stepped out of the room.

"Did he talk?"

"Oh, he talked, but nothing useful. Doesn't know where they took Watkins's kid. He did give us a couple of names." Spaulding consulted his notes. "He reports to Big D. Ricky Glover is the getaway driver."

Frank unlocked his phone and called Quinn. "Run down the name Ricky Glover and a nickname, Big D. See if Big D connects to anyone in Kozlov's circle."

"Yo!"

Spaulding turned back toward the room. "What?"

"Where's my lawyer? Big D usually sends the lawyer without our asking."

"You want a lawyer? You'll need to call one yourself, or we can get a public defender."

Mendoza's confident smirk faded. He sat back, skulking. When he leaned forward again, desperation had crept into his voice. "Wait. What if I give you another location? Can I see my brother?"

Spaulding winked at Frank, then faced Mendoza. "Let's see what it is. We have to verify it first."

"I don't know the address, but I can tell you how to get there. It's an office."

# CHAPTER 52

## THE SETUP

KC's foot pressed harder on the accelerator as she headed home. Time was ticking. The car came to an abrupt stop in her driveway, no time for proper parking. Pulse drumming, she ran inside.

Straight to the lockbox by the bedroom dresser. Combination spun, lid lifted. Her Glock remained where she'd left it, matte black, familiar, full magazine. Metal clicked as she slid the magazine home and holstered the weapon beneath her jacket.

A glance at her phone made her grimace. One hour to the meeting. No wiggle room.

At the sink, cold water hit her face. Hair secured in a no-nonsense knot, and then back out the door.

Traffic in Orlando was sluggish but not impossible. By the time she turned into the East End Market lot, the sun was lowering, the lot half full with weekend browsers. KC moved fast, head down.

Inside, roasted coffee and baked bread warmed the air. Voices rose and fell in cheerful waves. She wove through clusters of shoppers, past the coffee stall, to the general store tucked in back.

An older Asian man spotted her when she walked in. He hollered something in Chinese to someone in the back. A young Asian woman who resembled the old man, his daughter, came out and waved her forward. KC had no idea who she was, fellow officer? CI? No time to wonder.

KC followed her to a back room tinged with cardboard and dust. Boxes stacked high, mop bucket in the corner.

"Cassidy? ID, please." The young woman held her hand out.

KC displayed her badge and Orlando PD credentials.

The woman examined them like lab specimens, then returned them, and pointed to a plain brown paper sack on a counter. "Exit out the back."

"Thank you."

KC pulled the paper sack close and peered inside. Watch. Sunglasses. Earwig. A folded note.

She unfolded the paper.

*Watch = audio & mic. Sunglasses = POV camera. Earwig = one-way comms.*

She replaced her own smartwatch with the one provided, slid the earwig into place, and set the sunglasses on her face. The lenses felt heavier than ordinary shades.

She murmured, "Testing."

"Loud and clear." Jack's voice filled her ear, crisp and almost smug. "I see what you're seeing. Don't worry. Nobody can tell."

"Feels like they can." She adjusted the frames. "They crooked?"

"No, it doesn't matter as long as I can get the visuals."

"How's the feed?"

"Crystal clear. Audio's strong. Video's stable."

"Should I toss the bag and note?"

"Yes, but wait till you're out of the store. Toss it in a random trash can."

She put the note back in the bag, crunched it, and walked out the back like she was told.

Outside, the air smelled of jasmine and hot asphalt. She hurried to her car, tossed the bag in a random can, and slid behind the wheel. The dash clock offered twenty-eight minutes to hit Leu Gardens. Plenty of time under normal circumstances, but one never knew.

*Lord, please no accidents or traffic on the way, and I find a parking spot.*

She tapped her fingers on the wheel at a red light, glancing at the dashboard, wishing for a switch she didn't have. Even if her sedan had been equipped with lights and sirens, she couldn't have used them now. Not off the case on the way to a clandestine meet with a witness.

"You got a way to make the lights all green?"

She didn't think Jack would respond, but he did. "Sure, if I had the time and the authorization. Anyway, you'll make it. You should get there with about ten minutes to spare."

"What about parking?"

"Hang on. Let me look. All good. Might have to take one of those faraway spots."

At last, the destination was in sight. Leu Gardens spread across nearly fifty acres, all green paths and manicured beds. As Jack predicted, KC had to park far. She hopped out, ensured she had everything, and walked up the stone entryway. Beyond the gates, winding trails curved past roses, camellias, and towering oaks strung with Spanish moss. Families meandered with cameras. A couple strolled hand in hand.

She moved with purpose, scanning left and right.

"Nice venue. Why did he pick this place?"

"No idea. Damon is there. You'll be fine."

She slowed at a fork in the path. Ahead, a shaded garden opened into a secluded corner with wrought-iron benches and flowering shrubs. Not empty, but quiet. A perfect meeting spot. Public enough to feel safe, private enough for words that mattered.

She adjusted the sunglasses, taking it in. "Looks good."

"I have eyes on you and the surroundings. We can communicate. You're good."

KC drew a breath. The hum of cicadas rose in the trees. Somewhere deeper in the garden, a fountain burbled.

She didn't see Damon. But she knew. The slight rustle on the left where no wind blew, the faint glint of glass that disappeared the second she tried to place it. He was there.

*Where is Watkins?* A lone figure sat on a bench.

"Is that him?" she whispered.

"His sunglasses and hat make it hard to tell, but I think so."

KC strode toward the figure.

"Detective." Watkins stood. "I tried to warn you to leave this alone, but you wouldn't listen."

She frowned. "You sent the note? And the goon to hit me?"

"He was only supposed to deliver the message."

"So, now, you're doing it yourself. And this is what you wanted to tell me?" She shook her head.

"You don't understand."

"Then help me understand."

"I did something stupid. It was an accident—"

"What—"

But once he started talking, he wouldn't stop. "I didn't mean to hit her. Just lost my temper. I don't even know how, but it turned into a fight. Then… I didn't know what to do. I remember this jerk I prosecuted. He hooked me up with Kozlov—"

In her ear, she heard Jack's voice. "Figure approaching from the east."

Then Damon's voice, "I'll check it out."

"You need to find my son," Watkins pleaded.

KC wanted to see for herself, but her eyes saw what her brain hadn't processed. Her body got lifted by the blast, and she landed in a heap some feet away. She opened her eyes, but everything was blurry. Sounds were thin and far away. Darkness rushed up, swallowing the world, until there was nothing at all.

# CHAPTER 53

## BREACH

"Report!" Frank gaped at the screen as Jack cried out KC's name.

A bomb went off, but where was it? Frank couldn't blame Damon for not noticing. Nobody could know where Watkins would be. It had to be remotely detonated. Someone was monitoring Watkins. As soon as he was about to spill his guts, they took him out.

"KC is gone." Damon's voice came through.

"We saw someone take her. They sped off in a golf cart."

Damon scanned around. "Did you see which way it went?"

"West," Jack answered. "But I lost them somewhere in the tree line."

"I should have checked—"

"No," Frank interrupted Damon. "No, you were short on time, and nobody had expected this move." He closed his eyes. Watkins dead. His last words were to find his son. They were using Joey as leverage to force Watkins to cooperate.

"Joey is our priority now. With Watkins dead, they no longer need him alive." Frank tapped his phone. "Jack, continue to track KC's signal."

"Yeah, that's what I've been doing. Signal's cutting in and out. Don't know if I told you, but the watch also tracks her heart rate. For what it's worth, she's breathing."

Frank nodded, his mind pulling in different directions.

"Boss." Quinn's voice crackled through comms before she appeared in the lab doorway. "I found Ricky Glover on IRIS. He's walking into the office building. The same one you guys got out of Mendoza."

"This is where they're holding Joey." Frank's head snapped up. "Damon, Claire, Quinn, let's hit it. Jack, do everything you can to track KC." He finally pressed *Call* on his phone.

Spaulding answered right away. "Commander, we ready to hit the office?"

"Yes, but I need you on KC."

"What do you mean?"

"No time to explain." He headed to his desk for his gear. "She's hit and abducted. Jack is tracking her."

"Boss," Jack's voice cut in. "Sorry to interrupt. Signal's fading fast. GPS is gone. Now I've lost everything. Her new watch is either smashed or dumped, or she's underground somewhere. I'm pulling traffic cams near Leu Gardens."

"Keep at it. Spaulding, Jack just lost her signals. You have full access to our resources here to locate her. Find her. Call me as soon as you have a location."

"Understood."

"When you're ready to move, I'll send Damon."

"No need, Commander. I'll alert Tanner. Er, FBI SSA Nathan Tanner."

Frank frowned. "This is not a Bureau case."

"No, but this is personal to Tanner."

No time to dwell on that. "Okay, keep me posted." He disconnected and hurried out the door.

—•⫶•—

The building crouched at the edge of an industrial strip, a block of gray concrete squatting under the failing buzz of a neon sign. From the outside, it looked dead, two stories, windows blacked out, parking lot empty except for a pair of semitrailers. But Frank's gut told him differently.

He studied the façade through binoculars. "Damon, point. Claire, with me. Quinn, cover our six. Tight formation. We clear it all."

They approached in tactical formation, weapons drawn. Damon tested the door handle, then gave a sharp shake of his head. Locked.

Frank raised three fingers, dropping them one by one.

Damon's shoulder hit the door hard, splintering the frame around the dead bolt. They surged inside, Claire sweeping left, Frank taking center, Damon moving right.

The stench hit first—stale coffee, old smoke, sweat soaked into carpet. A reception area opened before them, littered with outdated magazines and a desk piled with unopened mail. Fluorescent tubes buzzed overhead, one flickering erratically, casting a sickly half-light across water-stained ceiling tiles.

Movement flashed across the hallway to the left, a figure ducking behind a doorframe.

"Contact left!" Claire called, adjusting her angle.

Gunfire erupted. Muzzle flashes lit the dim corridor as rounds chewed through drywall, sending plaster dust floating through the air. Frank dove behind the reception desk, particleboard exploding around him. Quinn hit the deck, rolling behind an overturned filing cabinet.

"Suppressing fire!" Frank shouted.

Quinn rose, laying down controlled bursts that forced the shooter back into cover. Brass casings clinked against the linoleum as Claire moved along the wall, using the doorframe for protection.

"Moving!" Damon advanced through a side corridor while the others kept the gunman pinned.

A second shooter appeared from behind a cubicle partition, assault rifle chattering. Rounds sparked off metal desk frames and shredded fabric dividers. Frank rolled right, coming up with his Glock extended, and put three rounds center mass. The man dropped hard.

"Forward!" Frank commanded.

They pushed deeper into the building's maze of cubicles and half-cleared offices. The place felt abandoned but recently used. Papers still scattered across desks. Coffee cups held rings of mold. A jacket draped over a chair. Emergency lighting cast long shadows between the partition walls.

Claire moved methodically, checking each angle before advancing. A door slammed somewhere ahead, followed by running footsteps on concrete.

"Runner, moving east." Quinn tracked movement through the maze.

They reached a central hub where several corridors intersected. Office chairs lay toppled, filing cabinets hung open, their contents spilled across stained carpet. The air-conditioning hummed overhead, but one vent rattled loose, adding to the building's decay.

A gunman burst from behind an overturned desk, firing wild. Claire dropped low, her return fire precise. Two rounds sent him spinning into a watercooler with a crash of plastic and splashing water.

"Clear front!" she called.

Damon checked a side office, kicking the door wide. "Storage room clear!"

They advanced toward the building's rear. The fluorescent lighting grew sparser, replaced by dim emergency bulbs that left pools of shadow between the cubicles. Somewhere ahead, metal clanged, like a chair hitting concrete.

Frank held up his fist, and the team froze.

Then they heard it. A muffled cry, strained and desperate.

"South corridor," Claire whispered, tilting her head toward the sound.

They moved with renewed urgency but maintained discipline. Each doorway was a potential ambush, each corner a threat. Quinn covered their rear as they advanced, watching for flanking movements.

The corridor narrowed, lined with offices more permanent than the cubicle farm. Real doors, frosted glass windows, nameplates long since removed. At the far end, a heavy door marked *Conference Room* stood ajar, yellow light spilling from the gap.

The sounds were clearer now, struggling, the scrape of chair legs, gagged shouting that could only be human.

Frank's heart rate spiked. *Joey.*

But training kept him cautious. It could be a trap. The sounds could be bait to draw them into a kill zone.

He signaled for a stack formation. Claire took point beside the doorframe, Damon opposite her. Quinn maintained overwatch down the corridor.

Frank checked his weapon one final time, then raised his hand. The team tensed, ready.

Three. Two. One.

Damon hit the door with his shoulder. It flew open, revealing—

# CHAPTER 54

## THE TIP

After the call with the commander, Spaulding called Tanner, who answered right away.

"It's KC." Spaulding wasted no time filling Tanner in. He pictured the agent's concerned face. "She was at her aunt's. No idea when she came back in town. She promised not to do anything stupid."

"I knew she wouldn't stay put. Let me check her watch." A pause. "Stationary at Leu Gardens."

"That's where she went. I heard Jack had a special watch for her. You think she still has her own?"

"I don't know. Maybe she locked it in the car. Let me ask Deanna—"

"Hang on. I have another line." Blocked number. Spaulding hesitated, then accepted the call. "Spaulding."

A distorted voice said, "Detective Kylie Cassidy is heading to Mission Grounds. Hurry."

Click.

Spaulding stood frozen for a breath, phone still pressed to his ear.

*Mission Grounds. And who is this? A trap?*

He switched back to Tanner. "I just got a call. Blocked number, voice scrambled. Said KC's at Mission Grounds. Said to hurry."

"Could be a trap. Mission Grounds… Let me check our intel on that."

While Tanner ran his search, Spaulding grabbed Kozlov's thick file and started hunting through the property holdings. The timing felt too convenient, but if there was a legitimate connection… His phone rang as he spotted the relevant LLC.

He swiped to answer. "Hey, Tanner, one of Kozlov's LLC—"

"Has financial interests in Mission Grounds." Tanner finished Spaulding's thought. "I also had Deanna check for cameras in the area. Nothing yet."

"We can't ignore it, though. Before we go half-cocked, let's check with Jack." Spaulding clicked to enlarge the video-call window. "Jack, any luck?"

"Depends on what you call luck. Signal popped up a minute ago, but it's in and out."

"Is it anywhere near Mission Grounds?"

"Yeah, how'd you know?"

That was all the confirmation they needed. Spaulding thanked Jack, and Tanner said, "I'll meet you there."

Thank goodness it was a Saturday, and the lieutenant wasn't in. Spaulding wouldn't have to tell him KC's dilemma.

Travers, who asked to be looped in, would send Damon over. But they were tied up in the office raid, and time was critical. Every minute KC was missing was another minute for Kozlov's people to move her, hurt her, or worse.

Spaulding ground his teeth. So… going in undermanned versus letting the trail go cold? The choice made itself. He'd head out with Tanner and update Travers if they found KC.

# CHAPTER 55

## MISSION GROUNDS

K C clawed her way back to consciousness through layers of fog. The hum of an engine beneath her, steady and low, registered first. Then, the hard ridges of a van's metal floor pressed into her ribs. Cargo van.

She kept her breathing shallow, eyelids heavy, feigning unconsciousness. The vehicle slowed, gravel crunching beneath the tires. Then a lurch, brakes squealing enough to jolt her head against the wall. Pain flared behind her eyes, a migraine pounding at the base of her skull.

The side door screeched open. Cool late afternoon air rushed in, carrying the scent of earth baked under the Florida sun, tinged with mildew and something older—stone, moss, decay.

A man's hands hooked beneath her arms and hauled her up like she weighed nothing. She let her body hang limp, counting each step as he carried her out. The light shifted across her eyelids, sun, then shade, then the hollow cool of shadow again. Grass brushed her boots. Dirt shifted underfoot. The faint echo of birds startled from the trees rang overhead.

He carried her a distance before dumping her onto the ground. Her cheek pressed into brittle weeds and chalky soil, dry and sharp against her skin. She kept still, breathing through the ache. A phone clicked on.

"She's here, boss." His voice was low but carried, the words sharp against the stillness.

KC strained, forcing her blast-deafened ears to catch every thread. Silence. Then a reply filtered through, so faint she couldn't make out the words.

"All right." The call ended.

She lay motionless, pulse thudding in her ears. The air was different here—open, uncontained. A shift in the wind carried the creak of old wood, the groan of rusted metal. She cracked her eyelids the tiniest fraction.

Through her blurred vision, she made out jagged silhouettes against the sinking sun.

Footsteps receded, crunching across gravel. A door banged shut somewhere off to her right, the sound echoing through the hollow ruin. Then quiet.

Crumbling stone walls rose around her, arches half eaten by time. A toppled cross jutted sideways from the weeds like a broken bone.

KC let out the smallest breath, sinking deeper into the weeds, conserving what little strength she had. She'd need it. They weren't leaving her here to nap.

Every instinct screamed at her to lift a hand, probe her head, confirm the dampness she feared might be blood. But she didn't move. Not yet. She tested her fingers, toes, rolled her tongue against her teeth. Nothing broken. Just the massive headache.

Beyond the cross, what might have been a bell tower was nothing more than a skeleton of beams, cloaked in vines. An old mission. Abandoned, forgotten, and now her cage.

The commander would know she'd gone missing. He'd have people looking for her. And he'd loop in Spaulding, who'd let Tanner know. And that meant Tanner would find her.

But until then, she'd be her own backup.

The moment his footsteps faded, she pressed her palms against the ground and tried to push herself up. Her arms shook. The world swayed, and she sank back down, jaw clenched against the nausea.

She scanned the grounds around her, too much open space, too many places for him to corner her. Better to conserve what little strength she had. She searched for her phone and her weapon. Gone.

After what seemed like hours, the man's footsteps crunched back toward her, slower this time. Her cheek burned where it had kissed dirt. Somewhere under that ache, adrenaline hummed awake.

He didn't come alone. Another set of footsteps echoed off the crumbling stone walls. And this one turned her over. "Detective." He shook her head from side to side. The ache in the back of her head made her wince. "There, you're awake. Time for us to chat."

*Kozlov!*

She opened her eyes and managed to sit up. Beside him stood the man who must've carried her.

"Detective, you don't know how to quit."

"Quit what?" she rasped, forcing her voice low and steady. Let them hear her. Let them underestimate the steadiness under the pain.

Kozlov laughed, a practiced chuckle. He smirked at the man with fond mockery. "I like her. So spunky. What about you, Big D?"

Big D nodded once, slow. "She's got a mouth."

Kozlov's smile cut back to her from the shadow of a broken archway. "Do you know how much your poking around is costing me?"

"No idea."

Kozlov's expression hardened into a lecture. "I lost a surgeon because of you."

"Good."

"A warehouse. A safe house." His voice hardened. "And if my intel is correct, I'll soon lose another base. Not to mention the tens of thousands of lost revenue."

A breeze stirred through the hollow mission, carrying the scent of decay. "You're forgetting the assistant state attorney," she said before she could stop herself. The words tasted like accusation.

Kozlov made a show of considering her, as if her interruption were an amusing interlude. "Ah, but he wasn't an employee, nor was he a partner."

"What do you call it? You took his son to blackmail him."

The smile returned, colder. "You don't know anything. The boy is sick. He needs a kidney. And he has this rare genetic marker that makes finding a donor difficult."

Kozlov leaned in as if he were gifting her a truth, his back against the weathered stone wall scarred by years of neglect. "Your saintly attorney came to me for help. But guess what? The boy's mom didn't like the idea. He pushed her and almost killed her. And then he came to me a second time."

That didn't line up. "Then why take his son? You were using him as leverage."

His nostrils flared as if she'd asked a rude question. "I wouldn't call it leverage. Insurance, maybe. See? Dr. Chandler grew a conscience. I can't have the attorney do the same."

Pieces clicked into place with the wrong edges. Bits of Watkins's confession returned. He'd said he'd made a mistake. Foley, the ex-wife, didn't fit the pattern. "So, you had Chandler mutilate his ex-wife's body to hide the crime?"

Kozlov's face was all calm execution. "I wouldn't call it mutilation. I regretted that her organs weren't viable. I would've made good money off that. Have I answered all your questions? I wouldn't want you to be unsatisfied before we said goodbye."

"But you did kill those other girls. You harvested their organs!"

He sighed. "They were desperate. They wanted money and answered the call. We didn't invite just anybody. Only the ones who wanted to help."

*What twisted logic!*

"If you had told them you would kill them, they would've thought twice about 'helping' you. You're sick. Both of you."

The skeletal bell tower cast long shadows across the weeds as Big D raised his arm, ready to strike. She was prepared, but Kozlov stopped him.

"Not yet. Need to be clean." His words echoed through the hollow grounds. Kozlov stepped back. "You know what to do. Make it look like an accident."

"Yes, boss."

Big D put his arm down and grinned, a hunger in his eyes. He was a man who liked danger. This was the moment he'd been waiting for. He leaned so close she could smell him—sweat, tobacco, something metallic.

She pressed against the chalky soil, surrounded by crumbling walls with nowhere to run. Her pulse thudded, loud and useful. The ancient stones seemed to crowd her, waiting. Every fiber of her being wanted to launch herself at them, to lunge, to bite. Her vision bounced. The migraine thumped at her focus. No gun. No obvious cover. But she had fists and teeth and a spine that refused to be negotiated with.

This was it. Now or not at all.

# CHAPTER 56

## DEALS WITH DEVILS

The door exploded inward with a hollow crash that reverberated through the converted conference room like a gunshot.

Frank swept his weapon across the space, taking in everything in one tactical heartbeat. Joey slumped in a chair between server racks, zip-tied and gagged, and a figure hunched over a keyboard at the far workstation, fingers flying across keys with desperate urgency.

"Police!"

"Show me your hands!"

"On the ground now!"

The guy ignored them. A second later, Damon yelled, "Drop it!"

His gun cracked once. The suspect crumpled, his final keystroke echoing in the sudden silence. The sharp smell of gunpowder mixed with ozone.

Damon moved to kick the pistol away from the still form, checking for a pulse with two fingers to the neck. "He's gone."

"Call it in." Frank nodded toward Joey. "And send paramedics."

"Clear," Claire called, sweeping behind equipment towers.

Frank kept his weapon trained on the room's remaining shadows, cables snaking across the floor like black arteries, dead monitors casting angular silhouettes, server towers blinking with nervous green eyes. The air tasted metallic, heavy with ozone and the acrid smell of overheated circuits.

Claire was at Joey's side, holstering her weapon as she dropped to her knees. She yanked the gag free in one swift motion.

With the room secure, Frank lowered his weapon and looked at Joey for the first time. The kid, man now, scanned the room with confused eyes.

Joey wouldn't recognize him. Why would he? Frank might have seen him once or twice over the years, maybe at some social events where Watkins brought his family.

"You're safe now. Just breathe." Claire cut the zip ties off.

Joey's arms fell to his sides like dead weight. He doubled forward, coughing until tears streaked down his bruised cheeks. A split lip had crusted with dried blood. One eye was swollen nearly shut.

"Thank you," he managed, voice like gravel scraped over broken glass.

"I'm Detective Santos, or you can call me Claire." Claire tipped her head toward Frank. "That's Commander Travers."

"And I'm Damon." Damon stood by Quinn. "Let's hope we get something."

Quinn sat at a workstation where the suspect had been typing. Her ponytail swayed as she leaned into the pale glow of monitors, fingers dancing across blood-spattered keys.

"System's been wiped." She slapped her hand on the table. "Professional job. This guy knew what he was doing. Everything's gone. They torched the whole thing."

Frank moved closer, stepping over the tangle of cables and

approaching the nervous blinking of status lights. "Any chance of recovery?"

She tossed her ponytail back over her shoulder. "I don't know. We'll have to get it back to the Hub. Jack and I may be able to salvage something. But it'll take time."

"Do it." He knelt by Joey. "Are you up to answering some questions?"

Joey nodded.

"Can you tell us what happened? From the beginning."

The kid closed his eyes, and when he breathed in, the coming words appeared to cost him something. "For background, I have PKD, polycystic kidney disease. It's congenital. On top of that, I've got a rare tissue type. My body rejects most donors. I've been on the transplant list for years. Doctors told my parents I'd need a new kidney before I turned thirty."

The telling seemed to drain Joey, obvious in the way he blinked hard and swallowed.

Frank cleared his throat. "You can tell us later."

Joey shook his head. "No, I'm okay. A few months ago, I got an infection. Dad freaked out. He never told me what he did, but I figured it out. He contacted their boss." He jerked his head toward the dead guy. "I think they're part of some organ-for-pay network. The boss must've promised Dad I'd get a kidney if he'd do whatever they wanted."

A shaky hand rubbed at his swollen eyes. "This is the part I don't know. I heard him talking to Mom about me. Then, one day, Mom didn't pick me up after dialysis. Dad showed up instead. I never saw her again."

"So how did they get you?" Frank asked.

"I don't know. I went through my dialysis like normal. The tech wheeled me out and then nothing. I woke up in a room. They'd sedated me. There was a medical person, a doctor or a nurse, somebody who checked me over." He swallowed hard. "They said I'd be 'taken care of.'"

So, Watkins made some deals with the devil. The thought Frank had been avoiding crystallized. Watkins had probably killed his ex-wife. Frank sighed as his phone buzzed against his ribs.

Jack's name lit the display.

Frank answered on the first vibration. "Talk to me."

"KC's signal pinged. Near Mission Grounds. Spaulding's already en route."

"Confirmed location?"

"Best we've got. Signal's intermittent, but it's something."

"Copy." Frank pointed two fingers like a gun, air-tapping Damon and Claire. "KC's at Mission Grounds. Spaulding is on the way. Move."

"On it." Damon headed out.

Claire gave Joey's shoulder a final squeeze. "Medics are seconds out. You're going to be fine." Then she was gone, boots pounding after Damon.

The room settled into a strange quiet once the door shut, broken only by the electronic hum of overworked servers and Joey's ragged breath as he steadied himself. It all closed in—the slumped suspect, the blinking towers, the boy's battered face. They'd pulled Joey out alive, but the intel they needed was ash.

"Would it help," Joey rasped, "if you knew who their boss's attorney is?"

Frank's head snapped toward him. "You know?"

"Not positive." Joey's voice was thin, but steady. "I overheard them once. The name came up, T. J. Simms. I know he's an attorney because Dad had a case against him. Called him a scumbag."

Frank froze. *Simms.* That name been whispered in corruption cases that never quite stuck, evidence that always seemed to disappear. If Joey was right, this thing went all the way to the top.

# CHAPTER 57

## EEYORE

K C's pulse hammered in her ears, every nerve screaming at her to move. The weeds scratched her palms, dirt grinding into her cheek. She forced herself upright, swaying on unsteady legs.

Big D launched at her.

She twisted hard, rolling across the brittle weeds.

His boot slammed where her ribs had been. The ground shook with the force of it.

She staggered up to one knee, vision swimming, and drove her shoulder into his midsection. The impact rattled her skull, nearly dropping her, but it rocked him back half a step.

"Feisty." He recovered with a grin.

KC swung a fist.

He caught her wrist in one meaty hand and wrenched it hard, spinning her until pain seared up her arm.

She gasped, twisted with the momentum, and drove her heel down on his instep. Bone met bone with a crunch.

Big D cursed, shoving her back.

KC staggered, nearly going down. The edge of the mission

grounds yawned just behind her. She glimpsed a slope of broken stone and jagged brush. One more step and she'd tumble.

Her head throbbed. Her breath came shallow. But her fists rose again.

He laughed, low and eager, and advanced.

KC darted in first, aiming for his throat. He blocked with his forearm, swung his elbow down hard into her back. She dropped to her knees, breath knocked out in a sharp whoosh. His hand clamped on her collar, yanking her upright like a doll.

Her pulse roared in her ears. She clawed for his face, fingers digging, nails raking skin. He roared and shoved her away. She stumbled, hit the ground hard, dust and weeds scraping her cheek.

*Stay down!* her body screamed.

*Get up!* her head commanded.

She rolled just as his boot crashed down where her skull had been. She forced herself to her feet, swaying, fists trembling but raised.

When he came at her again, arms wide, ready to crush, she ducked, slamming her forehead into his chin. White-hot pain burst across her skull, nearly dropping her, but he staggered back this time, jaw snapping shut with an audible crack.

She tried to follow through, throwing a kick. Too slow.

He caught her leg midswing, ripped her off-center, and tossed her to the ground like she weighed nothing. Her back hit the dirt, all air driven from her lungs.

She blinked up at the bell tower's skeletal outline against the twilight sky. The world tilted, sliding sideways.

Bootsteps thundered. Big D loomed above, grin splitting his face as he charged, all brute weight bearing down, straight for her.

She braced for impact, too slow to roll clear.

A blur of black and tan streaked from the shadows. The

German shepherd charged into Big D's side, jaws clamping on his leg with bone-crunching force. His roar ripped through the ruins as he staggered, dragging the dog along with him, boots skidding in the gravel.

KC scrambled back, heart hammering against her ribs.

The dog snarled, deep and furious, dragging him off-balance.

Big D swung wildly, trying to kick free, but the shepherd held fast, teeth buried deep.

With a last surge of strength, KC shoved herself forward and drove both palms into his chest. The combined force sent him stumbling back, heel catching on broken stone at the cliff's edge.

His head cracked hard against the jagged wall as he went down. The shepherd released at once, stepping back, hackles high.

Big D collapsed in a heap, groaning once before going still. Unconscious.

KC dropped to her knees, breath ragged, staring at the dog now standing guard between her and the fallen brute. Its chest heaved, ears sharp, eyes burning with focus.

Not wild. Not random. Trained. Could this be…?

Somewhere behind the silence, a new set of footsteps approached, deliberate and steady.

"Guard, Eeyore!"

The German shepherd froze, then backed off Big D, hackles still high, eyes locked on his fallen target.

"Are you okay?"

KC blinked hard. Maybe she'd taken one hit too many. Maybe she was hallucinating. But she saw the dog, heard the name.

"Jagers?" Her voice emerged raw, half breathless.

He crouched beside her, steady hands helping her sit up. His touch was quick but efficient, fingers checking her head, probing. "No fracture. Concussion, maybe. Nothing life-threatening."

She swallowed. "You're real?"

A faint smile tugged at his mouth. "Your aunt alerted me. Glad I got here in time."

"Aunt Mae? How'd she know?"

He shrugged, scanning the shadows as though expecting movement. "Said you called her, but you didn't say anything. She tried again, no answer. So she sent out a Bat signal." He chuckled under his breath. "Inside joke. Anyway, I'm never here. Got that? Your partner should be here any moment."

During the ill-fated meeting with Watkins... She must have speed-dialed Aunt Mae just before the blast without realizing it.

She pushed against the ground, fighting to steady herself. "But how'd you find me?"

Jagers smiled. "Thank your aunt for giving you that ring. It's a tracker."

The ring? Her fingers flicked along it. Graduation day at the academy. Aunt Mae had pressed the tiny piece of jewelry—a ring that resembled any class ring with her initials on top—into her hand. *"Kylie, I don't want to stop you from becoming a cop. It's your dream. But we lost your dad in the line of duty. Please keep this with you. Just a reminder to be careful."*

Now it made sense. KC wore it everywhere.

But Aunt Mae was a lawyer, not an engineer. How had she known about an embedded chip in a ring? And Jagers—

"Wait. Who are you? *What* are you? A spy?"

His smile deepened, but it didn't reach his eyes. "Not important. Tell my Mayflower I got your six."

*Mayflower?* KC's head spun, and it had nothing to do with the hit she'd taken. "You mean Aunt Mae?"

But he was already rising, calling Eeyore to heel, fading toward the ruined arch.

"Not so fast!"

The voice rang out like a crack of thunder.

KC's stomach dropped. She turned her head toward the stone wall.

Kozlov stood there, gun leveled steady, silhouette etched against the twilight sky.

# CHAPTER 58

## AFTERMATH

Spaulding rolled to a stop beside a black SUV half hidden in the weeds. Tanner was out before the engine settled, his weapon low, eyes raking the sprawl of ruins ahead.

Mission Grounds was bigger than Spaulding had imagined. Crumbling stone walls half swallowed by vines, terraces sunk into shadow, hollow arches yawning as the last of the daylight bled away… Too many places to hide.

"No car here." He joined Tanner at the edge of the main lot. He eased his Glock free, the grip familiar and steady, and his gaze swept the cracked asphalt. Weeds pushed through faded lane lines. A rusted lamppost leaned like a tired sentinel. "Where do you think she is?"

Tanner shook his head, jaw tight. "No idea. Let's start sweeping. You take west. I'll take east."

"Copy."

They split, boots crunching over gravel and broken glass as they canvassed the grounds. Spaulding checked the chapel ruins, peered through dark archways, cleared shallow alcoves, the whole front face of Mission Grounds. But found nothing but echoes and the hiss of wind through tall grass.

When they regrouped, Tanner pointed toward a narrow service drive that slipped away around the chapel's rear, half hidden by a stand of scrub oaks. "Back lot. They'd use that to stay out of sight."

They moved fast, angling into the trees. The air cooled under the canopy, and the shadows fell thicker. The service road opened onto a forgotten staff lot, gravel packed thin, moss at the edges, a sagging wooden sign, *Employees Only* in faded red paint. Half-buried tire ruts freshened the gravel where someone had turned recently.

Two vehicles were parked in the gloom, positioned in the weeds to stay out of sight. A cargo van with one side door ajar and a dark sedan close beside it. Oil had left a damp sheen beneath the van. The smell of warm rubber and a faint exhaust ghosted the air.

Spaulding's jaw tightened. "There. Fresh."

Tanner eased forward, eyes narrowing at the van's scuffed side panel and the smear of recent footprints trailing away toward the ruins. "Keep your head on a swivel. Could be hot."

They closed the gap, weapons up, every step deliberate. The van's open door revealed nothing but shadows. Spaulding nodded toward the footprint trail into the grounds, still fresh in the damp earth.

That's when they heard it. A growl, coming from deeper in the complex.

"You hear that?" Tanner asked.

Spaulding cocked his head. At first, only the sigh of wind. Then low, guttural. A snarl.

Dog.

Before he could process, two sharp cracks split the ruins.

Gunfire.

Tanner took off at a sprint. "Come on!"

Spaulding pounded after him, weaving through a collapsed wall. They rounded the corner—

And froze.

KC knelt in the weeds, pale and shaking. Blood had dried at the corner of her mouth, and her left eye was already swelling shut. She held the gun with both hands to steady the tremor in her grip. Ten feet away, Kozlov sprawled against the stone wall, blood pooling dark beneath him.

Spaulding swept the scene. Two bodies. Tanner approached Kozlov, signaling Spaulding to the other body. He stooped over the big guy. Still breathing. He yanked the suspect's arms back and cuffed him.

"This one's gone," Tanner called, then went to KC.

Spaulding joined him. His gut clenched. Her face was a mess of bruises, her shirt torn at the shoulder.

The acrid gunpowder odor still hung in the air. His partner fought to keep it together, her breathing too quick, her body swaying to stay upright. "Geez, KC…" He exhaled. "How bad are you hurt?"

She put on a weak smile. "Just look at the other guys."

Tanner checked her head for injuries and administered the field concussion test while Spaulding asked, "What happened? Where's the dog? That guy's left leg looks like it's been mauled."

"A wild dog. I don't know where it went."

"So, what happened? I heard about the blast." Tanner squatted down.

"I'm not sure. I woke up here. Kozlov and I had a chat. I'll have to debrief the commander. Anyway, I thought he'd left after the talk. Big D, that's the sleeping one there, started a fight. He came at me, and that dog lunged out of nowhere. I managed to hit him back, and he hit his head."

Her tone, the bruises, the way Big D's bulk lay crumpled where she said he'd fallen… The story fit together, mostly. No missing the inconsistencies. But Spaulding trusted her. Whatever details she was keeping for now, they could sort it out off the record. "And the dead guy?"

"I was catching my breath after Big D went down when Kozlov showed up. He hadn't left after all. Probably watching from behind those stone pillars. Anyway, he had a gun pointed at me—"

"How'd you get this gun?" Tanner secured it in an evidence bag. "It's dirty. Serial's filed off."

Spaulding leaned closer. "Not OPD issue. Not Bureau either. Street import, maybe Russian."

"It was Big D's. He dropped it when he went down. Figured I better arm myself in case more of Kozlov's guys showed up."

Running footsteps startled him. He and Tanner blocked KC, faced the noise, weapons raised.

Two figures ran through the ruins. Damon and Claire, weapons drawn, scanning for threats on approach.

"KC?" Claire called as soon as they were in sight, voice sharp. She took in the scene, the bodies, the blood, KC kneeling in the weeds, and her shoulders relaxed. "Looks like we missed all the fun."

Spaulding took a step forward. "KC's okay. Need paramedics, though."

"On it." Claire pulled out her phone to make the call.

"Kozlov dead?" Damon asked.

"Yes." Tanner extended a hand. "FBI. Nathan Tanner."

The detectives introduced themselves.

Damon walked toward Big D. "This cuffed one. Alive?"

"He was a minute ago." Spaulding shrugged.

Damon checked Big D's pulse again. "Still breathing. Good." His grim expression flatlined. "With everything we lost in that server room, he's our best shot at mapping Kozlov's operation. Time to find out who else is in this thing."

# CHAPTER 59

## WHAT WATKINS HAD

The hospital smelled of antiseptic and tired coffee. Frank had gotten used to it, having seen too many burn victims, gunshot wounds, suspects cuffed to gurneys. The same fluorescent buzz. The same shuffle of nurses moving on weary feet.

Reports had trickled in. Quinn and Jack were back at the Hub, sifting through the burnt drives to salvage something. Damon and Claire had sent updates. KC was alive, banged up, admitted for observation. Kozlov was dead. Big D was here, being taken care of, under guard.

Frank avoided the police headquarters, which would be a zoo since the blast this afternoon that killed Watkins. His time was much better spent wrapping things up.

He had Damon on the phone. "I'm at the hospital now. Will stop by to check on KC. Then I'll see if I can talk to Big D. Give me everything you have on him."

"Will do. Claire and I can start on the attorney."

"Do it." Frank flexed his grip on the phone. "Just be careful."

He ended the call, headed down the hall to KC's room. Bruises mottled her cheek, and her left eye had swollen, but her spirit hadn't dimmed.

She cracked a smile when she saw him. "Commander."

"You look rough, kid." He stepped in. "But I'm glad to see you're okay. Good work."

"Thank you." She smiled. Her gaze went to the man standing by her bed. "Spaulding just left to start on the paperwork. Er, this is FBI SSA Nathan Tanner."

Frank shook hands with Tanner. "You work with Ron Peters?"

"Yes, my boss. He got bumped up to SAC not too long ago."

"Yeah, I heard. We worked together on a couple of joint ops. Good man." Strange, Ron accepted the SAC position. Ron always said he belonged in the field, much like Frank himself. Then again, Frank also accepted the governor's offer to lead Orlando Prime.

"Great boss." Tanner smiled.

By the looks of the agent and the detective, Frank now understood what Spaulding referenced when he said it was personal to Tanner.

"I just wanted to stop by to thank you. Take care of the paperwork later. Now rest up." Frank nodded to the two of them and backed away. "Again, good job."

Just as he was walking out, a woman brushed past him to go in. Behind him, KC greeted her as Aunt Mae.

One down, one to go. Big D wouldn't be as cooperative as KC, but Frank had leverage now. The suspect was hurt, isolated, and facing serious charges.

The suspect's room was a few doors down. As he approached, a young, harried doctor walked out. Frank showed his badge and asked how Big D was doing.

"He's stable now. A scalp cut and a concussion. Got a nasty bite wound on his left leg. Otherwise, he's good. Take it easy."

Frank frowned. "Bite wound?"

"Yeah, he said it was a German shepherd."

Nobody mentioned a dog. Maybe it was a wild dog roaming

the abandoned grounds. No time to waste on that. His phone vibrated when he was ready to step inside. Damon.

He scanned the message. Big D's real name was DeShawn Carter. Did a stint in Raiford. Mostly assaults. Now Frank had some basic information on the suspect.

Big D was propped on the bed, cuffed at the wrist, face pale under the harsh light. His head and left leg were bandaged. He scowled when he saw Frank.

"Evening, Mr. Carter." Frank pulled up a chair. "How's the leg?"

"Huh? Nobody calls me that. And it hurts! Y'all need to put that beast down."

"We'll consider it." Frank set his phone on the tray, recording light blinking. He stated the date, time, his name, rank, and other pertinent information. "Before we start talking, let me inform you of your rights. You have the right to remain silent—"

"Yeah, yeah. I know my rights. Just get on with it."

"Okay. Here's your problem. Kozlov's dead. And when the boss is dead, the heat rolls downhill. All that organ harvesting, the abductions, the safe houses, someone's gotta pay. Right now, you're the last man standing."

Big D's jaw worked, his cuffed hand clenching the sheet.

"Makes my job easy to pin everything on you. The state attorney will throw the book at you."

"Save your breath. I didn't do n'thing."

"Here's where you're wrong. Florida is a felony murder state. That means if a death happens during the commission of felonies, you know, like kidnapping, everyone involved can be charged with first-degree murder."

He settled back, crossed one knee over the other, and locked his hands on the top one. "Let me explain. An assistant state attorney was blown up today. A police detective was abducted and assaulted by you, Mr. Carter. So, you see, there's kidnapping and there's a death, and you are involved. So, the state can charge you with first-degree murder. In case you're not aware, Florida has the death penalty."

Big D's breathing turned rough. His eyes shifted.

Frank let it gnaw at him, then said, "However, if you cooperate, I can talk to the prosecutor."

"So what are you saying? I tell you about Kozlov, and I'm off the hook?"

"Whoa, now you're dreaming. Not off the hook, but maybe life instead of death?"

"But the boss man is the one behind everything."

"I understand, but did you not hear what I said? It doesn't matter if you're the boss or not as long as you're involved—*and you are.* We can prove it. There's a death, and there's a kidnapping, today alone. You're on the hook."

After a few minutes, Big D sighed. "What do you want to know?"

An hour later, Frank walked out of the room to check his messages. Mayor Porter left an urgent message for him to call.

"Frank Travers for Mayor Porter," he said when an aide answered the call.

"One moment, please."

"Frank, you need to get here now."

"Not the press—"

"Not that. You need to see what Watkins had. Get here now."

*What Watkins had.* "On my way!"

# CHAPTER 60

## BAT SIGNALS

The monitors ticked steadily, a counterpoint to the ache in KC's skull. Tanner had gone to the cafeteria to grab food, leaving her with Aunt Mae perched in the visitor's chair, purse in her lap like she might scold the entire hospital into order.

This was the time to get the truth out. KC shifted, the blanket rasping against her skin. "Aunt Mae, who's Cyrus Jagers? The truth, this time. He talked about a Bat signal. And he called you 'my Mayflower.'" She held her right hand up. "And the ring. He said it was a tracking device."

Her aunt exhaled through her nose, a sigh that carried more years than KC wanted to count. "It'll take too long to explain."

"Try me."

"You called me, but when I answered, you didn't say anything. Then I heard that blast... and silence. I called and texted back, nothing. So I—"

"What? How'd you send this Bat signal? Did you call him?"

Her aunt chuckled, shaking her head. "I don't have his number anymore. But I still have the music box. That's the Bat signal he was referring to."

KC frowned. A music box. "How does that work?"

"I have no idea. I just wind it up. A moment later, my phone rings. I leave a message. That's the Bat signal."

Like one of those old-school pagers. Just fancier. "And the ring? How'd you know how to turn it into a tracker?"

"Oh, I didn't. I special-ordered it. Just because I was a lawyer doesn't mean I don't know certain people in certain professions." She capped it with a wink.

KC tilted her head, viewing her aunt with a new lens. Who was Mae Cassidy Reeves? Could her aunt have been more than a corporate attorney? And that Jagers character. "Were you two ever…?"

Aunt Mae laughed outright, the sound warm and dismissive. "Oh, that was so long ago. And I loved your uncle." She put a hand on her heart. "God rest his soul."

KC leaned back, unsettled. Her aunt was still holding something back. Still, Aunt Mae was family. Nothing would change that.

After another few minutes, Aunt Mae stood. "I'll find some coffee and a snack." She squeezed KC's hand before slipping out.

The room quieted, leaving only the steady monitor beep and the faint hum of air vents. KC stared at her ring. How many secrets was her family keeping?

The door opened again. Tanner stepped back in, a takeout bag dangling from one hand. He set it on the tray table by her phone. "Now that you seem to be better, you want to tell me the truth about back there?"

"What do you mean?" She reached for the bag.

He scooped it away and gave her a look. "I'm an investigator. You weren't telling the whole truth. Even Spaulding picked up on it. He and I heard a dog growl, but it was gone by the time we got there. If it were a wild dog, I'd expect it to either stick around and maul the guy some more or roam about and run into us. He said something about a witness with a dog."

No point in lying anymore. She let out a slow breath. "Yeah. The witness is Cyrus Jagers. He has a German shepherd."

"Okay." He put the bag back in reach but nodded for her to continue.

She unrolled the top and dug out a chicken wrap and passed him one. Then she told him how Aunt Mae somehow alerted Jagers and he tracked her to Mission Grounds. "Eeyore, the dog, charged Big D at just the right time. Saved my life."

"And Kozlov?"

"Jagers had Eeyore growl to distract Kozlov. He grabbed the gun and shot him. He put the gun in my hand and took off."

"Who is this character?"

She peeled back the paper wrapping, exposing rolled-up avocado, chicken, and tomato. "He's a Brit. Supposed to be retired, doing some consulting gigs. Spaulding was going to ask Ron about them, but maybe he got sidetracked. But we told the commander and that outfit. He said he'd look into it. Not sure what became of it."

"It sounds a lot like this guy is a spy. I wonder if Olivia knows him."

KC remembered Olivia and Simon's wedding. Was that only last week? Seemed like ages ago. "Well, you can't ask her now. They're on their honeymoon." She held his hand. "You can't report this. We need to keep this between us. The man and his dog saved my life. I owe him this much."

"Of course. Why do you think we didn't press you at the scene?"

"Thank you." Her phone danced on the tray. She picked it up to scan Spaulding's message.

> Be prepared. Coleman wants to see you as soon as you're cleared for duty.

# CHAPTER 61

## DAMAGE CONTROL

City Hall after dark always felt wrong. Too much glass, too clean, like the city had tried to scrub the grit off its hands. Frank expected to meet the mayor in her office, but the aide led him to a second-floor conference room.

The voices hit him before the door even opened, low, tense, overlapping. When he stepped inside, every head swiveled.

Mayor Elaine Porter sat at the head of the long table, posture crisp, her suit jacket immaculate despite the hour. Beside her, Chief Ed Hamilton, OPD, leaned forward like he was about to come out of his chair. Byron Williams, state attorney, Ninth Circuit, sat opposite, flanked by Watkins's division chief, Anita Myers. Both looked tense. A few other staffers and deputies rounded out the table.

The argument cut off the moment Frank entered.

"Commander, thank you for coming." Porter gestured to an empty seat. "We were just reviewing developments."

He nodded to those gathered and sat.

Porter folded her hands. "State Attorney Williams and Division Chief Myers received an email from Watkins earlier today. A resignation letter with a secured attachment. The attachment was evidence. A collection of files implicating Kozlov and his network."

Frank didn't react. Watkins's strange visit now took on new meanings. If Watkins was blackmailed, as evidence seemed to support, was he trying to make the best out of it? But then, he told KC he had made a mistake, and something had been an accident. Presumably, he'd accidentally killed his ex-wife, but could he be referring to something else?

"Anita." Porter gestured to Myers. "Why don't you give us a summary of what the evidence shows?"

"Of course. The email and attachment were sent through the usual encrypted channel. We haven't studied it in detail. What we can say is that Watkins assembled an extensive file on Kozlov, his organ harvesting, and his adoption network. Accounts, names, etc." She drew an unsteady breath before launching in faster. "Gavin was my ASA. He wasn't perfect, but he worked cases hard. I don't want his last act dismissed out of hand." She leveled her gaze on her boss.

Williams steepled his fingers before his face. "We'll be forwarding the pertinent information to the Bureau. Technically, Watkins was assassinated since his resignation wasn't in effect then. Our office has to maintain credibility, especially now. The public needs to see one of our own acted responsibly—"

"Now, wait a minute," Chief Hamilton interjected. "He killed his ex-wife—"

"We don't have evidence—"

"A confession?" Hamilton cut Myers off. "He basically confessed—"

"What he said," Williams chimed in, "was 'I made a mistake' and 'it was an accident.'"

"There you go." Hamilton raised his voice.

"He never said what 'it' was," Williams retorted.

"All right, people." Porter raised her hands to calm everyone. "Let's all take a breath. We won't solve this debate tonight. The

FBI will take over dismantling Kozlov's networks." She met Frank's eyes. "Prime has done its job. Your team will stand down."

He inclined his head. "Yes, ma'am. Chief Myers, if it's all right with you, I'd like a copy of the evidence file so we can wrap up our own cases."

"I'll send it to you."

"Thank you." He stood. "And if there's nothing else, you all have a good evening."

Porter's nod signaled her dismissal. "Oh, if the Bureau needs Prime's help, feel free to join forces."

Frank nodded and moved fast to get out of there. He didn't trust himself not to speak his mind if asked.

Watkins was dead. Kozlov was dead. Did Joey need to know his father might have killed his mother?

# CHAPTER 62

## LOOSE ENDS

The Hub smelled like bacon and coffee instead of gun oil and ozone. Frank stood at the stovetop tucked into the corner of the kitchen, spatula in hand, turning a skillet of scrambled eggs like he had a hundred times before. Sunday had been for rest. Monday was for wrapping up.

"Boss," Quinn called over from the table where she was buttering a biscuit, "you ever think about retiring from police work? I hear the diner is hiring."

Damon snorted into his mug. "Careful, Quinn. At least his food doesn't come in shrink-wrap."

Frank slid eggs onto a plate, handed it across the counter to Claire, who accepted it with a quiet thanks. He nodded toward Quinn. "Eat. It'll keep you alive longer than those donuts you bring in."

Jack wandered in, tablet under one arm, sniffing at the air like a bloodhound. He'd combed his hair this morning. Wouldn't stay in place long. "Smells… edible. Amazing. Next time you retire, you can open Travers's All-Day Breakfast Shack."

Claire arched a brow. "Don't encourage him."

They gathered around the long table with their plates. Forks clattered, and muted chatter warmed the space. For a rare moment, the Hub felt almost normal. Like a family kitchen instead of the nerve center of an elite team.

When the plates were mostly cleared and Quinn was licking butter from her thumb, Frank allowed himself one more moment of normalcy. Then he wiped his hands on a towel, and the weight of command settled back onto his shoulders.

"All right, time to close the books."

The transformation was immediate. The relaxed chatter faded as they moved from the kitchen to the bullpen. The morning light spilled through the high windows, catching dust motes that swirled above glowing monitors. He notched a hip against the wall, coffee mug in hand, scanning his team's faces.

"Mayor Porter gave me the rundown Saturday night." His voice carried across the open space. "FBI will take over dismantling Kozlov's networks, both organ trafficking and adoption. Prime's job is done. We just need to wrap our files, make sure nothing slips through."

Nods circled the room. Damon tapped his pen against his notepad. "Then I'll start. Adoption network."

He flipped a file open, pages bristling with notes. "Kozlov bought infants and toddlers from poor families overseas, mostly in the Middle East. He then 'placed' them with families here in Florida. Watkins's files back that up, and Big D corroborated it. Kozlov was looking at expanding to Georgia and the Carolinas. We've got enough documentation to forward it up the chain."

Claire's mouth tightened. "What happens to those kids now?"

Frank didn't answer right away. The question hung like smoke. "Not our case anymore. That'll be for the Bureau and the courts to decide."

But deep down, he knew the truth. Whatever else Kozlov was, he'd placed those kids into homes where they'd grown up believing they belonged. Ripping them out would feel like a second crime. Frank only hoped someone in a higher office had enough sense to weigh mercy with the law.

"Organ harvesting." Claire picked up, scanning her notes. "Watkins had reason to believe Kozlov could arrange a kidney for Joey. But only if Watkins returned the favor—"

"Which we now know he did," Quinn cut in.

Frank gave a single nod. "We can close the cases on the serial."

Jack had been waiting his turn, bobbing with barely contained energy. "And speaking of Joey—"

Claire leaned forward. "He's still waiting on a kidney?"

"Well… about that. I might've gone a little overboard while running his DNA."

Damon groaned. "What did you do?"

"It's heartbreaking watching a kid waste away on dialysis, okay? So I cross-referenced. And guess what? Joey has a familial match. Twenty-five percent." He held up two fingers. "That means half-sibling, aunt, uncle, or grandparent. In this case, half uncle. Lives in Australia. Watkins's half brother."

Quinn whistled low. "You're telling me the poor kid's got an uncle halfway around the world and never knew it?"

Jack nodded, a little sheepish. "Apparently, the family fractured a long time ago. The uncle knew about Watkins, but not Joey. Always wanted to meet up, though."

Claire's eyes softened. "So… is he a match?"

Jack's grin spread. "He also happens to have that genetic marker. So, perfect match. I may have made a call, just to, you know, explain the situation. And then Deanna's boss, the SAC, pulled some strings. The guy's on a plane right now. He's coming."

Something loosened in Frank's chest, a knot he hadn't realized he'd been carrying since he'd seen the kid hooked up to that dialysis machine. Joey would live. Really live, not just survive.

Quinn grinned. "Jackpot. Kid might get a shot at a normal life."

Damon shook his head, though there was a glint in his eye. "Jack, you should rein yourself in. One of these days you'll cross a line."

"Yeah, but today wasn't that day." Jack rocked back in his chair, satisfied.

"Look who the cat dragged in?" Claire smiled as Eli walked in.

They all turned to the profiler/consultant, who nodded. "Have I missed breakfast? I heard Frank was quite a cook."

They laughed. Frank tilted his head toward the kitchen. "I'm sure you can find some leftovers."

Eli waved a hand and sat. "Don't bother. I also heard you solved your cases."

"You helped." The mention of Eli's help reminded Frank that someone else had also helped. He fished his phone out of his pocket. "Excuse me."

He went out to the small garden and made a call.

# CHAPTER 63

## PARTNERS

The squad room buzzed the way it always did on a Wednesday morning, with phones ringing, keyboards clacking, voices low and sharp. Familiar. Comforting, almost.

KC paused just inside the door, inhaling the smell of burnt coffee and toner. She'd been cleared for duty, bruises fading, headache dulled to a ghost. The department shrink signed her off yesterday. She was back.

Spaulding looked up from his desk, the corner of his mouth twitching in what passed for a smile. "Welcome back!"

"Thanks. Let's hope it's not short-lived." She sat, setting her second cup of coffee on the desk. "So, what'd I miss?"

"Quite a lot. Commander got Big D to cough up a lot of intel. Watkins assembled a treasure trove of evidence. The Bureau has the ball now."

"Yeah, I was gonna ask you. The news made it sound like Watkins was in some classified operation that led to his death."

"That's called politics. At least, his kid gets to think his dad died a hero."

She almost forgot Joey. "I guess, small consolation. What else?"

"I did all the paperwork." He mocked a bow. "You're welcome. Copied them all to Prime, as instructed. Oh, remember Jesse Bell, the sponsored student?"

She stirred her drink. "Right, Kozlov's company paid for his tuition."

"That's the one. He's, for lack of a better word, a victim of Kozlov's adoption network. They buy infants or kids from poor families overseas and sell them to families here. They're all in Watkins's files and confirmed by Big D."

"What about that tutoring place? Elite something?"

"Yeah, Elite Prep Solutions. Owned by another of Kozlov's LLCs. So, whatever the guy was, he did some good."

She glanced back at Coleman's office. "Guess I can't put it off much longer." She stood. "Wish me luck," she whispered.

"It's gonna be okay."

KC took a deep breath, squared her shoulders, and crossed the room. The squad quieted enough for her to feel the weight of eyes on her back. Everyone had heard the rumors. Kozlov. Watkins. The blast.

Coleman was at his desk, putting his phone down. "Come in."

She stepped inside. Shut the door behind her.

"Cassidy, you were off the case. That was an order."

"Yes, sir." In her defense, the commander had his profiler call her. Did that count since she'd already planned to confront Watkins on her own?

"I can't have a loose cannon in my squad."

"No, sir." She bit her lower lip. She could always go back to the Sheriff's Office. Ouch.

"Do you know how long I've worked with Spaulding?"

"No, sir."

"Coming on nine years. He doesn't trust anyone easily, and it takes a lot to earn his respect."

*Just where is this going?*

"You've been here a short time, and he's already willing to go to bat for you. That tells me you've got something."

She remained silent. *Spaulding went to bat for her?*

"The commander called. He claimed it was all his idea for you to go see Watkins, even though you were off the case."

*Wow. She didn't expect that.*

"He also mentioned nominating you for a commendation for valor and bravery."

Her eyes went wide. "Sir?"

"You went off script. That can't happen again. But you did good work. Prime couldn't have wrapped it without you. Consider this your second chance. Don't make me regret it."

Her knees wobbled. She breathed in relief like a breath after drowning. She straightened. "Understood."

"Good. Dismissed."

KC stepped out into the squad room, pulse still quick. The moment her foot crossed the threshold, her coworkers' gazes darted away, detectives scattering back to their phones and keyboards like they hadn't been watching.

Spaulding leaned against his desk. "Well?"

"I still have my job."

He exhaled, long and heavy. "Good. Because we've got a case. Sexual battery. And I'd hate to break in another new partner."

The corners of her mouth lifted a little. Bruises or not, she was ready. "Well then, let's go, partner."

In case you missed it, download *Christmas Murders*, the prequel in the KC & Orlando Prime series.

Interested in learning more about Tanner's team? Check out the Mirror Estate series.

# THANK YOU!

Thank you for diving into *Fatal Invitation*! Writing this story has been such a wild ride and knowing that you've spent time with the cast means the world to me.

I hope you loved reading it as much as I loved writing it. If you'd be so kind as to leave a review on Amazon and/or Goodreads to share your impressions with others, I would greatly appreciate it. Your insights will help other readers find the book.

# ABOUT THE AUTHOR

S.F. Baumgartner writes fast-paced Christian suspense thrillers. Book 1 of her Mirror Estate series, Living Secrets, was selected as one of the Top Picks in the thriller category at Killer Nashville, 2024. Her love for writing comes second only to her love of reading.

When she's not busy writing about complex characters, secretive operatives, and relentless agents, she spends her time binge-watching crime TV shows, such as NCIS, or playing with her cats. If you enjoy James Patterson's style—specifically short chapters—you'll love her Mirror Estate series.

To be the first to know about any sales, promotions, and new releases, sign up for our monthly newsletter. By subscribing, you'll stay informed about all the latest happenings and never miss an opportunity to explore this captivating world.

# ALSO BY
# S.F. BAUMGARTNER

**Mirror Estates series**

Buried Secrets, book 1

Living Secrets, book 2

Forgotten Secret, book 3

Tangled Secrets, book 4

Hidden Secrets, book 5

Shadowed Secret, book 6

Stolen Secret, book 7

Box Set (Books 1-4)

**KC & Orlando Prime series**

Christmas Murders, a prequel

Fatal Invitation, book 1

# ACKNOWLEDGMENTS

Publishing a novel is not a solo endeavor, and I'm deeply grateful to those who made this book possible.

A heartfelt thanks to Deirdre Lockhart at Brilliant Cut Editing and Chelsea Lauren from Represent Publishing for their invaluable guidance and support. To the team at 100Covers.com, your stunning cover design perfectly captured the heart of this story.

I want to extend my thanks to Gabe & Amy Baumgartner, CPAs, for their helpful suggestions.

I also want to thank the amazing beta and ARC readers—your feedback and enthusiasm were crucial in refining this novel.

To my family, your unwavering support has been my greatest strength. And finally, to you, dear readers—this book is for you. Enjoy the journey!